Trajen

The Loren

....
....

J.S. Samuel

theloren.com

Print Edition Copyright 2016

For my friends,

never stop dreaming

&

for my family,

I am here because of you,

for that I can never truly thank you.

Prologue

An alarm screams, echoing down the endless corridors. The compound has become a hive of activity, guards and workers all travelling to their appropriate positioning. Some run up an eastern stairwell, others run down the southern. Many make their way calmly out the front door. None share more than a glance as they pass, but that is all that's needed to communicate. Some consider the alarm a fire drill, others know better. This alarm can only mean one thing.

A cage is open.

Two hundred feet below the entrance level of the compound, the bodies begin to pile as they fall. Every few steps gives way to another unconscious form, some barely clinging to life as they land, though each man that falls will surely survive the battle. Many have wounds which have already begun to heal, more than one nose self-corrects a recent slant. One guard remains barely conscious, so concussed that the world around him feels more like a fever dream than reality. He attempts to stand, unable to perceive that he is not alone. His effort is met with a swift blow to the abdomen, delivered by a force he will never remember. The form continues its onslaught, a dashing blur of red and white on the cameras that track its path.

Only yards away, as the guard falls fully into unconsciousness, another man's world comes back to life. His joints feel stiff and his vision is blurred. No single smell stands out to him. His world is a mess of noise and static. The restraints around his hands and feet loosen and disengage, a primal urge to run threatening to overtake him.

His throat hoarse from inactivity, his vocal cords struggle almost more than his mind to come together. The sound coming through them feels like sandpaper on his insides. Unsure if he'll even be heard above the noise, he manages to address the grizzled figure setting him free. The man opening his restraints is old, salt and red pepper hair on his head and face.

"Where...am I?" speaks the teenage man.

"There's no time for that now!" The old man says, almost gleefully. "We have to get you out of here."

The last strap comes free of the waking man's ankle and he stumbles forward, unsure if he remembers how to walk. The pair exit the cage into a corridor filled with fluorescent lighting, scattered bulbs flickering in spite of their guaranteed lifespan. Somehow, the alarm manages to become even louder as the sound reflects off the walls of the hallway, so narrow is the passage. Thirty feet away, at the end of the hallway, two more guards enter through double doors, stepping over their seemingly sleeping companions. Long hairs threaten to break through from under the guards' uniforms, their hands imperceptibly turning to claws. Their nails grow and become natural razors.

Still groggy, the young man's instincts take over. He does not notice the gray hairs now sprouting from the hand of the man in front of him. He's unsure what's happening as his muscles come fully to life and his awareness of his surroundings becomes acute. The incessant pulsing of the alarm slows nearly to a crawl, and he finds himself bounding towards the guards. Seeing there isn't enough room to easily run past his new companion, it feels natural as his feet make their way up the wall. His form becomes completely horizontal, then vertical once more as he runs across the ceiling. Coming near to the guards, he simply stops running, instead flying towards the furthest opponent. His body turns naturally in the air as he looks forward, back towards his companion. His arms reach themselves outward as he flies behind the farthest guard, his body positioned like a spear with his legs straight out behind him. His hands grab onto the hairy man's shoulders, the inertia from his flight throwing the guard on his back. As they land, the guard's head bounces off the tile like an overly compressed basketball. The young man is back on his feet as quickly as the guard enters his concussion.

The older man screams as the world comes back to full speed. His legs again propelling him forward, the younger man reaches out to grab the remaining guard by the sides of his shoulders, lifting the man's robust frame almost completely from the floor. The guard is slammed twice into the nearest wall before his legs crumple and he slides down into a sitting position. His head falls lightly onto his own chest, which appears less hairy with each breath under his uniform. As he turns, the young man sees his now wounded companion sitting in a similar fashion, his head back against the wall. The man's breathing is labored.

"That's it for me," he says, a blood-filled cough soon stealing the momentum of his words. "Bastard got me good out of nowhere. Here, take this. Whatever you do, just keep going. We'll find you."

The man seems even older than before, the features on his face becoming softer as he hands the young man a keycard with the word LYRACORP across the front in bold, green lettering. As the card passes from one to the other their hands brush up against each other and the wound on the older man's chest looks noticeably smaller. They share a meaningful look, albeit brief, before the old man pushes him away.

Placing the keycard in his pocket, the young man is through the double doors in an instant. A glance back shows no sign of his would be savior. In a flash a solitary guard turns the corner at the end of the hall, stepping directly underneath a flickering light. With one step, the young man is in his own area of light and dark fifty feet in front of the guard. With the next, he is behind him as his form is released from the shadows. His arm reaches back as he palms the guard's head, turning and rolling the man's skull in his hand as the guard stumbles and is turned from the force. The young man continues the motion, bringing the guard's back against his chest, planting two powerful blows onto each of the guard's temples simultaneously. Gravity is unable to finish pulling the guard to the floor before the young man is moving again.

Each of the hallways looks the same as the one before it, white and covered in plaster. Smells have begun to return to the young man's adrenaline-filled body. The scents sting his nose, a mess of cleaning products and strong sweat.

With his senses now more fully within his control, he tunes out the blaring of the alarm, the sound of his breath now louder than anything else. Each exhale is another ten feet. Every gasp for air is a firmer grasp on his freedom. He comes to the end of another hallway after having wound around two more, facing two possible directions to choose from. He stops for just a moment, unsure of which way to go. The air comes in sharply through his teeth. His sense of urgency is telling him there is no time for such deliberation. The decision is made for him as the scent of daffodils and fresh air slips onto his tongue and into his nose. For reasons of which he is unsure, he trusts his sense of smell on the matter, and he continues on once again. The daffodils break the taste of ammonia in his mouth so beautifully, he feels like only a fool would avoid them.

The man comes to a plated-glass door, a unit on the right waiting for a swipe of his keycard. For a moment he cannot figure out what he is meant to do, keycard still clutched in his left hand. Eyeing the slot designed for the swipe of the card, he brings his hand forward and thrusts the card down through the reader. As the light next to the door turns green and the glass slides to let him through, the smell of the outside becomes magnified. Navigating his way through the rest of the compound is done without so much as another thought, his nose guiding him to an emergency staircase. He takes the steps three at a time, his feet landing so lightly he seems to have wings as he propels towards the surface. As comes through the final door, he is greeted by the snow's sobering coldness. His feet press down on top of the fresh powder, deep holes marking clearly his path as he takes it. He can see a wall many yards away, the barrier he knows to be between him and freedom. Several stories above him, the barrel of a rifle pokes through an open window. Another guard in a much darker uniform holds his breath as he steadies his shot. A practiced finger squeezes a familiar trigger just as the young man approaches the wall at the edge of the compound. The bullet enters through the back of his right shoulder, exiting through the front under his collarbone. The pain calls forth an angry cry as he propels himself over the wall's twenty foot height. He stumbles as the lands on the other side, spotting the tip of the daffodils that led him to the outside world just across the road, covered almost completely by the falling snow. For the first time in longer than he knows, he remembers how to smile, standing like an idiot in the middle of a poorly lit stretch of road.

The car screeches as it tries to stop, the icy path it travels preventing the anti-lock brakes from properly halting its metal form. The woman inside manages a muffled curse before the young man's body is forcefully struck by her bumpers. She wasn't driving that fast. She never drives that fast in the snow. *Oh god, please be okay,* she thinks. She steps out of her car to see the smile still spread across her victim's face. More than anything else, he looks peaceful. She knows better than to move the body, but there isn't any blood. An ambulance would likely mean police. *The city isn't so big,* she remembers her husband saying. She would probably know the officer that showed up. That's just how it had been since they moved here. For all of the people, it wasn't hard to seem like you knew everybody.

She could handle going to jail. It was an accident and the road was icy. But in a city like this, her husband might lose his job. And when LyraCorp put you on their blacklist, you might as well try to find work on another planet. If only it hadn't been snowing, she could blame the car's guidance system. But the log would show it was being operated manually.

7

As her morals wrestled with her reasoning, the young man's eyes opened. She got a better look at him, then. His hair was matted, like it hadn't been washed in years. Parts of it had begun to dread. He looked to be well-built, his shoulders the most prominent feature on his body. She could see immediately that his shirt was stained with blood, a hole in his clothing staring her right in the face, though no wound was behind the tear. The young man blinks, her signal to come back to reality.

"Oh my god," she says. "Are you okay?"

The man rubs his shoulder. "I...think so. But I..."His voice cuts off, his eyelids suddenly feeling as if they're strapped to weights. He rubs his face to stay awake. "Please. Get me out of here." The young man immediately tries to stand, though he wobbles a great deal, nearly falling. The woman barely manages to both catch him and support his weight as she does. The boy doesn't look like he could possibly be so heavy, but her legs nearly buckle, as if she were trying to hold up her car.

"I don't live far," she grunts. "Do you want me to take you to a hospital?"

"I don't know what you're talking about. Please, I have to go. I can't be here. You have to...you have to help me."

"We'll go to my place." The woman staggers with the young man, taking them both over to her car, placing him as gently as possible into her passenger seat. She notices the man makes no move to buckle his seatbelt, though she imagines it's because he's just been hit by a car. She runs as quickly as she can to the driver's side, cranking up the heat as she sits down. The man's skin was so cold. She reaches for a blanket, telling him not to fall asleep as she steps on the gas. "Whatever you do," she says, "Just stay awake."

In the darkness of the forest to her left, a pack of wolves travels with preternatural speed towards her location. They exit the field of trees as a single-minded unit, with tactical grace and precision. The leader of the small pack saunters into the middle of the road, sniffing the ground and the air. He eyes the tire tracks angrily, an intelligence behind his eyes far beyond that of any natural canine.

The car is already gone.

A phone rings, the only audible sound to be heard in a corner office in spite of the facility's blaring alarm, which is at that moment being shut down. The man who answers is angry. He wants to hear good news. His suit is still freshly pressed, though he's been wearing it all day. For the right amount of money, it's an easy thing to have suits that never wrinkle. The man is large. The clothes he wears could easily fit two average-sized forms inside of them, though they fit his own form so snugly they stretch. Giant forearms flex, oversized teeth dig into each other in his large mouth as he listens to the news.

One of the residents of Level 9 has escaped. A young man is gone.

"Unacceptable," he says into the mouthpiece. His voice is low. The anger falls through his lips and down his chin in waves of heated breath, the smell of his last meal permeating around his office space. He has become not unlike a hot iron, so seething is his rage. The features on his face grow narrower as he listens. "Has the team been dispatched?" He growls as he's given his answer, the hair growing underneath his clothes as black as his dilated pupils. It is not often the large man becomes so angry that he takes on his altered form. A white stripe begins to appear in the middle of his head of hair, continuing down along his back. He feels more anger now than he has for some time. Somehow, his large form becomes even larger.

"Send the others." The words come now through fully sharpened teeth. "Release the hunters. *Find him.* Right now. I don't care how long it takes." The giant wolf turns to look at his reflection in the window beside him. His suit has torn from the strain of his over-sized form, the pieces perfectly straight as they lay on the floor.

The wolf stands from his office chair, his feet beginning a centuries familiar act, as he paces back and forth. So used to the confines of previous quarters is the wolf that he does not pace the full length of his office, which is as oversized as he is, but only strikes six feet one way before turning to walk six feet the other. His claws dig through his expensive shoes, scratching the carpet beneath his feet. Men will come in soon with new clothes. They'll come in with new carpet, as well. As he thinks of this, his rage intensifies, knowing it is unlikely the same men will come with the young man.

He had always been leader, though his surroundings had not always been lavish. He considers the varying levels of trouble the breakout may cause him, searching in his mind through the groups and singular individuals who might have even known there was anything in the building worth risking coming here to take with them. The usual names come to him, hatred dripping off of the letters now inscribed in his mind's eye. The names are then placed neatly, side by side in his mind, a technique he learned long ago from a man who knew how to manage his enemies. He thought fondly of how he destroyed that man when he used the tactic. It helped to keep his thoughts even, and remind him that no foe was too great. He was, and is, the greatest.

He begins to formulate a plan for each such individual or group as he paces. He will be satisfied only when he has all of his moves figured out, like playing multiple games of chess at once in his head. He doesn't sit again until he's finished. In life, as in chess, you must wait for your opponent to make their move again after you've made yours. Even though he did not start this match first, he will sit and play to see where it goes. He is secure, his own plans unaltered in spite of the young man's escape. It matters not in that moment who has come to try and take him down. He would wait for their next move before reacting.

There were so many other games he was playing. Moves he'd been making in the shadows of the world for centuries, and those could not be stopped.

The building was nearly completely empty. A few tall, lanky forms made their way not towards the stairs, but instead to the closest maintenance closet. The forms wobbled somewhat as they walked, their quick steps occasionally giving way to small hops as well. The tallest of them hunched over so as not to hit their head on the doorframe. Entrance ajar, the room looked much too small to fit so many of the tall people, their skin so fair it acted in sharp contrast to the darkness of the closet. Piling in like clowns to a car, the last body closed the door behind them quickly, the tiny space managing not to explode from the impossibly added mass.

Each of the long people's pupils dilated so wide their irises disappeared as they began to step down onto a staircase inside of the wall of the closet. A thin membrane slid over their eyes. The membrane acted both as protection against dust and as a lens for focusing the little to no light environment they were obviously made for. The staircase descended for several feet before the walls opened up, the group finally making their way underneath the ground level. Before long, they passed underneath the foundation of the building, the staircase unwinding into straight steps before coming to a straight piece of ground, the rock above them now far enough away even the tallest of them could walk comfortably.

The group traveled onward much slower now, their feet taking relaxed strides. Conversation had begun between them. This was their home, after all. They were away from the alarm. No one, *nothing*, would follow them down here on purpose. The group had gone far enough that electricity was an impossibility, though a dim glow continued to permeate along the walls, brought on by naturally occurring lichen. Bioluminescent plant life was not common in the natural parts of this

11

city, of course. The tall people brought it with them wherever they set up residence.

Soon the ground came to an end. The group stood at the precipice of a sharp decline, a few hundred feet into the earth. The woman at the front of the group stepped first over the edge, followed quickly by the rest of the group. Large wings materialized along the backs of each slender figure, catching the air easily and slowing their descent.

As they landed, the wings simply disappeared.

....

Bren pulled into her garage as her husband opened the door, ready for her arrival. She had held onto her fear of calling the police, a sentiment her husband thanked her for having. He said he'd be there to help her when she got home, and he was. It was the first time he'd done something he said he would since they had moved to the city, and all it took was a literal emergency to make it happen. *But what can you do, I guess,* she thought. The way their relationship has been lately, she couldn't tell if she was more relieved he kept his word, or surprised. Before Bren finished exiting her car, her husband was already unbuckling the young man's seatbelt. The man's eyes shot open as he stood up and showed completely black before appearing regular once more. As they walked inside, the young man's eyes began to glow, becoming purple, then green, settling ultimately on his natural color for the final time. The cold air of the garage felt nice as he was carried inside. His face had been resting directly in front of the air vent in the car, his driver unknowingly cooking his cheeks to a soft pink color. His legs are heavy, but he wills them to move. Bren's husband seems much less burdened by the young man's weight, though does not appear to be having a much easier time than she was. She makes a note to herself mentally to say something to her husband about how impossibly heavy the boy obviously is.

"It's going to be okay," Bren's husband says. "What's your name?"

The boy searches his mind for the first name he can think of. "Trajen. I think my name is Trajen."

"I'm Garrett, and this is my wife, Bren. You're going to be alright." Garrett walks Trajen over to their couch. "Sit down and don't fall asleep. I don't want you staying that way in case you have a concussion."

The boy's stomach growled intensely as the leftover adrenaline in his body finally subsided. "I won't. I...am very hungry." Trajen's stomach roared and gurgled audibly then, as if to accentuate his point to the room. His skin flushed again from the hunger, and his eyes again felt very heavy, a slight ache creeping into his head as his blood sugar dropped. Trajen looked at the couple, attempting to take his mind briefly off of how hungry he felt. They were both attractive, he thought. Bren's hair went down below her shoulders, straight the whole way, looking heavy and thick. Her thighs and arms were plump, and jiggled slightly as she walked. Her skin showed very few blemishes. Garrett's body was the opposite. His hair was short and cut close to his head, his face was rugged and full of the shadow of the hour. Garrett's body was lean, as well. He had a runner's body, though Trajen wasn't sure how he knew that.

"I'll get you some food," Bren said. "Honey, can you come help me in the kitchen?"

"Sure, dear." Garrett said. "Remember, kid. *No sleeping.*"

Trajen sat on Bren and Garrett's couch, his head tilted back, eyes on the ceiling. He was surprised he remembered his name. He couldn't remember much of anything else. He felt taxed to the point of drunkenness as he looked around the room. Part of him worried about being unable to run away if he needed to, but seeing the pictures above the mantle, with the dancing flames of a fresh fire in the hearth, he knew he was safe. Somewhere behind him an air freshener sprayed, the scent of cinnamon and apples meandering throughout the room. The smell was oddly comforting, even though he knew it was a manufactured scent and not the actual aerosolized form of any real apples *or* cinnamon.

Bren brought him stew. The meat was tender, its juices flowed delicately over the dryness in his throat. With each potato and carrot he swallowed, his body began to mend itself. He felt a rib painlessly crack back into place, the bone mending with a tingling sensation. One of his shoulders popped itself back into socket. He'd had no idea it had fallen out. Trajen began to lose himself in the food, it tasted so good. He was sure as he finished the bowl that it'd been much too long since the last time he'd eaten. When he finally looked up, Bren was taking the bowl and Garrett was handing him some clothes, directing him to the bathroom so he could change. It took him longer than it ought to as he tried to figure out how to disrobe his current garments. There was a zipper running along the back of his clothing, which was one piece in design. There was a zipper around his waist, as well, which would not undo itself until the zipper on the back had come down at least halfway. Trajen tried to shimmy out of the jumpsuit without undoing the zipper around his waist, but found the fit to be too tight. Unable to figure out the clothing he wore, he tore at the fabric, ripping it free of the zipper entirely. As it came away, the zipper unfurled itself, falling away in two separate pieces.

Trajen surveyed himself in the mirror, studying his form as is for the first time. His face was familiar to him, which he thought was surely a good sign. He examined his teeth, white and straight, and looked inside and behind his ears; they were clean. He flexed his nose and raised his eyebrows, turning his head every which way in the mirror. After a moment, he looked at the clothes Garrett had given him, hoping they would be easier to put on that the previous garment he had been wearing.

Garrett's clothes fit him a bit snug, but they were comfortable enough to make Trajen realize how uncomfortable his previous clothing had been.

Trajen walked back out to greet Bren and Garrett once again, who were standing only a few feet away from the bathroom door.

"Oh good," Garrett said. "We were worried you'd fallen asleep. I was only going to give you another minute before I came in there."

"I'm fine now," Trajen replied. "I am feeling much better. These clothes feel nice on my body. Thank you for giving them to me." Trajen smiled.

"Oh. No…uh…no problem." Garrett said. "It's good that you're feeling okay. Come on, let's go sit down. We can to know each other by the fireplace."

The three of them stayed up talking into the night, Trajen full of questions. Bren was too shaken up most of the night to wonder too much why Trajen seemed to know so much about one thing, and absolutely nothing about the next. More than once, she found herself staring at the young man, as well. It was impossible for her to tell Trajen's age. Sometimes the boy would make a face, and she would swear to herself he was only a child. Maybe seventeen, if that. In the next moment, Trajen looked well into his twenties, maybe even thirties. The three of them managed to have a great time getting to know each other. At one point, Garrett even made a joke that it took his wife hitting someone with a car for him to finally make a new friend in town. Bren's eyes nearly filled with tears as it her husband seemed to acknowledge so casually how alone they had both become, even from each other, in their new home. Eventually, Bren and Garrett felt sure that Trajen was without concussion and safe to shut his eyes. Bren was a nurse by vocation. While she might not have let an average patient go to sleep just yet, Trajen showed absolutely no signs that there was any real damage done. He wasn't even bruised or scratched from being hit. She looked at him again, laying on their couch, as she walked up the stairs. He looked so comfortable, she couldn't imagine him being gone in the morning. The boy just looked like he was where he belonged. She tried for a moment to rationalize the thought, knowing it to be beyond crazy, but Trajen had said more than once he wasn't sure if he even had any family. There was nowhere to take him when the sun came back up. Why not keep him?

Trajen turned over, the smile once again returning to his lips. The feeling of safety lingered as the fire cracked nearby, a fresh log fueling the flame. Garrett moved some of the coals around with a poker before following Bren up the stairs. The room was warm and comforting.

For the first time since they had moved into that house, Bren and Garrett fell asleep in each other's arms.

The alarm had long since been shut off. The lower levels of the compound were filled once more with only the whirring sound of air conditioning, which continued to pump warm air from the vents above. The smell of sweat had dissipated, only the ammonia remaining. On one side of the hall, a cage's door remained open. Bodies no longer littered the floor, each of the guards now awake and accepting their punishment for their failure. The sprays of blood had already been cleaned from the walls, many of the men now receiving fresh wounds for allowing their prey to escape.

Directly across from the open cage was another, though its door was still locked. Inside the cage, as if sleeping, is a young woman. She is strapped upright, the manacles around her wrists and ankles fused shut and made of something stronger than platinum.
Her next inhale is much slower than any that came before it. Her eyes open for the first time in centuries. The girl is smart. She knows she's been asleep for too long, she can feel her need for a proper meal and, her eyes lowered, takes stock of her surroundings. Her first instinct is to break off the manacles from her wrist, though her curiosity stays her hands. She focuses her hearing on the sounds around her, searching for the nearest bodies. She can see the cage in front of hers broken open,

and can hear that no one is nearby. Deftly, one swift motion all she needs, she forces her way out of her bindings. The girl takes one cautious step after another, her balance somewhat slow to return to her. She breathes in, getting her first good smell of the place. The scents around her sting her nose, the cleaning products doing nothing to keep the recently cleared blood from her nostrils. She decides it's time to leave, her instincts telling her, *compelling her*, where to go.

As she bends the bars of her cage, the alarm sounds once again.

She can already smell the dandelions.

Chapter I

Trajen's eyes open to the sun as it pours in through the windows of his lofty attic bedroom, the muscles in his arms and back seeming to drink in the sunlight as his body becomes invigorated by the new day. This morning begins his ninth month living with Bren and Garrett, the only people he trusts in the whole world. It had been a rough couple of weeks, getting started without an identity, but soon the group had begun to see some success in establishing Trajen as a person. The couple kept mainly to themselves, even before Trajen was there. The story they crafted was easy to sell.

Officially, Trajen had become their nephew, in town to get his life back on track. Much to Trajen's surprise, he found it was easy for people to believe he had been an addled youth, overtaken by drugs and bad decisions. Garrett knew someone who was able to get Trajen the right kind of paper trail, and the combination of easy story and documentation had sealed the deal. Trajen had become a person in no time at all. He was even enrolled in classes at the local community college as soon as was possible. Garrett went so far as to set him up with a job. If he didn't hurry, he'd be late for his first day.

Trajen brambled down the stairs, long-since comfortable enough to make noise in a place that now felt like home to the young man. According to Garrett, there had been a time when Bren had stopped making breakfast every morning. Garrett brought it up once when Bren wasn't around, during a moment of what Trajen could only understand as drunken clarity. Garrett didn't drink often, but on evenings that he did, the routine was to leave little sign of liquor left in the house. Trajen could tell it had made him sad when Bren stopped waking up to cook for the two of them. But since Trajen had been there, Bren cooked every morning. He couldn't remember ever eating eggs before he lived with Bren and Garrett, but he was sure if he had they weren't as good as the way Bren made them. This morning there was bacon, too. He couldn't remember bacon either, but he hoped he never forgot again. He spent a lot of time, his first few weeks, trying to remember anything he could. Thus far, his efforts had proven fruitless. He could only remember as far back as his first morning in the house. The night he arrived, and his life before, simply would not come to him.

"Good morning everyone." Trajen said as he entered the kitchen.

"Good morning, Trey," Bren said with a smile. "I've made you a plate. Do you have time to eat before work? I don't want you to be hungry while you're there."

"Ah, sorry Bren. No time! Garrett, can you give me a lift to Main on your way?"
Unbeknownst to the couple, Trajen had spent many nights his first few weeks walking throughout the city in the dark. Sleep was tough to come by until recently.

"Sounds like a plan. Let's get goin'." Garrett replied. "See you later, dear."

"Ok boys, have a good day." Bren and Garrett were the perfect picture of a modern-day working-class couple in that instant. Garrett's suit somehow blends perfectly with Bren's scrubs, the checkered pattern of her shirt not unlike the pattern on Garrett's tie. Trajen knows he'll regret his decision to forego breakfast, but he had decided to favor sleep over eating, or showering, that morning. The smell of the bacon still dances in his nostrils, even as he rushes towards the garage. After a quick kiss on Bren's cheek, Garrett makes his way with Trajen to the car. Bren is left with both a pile of food as well as dishes, though she does not seem to be bothered by either.

As the car leaves the driveway, Garrett locks eyes with a man at the end of the block. They've shared the same look almost every morning since Trajen arrived that night nine months ago, when Garrett would sneak out to take a walk with the rising sun, somehow never managing to run into

Trajen who had also been out walking alone. Garrett looked over then to Trajen, confirming the young man is unaware of the older gentleman's lingering presence. Trajen fiddled with the radio, settling first on the *Classic Rock* station, then switching to *Golden Oldies.*

"Are you excited for your first day, Trey?"

"I guess so. Don't know if I've ever had a job before. Not sure what it's like."

"Arnold is a good friend of mine. He'll treat you right. Just be courteous and do what he asks and you'll be fine. You'll be okay getting to school after work?"

"Yea. It's not too far. I think I'll have time to grab some food before class. I'll take the bus back from campus tonight."

"And how are your lessons going?"

"They're great, actually. Much better than the elective courses I was taking before. I guess there just wasn't much for me to learn when it came to interpretive dance or basket weaving. But this semester has been great!"

"Lots of lively discussions, then? That's what I miss the most about college."

"Mainly lectures, I guess. But I like those too. Each class is like a miniature documentary, and you know how much I like documentaries." Trajen smiled as he finished his sentence. He had spent nearly every moment of his free day time watching documentaries in his first month of residence with Garrett and Bren, soaking up the knowledge they had to offer with his unending thirst for their content.

As he stopped the car on the corner of Main Street, Garrett handed Trajen a cell phone. "Here, take this. It's got my number and Bren's in it. Call either of us any time if you need something." The phone is small, its case a level of shiny that seems to catch any surrounding light, no matter the original angle, and throw it back into a curious onlooker's eyes. It feels so light in Trajen's pocket, he silently tells himself to do his best to remember it's there, worried it could fall out any time. He'd have no idea it was gone. Trajen treasures the gift, a notion he makes no attempt to hide as his face belays his feelings.

"Thanks, Garrett. Have a good day."

Trajen takes stock of the store before him before he enters. He had been there a few times before with Garrett and Bren, picking up items the grocery store by their house didn't carry. Bren calls them 'specials.' Every few Sundays or so, she'll ask Trajen if he wants to go with her to "pick up the specials." A creature of habit, Bren starts each of those car rides the same, telling Trajen that her husband is a man of peculiar tastes, but the way his face lights up when she cooks the dishes with his special ingredients makes it worth it for her. Unlike the grocery store they frequent, this tiny shop makes almost no attempt to be seen. If not for the windows allowing any passerby to peek in, it would be easy for the world to have no idea food was even sold there. Opening the door, Trajen can smell the wonderful spices sat on shelves in the back of the shop, a smell he's never encountered anywhere else. Out from the back of the shop, struggling to carry a gallon of milk is his boss, Arnold.

Arnold is frail. Trajen's first thought when they met was that if he shook the man's hand too firmly, he might break something. As Trajen fully enters, Arnold is struggling to put the gallon of milk into a cooler.

"I got it, Arnold."

"Hey, thanks for that, kid. I'm so glad you're here. And with perfect timing. I've got another pallet of milk that I need put away, if you'd be so kind. Then I'll show you where the mop bucket is, give you a few quick pointers on the register, and you can just spend the rest of your day helping anybody who comes in. Sound good?" Trajen had watched a documentary once about the largest grocery chain in the country, of which there was a location near Garrett and Bren's house. He remembered the narrator saying how rigorously the cashiers – who were the unequivocal face of the company for customers – were trained by senior staff before being allowed to run their area alone. It seemed strange to Trajen that Arnold would let him run the store alone so quickly, but perhaps the owner would not be too far away, ensuring Trajen was still supervised.

"Sure," Trajen said with a smile. He liked the way Arnold talked to him. Arnold wasn't as nice as Bren, but he was respectful, and that made Trajen feel good. Garrett was respectful, too, but he had a musk to him that Trajen sometimes couldn't get past when they spoke. The musk made it hard to concentrate on their conversations sometimes. Especially after a long day, Garrett's natural scent would creep into Trajen's nose and stay there, in spite of the man's cologne or deodorant. Arnold smelled almost sweet. It made you want to be closer in proximity the longer you spoke with him. There was no attraction for Trajen to Arnold, but he'd be lying if he said he didn't want to be near the man.

The next few hours progressed as Arnold had said they would. Trajen performed some manual labor and spent the rest of his shift at the register, ringing up the few customers who came by. Arnold said most people came during the evening, and that he wasn't even normally open that early. He told Trajen he wasn't much of a daytime person. Arnold had spent almost the entire day in his back office, asleep on the couch. It wasn't the most exciting way to spend his morning, but Arnold was paying him daily, in cash.

After six hours, he left with about fifty bucks. Every time Trajen looked at paper money, it felt like he wanted to remember something. Sometimes the color of the paper, or the way it crinkled in his hands felt like it was drawing out a forgotten memory. When Arnold had handed him the cash, he was hoping that might be the instance the memory finally came to him. As with each other occurrence, though, he drew a blank.

"Enjoy your schoolwork. I'll see you tomorrow, same time." Arnold said with a yawn. The sun was just past the apex of its journey above. Trajen worried about Arnold being too tired to run the shop, but as he tucked his books under his arm, he turned back to see the CLOSED portion of the sign on Arnold's door facing outward; a sleepy shopkeeper turning off the lights to make his way back to his couch. Business was something Trajen hoped to learn more about in school, mainly because the goings on of LyraCorps was almost the only thing you could get Garrett to talk about for hours at a time. Still, it seemed to Trajen, keeping your shop open for business was the first step in making sure you had enough money to stay open. Didn't Arnold need customers bringing in revenue?

Trajen stopped into a diner at the midpoint of his walk to campus. He had almost an hour before his class began, and the breakfast he skipped that morning was starting to catch up to him. A burger from Sally's sounded great. Having been there before, he knew that all was not lost. He'd be ordering it with bacon. Their bacon was not as good as the bacon that Bren served, a comment Trajen had made the mistake of saying once in front of the daytime cook at the diner, Roger.

Roger was a big, burly man, often hunching somewhat as he walked, his huge hands making his normal-sized spatula appear to be made for children. Roger took pride in the food that he slung from his flat top at Sally's Diner, and Trajen had felt bad for insulting the man, even though he hadn't meant to. He was simply being honest. The bacon was better at home. Trajen liked it thicker, and chewy, as opposed to crispy and fried, which was the way they served it at Sally's. Bren had appreciated the comment, at least.

As he sat at the counter to order his burger, he was joined two seats away by an older man. For a moment, Trajen caught the same musky scent that he smells from Garrett. He turned to the old man and watched as he ordered a cup of coffee and a slice of pie before the waitress came to take Trajen's order. On a whim, Trajen asked for his burger medium-rare. Trajen's gaze lingered for a moment longer on the gentleman, sure he had seen him somewhere before, like so many other things he was unable to recall, Trajen decidedly lost interest and turned back to face front, soon opening one of his books to study. His first class that morning is Political Science. It's an introductory course, his first few sessions had been spent listening to lectures about the branches of government. Trajen found everything he was able to learn absolutely fascinating. Bren had jabbed at him playfully more than once that he was the only person she had ever known who could be happy watching documentaries all day on television, so it hadn't surprised him how often the other students in class would openly show that they had stopped paying attention. Though he didn't quite understand the reasoning, it seemed to Trajen that learning was not the first priority on many students' lists when they came to school. On his first day Trajen had tapped the shoulder of the girl in front of him as she was mid-doodle, reminding her that the professor was still lecturing. He thought he was doing her a favor; perhaps she didn't realize. When she glared at his reminder, he spent a portion of his evening pondering on the social misstep. Who would willingly forgo the chance to learn? It made no sense to him.

Even after his food arrived, the musk from the nearby man continued to permeate. Soon, just as when he is around Garrett for too long, the musk was all he could smell. He does not wait for his check to come before he places a twenty-dollar bill on the counter and leaves. The musk in the room proves too discomforting after there is no more food to eat. He had already been prepared not to enjoy the bacon as much as when he has it at home. The nearby man's smell had caused him not to enjoy his food at all.

Once Trajen is outside, he breathes deeply, ready for the fresh air to wipe the musk from his nostrils. He is given only a moment of freshness before the musk returns as he makes his way towards school. This musk is different, though. It sets his muscles on edge, the hair on the back of his neck standing completely straight as he continues onward. For a moment he wonders if a nearby gas line has sprung a leak, so steadily does the smell seem to follow him. There is an unsettling quality to the odor, as well. It sets Trajen's muscles on edge. For the first time in months, Trajen feels unsafe. His steps quicken as he prepares to turn the last corner before the straightaway that leads to campus. He can feel his vision tunneling, the muscular optical illusion reducing the light of the day, the street seeming to grow darker as he becomes more focused on his goal. The square of sidewalk at the end of the block is nearly all he can see, so intent is his focus.

He's ten feet from the corner, just in front of an alleyway, when he's pulled off the sidewalk. A large fist slams into his nose before he's thrown onto the ground. Instinctually, his hands and feet curl inward in an effort to protect himself. His books covering his eyes, snarls and growls sound all around him. Trajen's body rolls itself to the side, anticipating more kicks and stomps to come his way, his books now covering the back of his head. But there are no more kicks. Instead, he hears a roar, much deeper than the growls around him. The growls are then followed by what he understands to be yips, the sound a dog might make when it becomes injured suddenly. Through the stream of blood clouding one of his nostrils, he can again smell the musk from the diner. His eyes slowly become unglued.

As he peers out from underneath his books, he sees the old man, though his form is almost completely covered with white and red hair. The old man is a flurry of limbs, clawing and punching his way through Trajen's three aggressors. Now with his wits about him, one thing does stand out to Trajen as he makes his way to his feet.

The men all look like wolves.

"I could use some help, you know!" The older man yells to Trajen. At that moment the other men, much younger than Trajen's new companion, gain the upper hand. In spite of the hits the old man has landed, the younger aggressors seem undaunted. Trajen believes his eyes to be playing tricks, as he can see that each of the men, even the old man, appear almost doglike. One of them manages to grab the older dog's right arm with his left, landing a punch squarely to the old one's face. The old man staggers back a few feet, obviously dazed. Trajen drops his books to help, grabbing one of the men by his shirt. As he pulls him away, the man feels much lighter than Trajen thinks he should, gaining a better footing before shoving the man into the wall a few feet away, the force of his push strong enough to leave the man stuck against the wall for a moment before sliding down. Trajen wasn't trying to throw the man, but his opponent flew the four feet anyway. Trajen had moved him like he might a gallon of milk. Trajen slams his fist sideways into another man's cheek from behind, sending him tumbling over himself, before lifting the third man completely from the earth and slamming him into the ground. He had seen wrestlers do the same thing once, in another documentary about their sport. Trajen's form is ugly in comparison to the professionals, but the man might as well have been a pillow considering the ease with which Trajen picked him up and sent him into the earth.

Trajen's entire body is flooded with adrenaline. He can feel his heart beating faster than it ever has before. Expecting the fight to continue, Trajen turns to the first man he threw, only to find he has gone. As he turns back to the other men, he sees they are gone as well. Even his would-be companion has fled. Trajen's face portrays his confusion perfectly as he stands alone in the alleyway, his books on the ground to his left. If not for the blood slowly running from his nose, he'd be worried he hallucinated the event, so quickly had the others who were there left the scene. Even their scent had left him. The fresh air now all he could smell; he takes the phone from his pocket. Garrett's number is the first on speed-dial.

Chapter II

Bren didn't know what she was doing anymore. Having Trajen in the house had changed so much. Things were good again. Like when she'd first married Garrett. They were so in love in the beginning. If relationships truly happened in phases, as so many people seemed to believe they did, then by her estimation the "honeymoon phase" with her husband lasted for a few years, at least. Somewhere along the way, Garrett had grown distant. And when they moved to this town, Bren secretly had hoped that things would go back to normal. When they didn't, she found herself looking for something. She didn't know what at the time. Or at least, she didn't want to admit it to herself. The love was still present in her marriage. Even after Garrett had grown distant, Bren loved her husband with the same burning intensity as when they were first married.

But the passion was no longer there.

At first Bren thought she'd find a hobby. She had told herself that if she could take up something she could be passionate about, that at least having the output would help her to feel better. She and Garrett were just in a slump. That happened to everybody. Garrett had just been reassigned to a new place, his job had him learning to do all kinds of new things. The man came home so tired every night. But Bren told herself that her husband would acclimate, and that their marriage would bounce right back. She had gone to a craft store one day, just to look around. She had painted when she was younger. Maybe she would do that again. She liked to make things with clay, too. *I could spend a few months on a detailed piece,* she had thought, *and maybe by then things will have worked themselves out.*

Bren was looking at the different brands of clay when Kevin introduced himself. He was a stylish, well-built man. Not unlike her husband, though this man smelled like cologne. Bren stopped wearing perfume early into her marriage. Garrett said fake scents bothered his nose when he was around them too much. She always managed to forget how much she liked a good, fresh scent on a man. It was a guilty pleasure, that first day in the store, but Bren liked the attention so much that she had chatted with Kevin for almost half an hour. When she looked at her phone, seeing that she still had a few hours before Garrett would be home, she told herself that it was just coffee, and she'd made a friend. In that back of her mind, she knew from that first interaction with Kevin that the man didn't have any intention of being friends when he'd approached Bren in the crafts store. Kevin listened, though, when Bren talked. He asked her questions. Their dialogue only lasted a little over an hour that day, but she'd been able to talk about more with a stranger than she had with her husband for *months*. Where Bren had at first been telling herself that she just wanted to find an activity to do alone, to pour her overflowing reservoir of passion into, she found herself as she went home that evening entertaining the idea of *sharing* her passion. It was an idea she battled with, but more and more, she found herself running into Kevin again. More coffee. More talking. Before long, more than that, as well.

That was almost a year ago. The worst part was, she had been right about the slump. Her marriage was back to being great. Her *life* was back to being great. Running into Trajen on the night she did had truly been an act of fate. She had almost not gone home that night, so many months ago. When her and Kevin had finished, he had invited her to stay until morning. She had almost taken him up on the offer, contemplating what she might say to Garrett to make her story believable. But she was already worried at that point that she wouldn't be able to get the scent of Kevin's cologne off of her blouse. She had brought a change of clothes and left them in the car, but she knew Garrett's sense of smell was good enough that he might still pick it up on her. He could always tell where she'd gone on days she'd walked in the park, and that was just a casual stroll around a field of grass. She had known if she'd stayed that night, no amount of clever wordplay would convince her husband she wasn't cheating. His nose was just too good. She had taken the long way home because she could. Because she felt unwanted, then, in her own home.

Because she knew when she walked in she would get less than four words out of her husband; that Garrett wouldn't even leave his study to greet her, so common was it that her husband took his work home with him. And when she took the long way around that night, driving by LyraCorps, she hit Trajen with her car.

And here they were, so many months later.

And she was still sleeping with Kevin, sometimes.

But she didn't *want* to anymore. She had tried to break it off once a few weeks before that day, where she now found herself cooking lunch happily for her loving husband, who had been increasingly attentive in the months that Trajen lived with them. Kevin wouldn't let things end, though. Bren realized during the conversation that the man would say anything to keep the two of them from ending the times they spent together. She was ready to write the man off, and take the secret of their many trysts to her grave. But somewhere along the way, when she spoke with Kevin that day, Bren had started to feel like Kevin wasn't just going to *say* anything, but that he might *do* anything. What if Kevin told Garrett about their affair? Or worse, what if Kevin showed up at their house? Trajen was so overly friendly those first few weeks, this boy who seemed like he didn't know *anything* about life, he would probably still let a complete stranger in their house, even now. If you told Trajen you were a friend of the family, he'd ask you if you wanted anything to drink. Bren had just accepted that's how the boy was. She loved it, really. It made her want to take care of Trajen. So she had realized that Kevin had her cornered. She didn't even bother drawing their conversation to a close that day. She just hung up. Kevin texted her later on that night in the code they had developed. The text read, "Did you read that article about the fish last week in the Sun?" Translated, it meant that he wanted to see her at the hotel they went to sometimes, which was next to the newsstand downtown. When he said next week, he meant that weekend. Seeing the code on her phone had made her feel physically sick, she was so utterly finished with the man. But of course, she'd had to meet up with him. Maybe if she explained to him in person that they were through, he wouldn't act so crazy about parting ways.

Of course, it hadn't gone that way. Somehow, Kevin had managed to wear Bren down as they talked. It was a mixture of frustration, guilt, and raw giving up that led to them spending more of the time she had grown to loath together.

Bren was drawn away from her mind's eye then, as she made Garrett's plate. It wasn't anything fancy. Some peas and carrots, a little rice, fried together with some low-sodium soy sauce and an eighth of a chicken bouillon cube. She loved cooking fried rice during the day, though. It made the house smell just the right way to get her excited about cooking dinner later on, and the voracity with which Garrett always seemed to devour the midday meal made the whole thing really worth it for her. She set the plate down on the table, realizing Garrett had just gotten off the phone with Trajen. There was some sort of emergency, she could tell from Garrett's tone. She realized she was just as worried as her husband sounded. She knew in that moment she would do whatever she needed to when Trajen arrived, heading to the kitchen to grab the first-aid kid from her bathroom. As she sat back down, waiting for Trajen to walk in, her affirmation that this was the path she wanted her life to be taking was renewed all over again. She loved her husband dearly, passionately. And she loved Trajen dearly, like a son. This was her family now. If it were a picture, it would be one she'd want to hang in every room. She'd make Garrett bring a copy to his office. And when she looked at the picture, Kevin just wasn't in it. Bren didn't know what to do, but she was going to figure it out.

Chapter III

Trajen ran the whole way home. He kept thinking he'd get tired, but even as he opened the front door, he continued to wonder why he wasn't out of breath. The house could have been miles away still, and he knew he could have kept running. The thought that it might not be the adrenaline from the fight that had him going was worrying to him. When he woke up that morning, he felt safe. The world was starting to make sense to him.

Now, the safety seemed as fleeting as his dreams the previous night. His mind was an unending stream of questions. This was a state he normally enjoyed. Though, those questions had all been about the world around him. Now that the questions racing through his brain saw his life as their topic, he found his nerves completely on edge.

Why was he suddenly so strong? Was he always that strong? How did he run all the way here? Why did those men attack him? Who was the old man who stepped in? Why did they all smell the same way Garrett did?

Garrett and Bren were there to greet him. Bren had bandages and peroxide ready, as Trajen had told them he was in a fight. Trajen didn't feel right telling Bren how the fight had ended. But when he spoke to Garrett, and he thought of Garrett's musk, he knew it wouldn't come as a surprise to the man when he told him. Trajen had felt his nose snap itself into place on his run back to the house. He rinsed the dried blood off in the kitchen sink as Bren finished looking him over. She seemed happy there was no need for the bandages. For Trajen, it was just another question in his mind.

As they sat down at the table, Trajen went on to explain what happened. He recounted leaving Arnold's shop, and the musky smell in the diner that followed him as he walked. Bren's face was opposite to Garrett's as he relayed the details of the fight to them. Garrett's face changed only at the mention of the older man.

"And then I ran here," Trajen said. "The whole way. I practically sprinted. This is crazy, right?"

With a sigh and a look of reluctance, Garrett began to speak. "I can explain what's happening. I'm sorry, dear. Please don't be mad."

"What do you mean?" Bren asks. Her face is a mask of worry.

"Trajen, you're not human." Garrett allowed the words to sink into the moment before continuing, an almost inappropriate smile making its way onto his face. "Neither am I. I wasn't sure what you were until today, but Russel, the man who came to your rescue, called me after you did. You and I are Loren. You're a Peacebringer, I think. Russel and I, as well as the men that attacked you, are Lyra. No point in hiding it now, and we can't just ignore it if things like this are happening."

"What the HELL is a Lyra? Like LyraCorps? You're saying these are all men you work with!" Bren's face has gone fully from worry to confusion. Trajen had never heard her speak so loudly. *Is this what Bren sounds like when she yells?* Trajen wonders how she manages to yell and still sound so caring.

Hairs grow slowly from Garrett's face and arms as his features become more pointed, the ends of his nose and chin losing their curve to gain hard edges. "In a contemporary sense, a Lyra is a shapechanger. Though, many Lyra change into some form of canine. Changing into anything else now is a pretty infrequent occurance." Bren's eyes grow wider as she watches Garrett transform once again, back to his human form. "There are many races of Loren. Our history predates that of humans by a millennia or more. The Lyra, as you can imagine from LyraCorps' domination of the world market, have sat at the top of the Loren hierarchy for hundreds of years. But it wasn't always that way. There was a balance, once. It was kept by a race of dualities, the Peacebringers and their genetic mirrors, the Warmongers. I'm pretty sure Trajen is the former."

"Wait," Trajen said. "So there are more people like you?"

"There are many like me, yes. You're the first Peacebringer I've ever seen. Your race has been gone for a very, very long time." Garrett sat back in his chair, wishing for a cigarette in spite of quitting years ago. This, he thought, was a good time for a smoke.

"And there are other monsters?" Bren asked. She sat back in her chair, the emotion drained not just from her face, but seemingly from her entire person.

Trajen figured there wasn't really many other ways to react to finding out your husband was actually a dog-person. He knew he wasn't totally caught up on marriage or relationships. The whole romance thing still seemed so far off from his level of comprehension, but to him, it did seem like this was the sort of thing someone would be shocked to find out about their husband. Trajen recalled a documentary on couples that discussed the importance of pre-marriage topics. Money, life goals, and whether or not either person wanted children were definitely mentioned. He thought that maybe he should write a letter to tell the producers they neglected whether or not both people in the relationship were human.

"Oh, honey. We don't really like that word. But there are other types of Loren, yes. There are Dayrunners, Celebrants, Morkhavians, The Vampyr, Shadone, a race called The Wretched, and Golems who have been gone almost as long as Peacebringers and Warmongers. Honestly, I'm probably forgetting a few. This world is full of all kinds of things the average person has no idea exist."

"I...Jesus, Garrett. When were you going to tell me I married a werewolf?"

"Bren, relax. Lots of Loren marry outside their race. My line specifically is known to partner with humans. Less wolf and more dog, I guess. You know Suzy and Rick? He's a Morkhavian and she's a Celebrant. Celebrants can sprout shards of bone. That bracelet Suzy gave you for your birthday a few months back, I'm pretty sure she grew that and then carved it into that nice owl design for you. I think the paint she used is acrylic. Morkhavians eat necrotic flesh, which is why we never go to their house for dinner. I can't be *near* their fridge. Whenever Rick burps it takes everything I have not to leave the room."

"You said you knew the old man?" Trajen asked, trying to bring the conversation away from its current state. Bren was starting to look more troubled by the minute in spite of Garrett's efforts.

"Russel, yes. You don't remember, but he helped you escape LyraCorps the night Bren brought you home. Something isn't right, Trajen. It hasn't been for a while. LyraCorp's reach stretches into every industry. In the next decade, they plan to enact a global monopoly throughout all major avenues of business. Total world domination won't be far behind. I'm sure of it. Russel and I are part of the resistance. We've been working together for a long time to try and find a way to halt LyraCorp's plans. A little over a year ago, Russel heard about some holding facility built off the schematics at a LyraCorp location in some city we'd never heard of. LyraCorps has corporate headquarters all over the world, but we'd gotten information that the one here was different. I put in for a transfer after a little digging. It was blind luck that he found you that night; Russel was only supposed to gather information. A 'get in and get out' kind of thing. I'd gotten him a keycard and we'd mapped out the guard's rotations. But once he got to that lower level, the one that isn't supposed to be there, he refused to come back. Barely escaped after you did, too. It takes him a little longer to heal than the rest of us, age will do that. We've spent the last two months trying to keep The Hunters off your trail. They don't know you're here, in this house, we confirmed that before you got back. But they're obviously getting close. We got lucky again that it wasn't the primary unit you ran into. Those guys from the alley were grunts. Low-level Hunters, not even really on the proper Strike Team. When you put up a fight without their leader around, I'm not surprised they turned tail so quickly."

"That's something else I don't understand. How was I able to even *do* that? Those men felt like they weighed nothing." Trajen held up his hands for emphasis. The strength didn't feel like it was there any longer now that he'd calmed down, but he was worried if he didn't set his fists down gently he'd break Bren's kitchen table.

"The way I understand it, your race kept the balance between the others. I've always heard it was because they had the powers of all the other races. Certainly explains your strength and agility. The rest of us have weaknesses, too. Silver is a real thing for my kind. It's fatal if it gets into our bloodstream. Your kind are said to be without traditional weakness. You must have accessed some set of powers when you fought earlier."

It was a lot to take in. Trajen woke up that morning under the impression he understood the world around him, at least to a point. He was almost finished with the documentaries on his streaming service. He could speak at length about plenty of things. Then it took all of a day to wipe the slate clean again. He wasn't human, Garrett wasn't human, and for some reason Bren, who had gotten up from the table as he was talking with Garrett, was making coffee as the sun was setting. Coffee was meant for the morning. His life had gone completely upside down.

"So what happens now?" Trajen asked.

"For the time being, Russel and I keep working to make sure you're safe. Maybe your memories come back, maybe they don't. You've got to have some kind of precious info up there for LyraCorps to keep you so well hidden and off the map. But for now, everyone keeps up appearances."

"That's…that's it? I just go to class or something?" To Trajen the idea seemed ridiculous. He looked to Bren for affirmation that he wasn't wrong. The woman's back remained turned as she continued to fiddle with the coffee maker.

"We're pretty good with scents. The night you arrived, Russel put up a fake that led to the next state over. Other members of our team are already doing the same, so The Hunters, even the Strike Team, will be off your trail for now. If we break from character before we're ready, you never know who might notice. Write your professor an email and tell them you're sick today, but tomorrow you're back to work at Arnold's."

After Trajen had left the room, Bren poured the coffee for herself and her husband.

"You know," she said. "I think, somehow, I always knew you were different."

"Oh? So, how are you handling it, now that it's out in the open?" Garrett was worried. He and Bren met on a website for singles who wanted a childless lifestyle, but he saw the way she had taken to Trajen over what had almost turned into a full year. The change had happened so slowly, he almost didn't want to notice, knowing eventually she might have to learn that Trajen wasn't human, and likely would not age. The Resistance didn't have a solid plan for the Peacebringer just yet, but they were considering many things which involved taking Trajen to another city, utilizing him in any way they were able. Garrett tried not to think about how that would make Bren feel, as she had so obviously come to love and care for the boy.

"Ah, I think our marriage will make it," Bren said with a smile. "And honestly, Rick's breath always does smell *horrid*. How does Suzy put up with that?"

"Celebrants are known for their lack of most senses," Garrett said with a laugh. "But you're right. Rick can get pretty ripe here and there."

"Seriously, though. Are we going to be okay? Are we…safe?" Bren put her hand on Garrett's shoulder. She thought about how invigorated their marriage had become since Trajen had been there. Suddenly the distance between them before made sense to her. Her husband was trying to take down an *empire*. Looking in his eyes, all she wanted was for him, and she realized *only him,* to comfort her.

"Hey," Garrett said as he drew his wife's chair closer to his. "I won't ever let anyone hurt you. I promise. No one knows Trajen is here, I've made sure of that. I will *always* protect you, and I'm watching out for Trajen the best I can. Though it looks like he can do okay on his own." Garrett stopped to kiss Bren on the forehead before he continued. "There may be one problem, though. It's a small one right now."
"What's that?"

"Trajen's race, which includes the Warmongers, is naturally curious. And he wasn't the only one who broke out from the facility that night."

Chapter IV

Edie and Finley had finally made a name for themselves. It wasn't just any mercenary group that got the chance to speak before The Reach, the ruling house of Celebrant nobles. Celebrant culture was a mishmash of different traditions. There were three ruling houses left, The Reach, The Far, and The Breadth. Edie often wondered if it was a coincidence that there seemed to be a unifying theme behind the names, and was sure many other Celebrants had often wondered the same. Finley was his best friend. They had come up together, training since they were ten in as many styles of fighting as they could. Because of the haphazardness with which their race seemed to draw influence from the many different peoples the world had to offer, there was no shortage of styles of self-defense available to the budding mercenaries over the years.

Edie and Finley had managed to work hard enough, watching each other's backs well enough, that they were the top men for one of the most well-known Celebrant mercenary bands in the world. The two had traveled everywhere twice over, first to learn how to handle themselves, then for work, more than once being asked to protect the very people who had taught them. It was only recently the two had branched off to start their own band. It had apparently been a wise move, as they were now being summoned by The Reach.

The two men, who were similar in build and disposition, slowly grew bone around their vital areas. A noble summons is an exciting thing, but they were no amateurs. Even the larger bands, like the one they had recently left, were required to prove themselves before being given a contract. This was not their first time in the residence of The Reach. They'd been out before with some of the men and women they may be facing today. Secretly, Edie hoped he'd have to fight Sandra. She was a spritely woman, much thinner than the average Celebrant, her bones somehow sharper than many others he'd run into. They had fought once before, her skill almost equal to his own. She could drink like he could, too, in spite of her diminutive size. He still remembered the way she-

"Welcome, gentleman." The houseman said, as the two entered a magnificent library. A sea of books lined shelf after shelf, surrounding the entire space. In the far end of the library was a luxurious sofa.

On it sat Lady Reach, ruling matron. Lady Reach was a picture of pure regality and class, one leg crossed over the other as she waited for the men to enter. She sat in stark contrast to everyone around her, including the other nobles in the room. Her dress was an eggshell white, matching her hair and the shards of bone strewn through it, shaping it into a hairstyle which made it nearly impossible to tell where the hair ended and the bone began. Each of the small shards, the men knew, were more than simple clips. Like other Celebrant ruling nobles, Lady Reach's deadliness was well known. The houseman pointed to where Edie and Finley were meant to stand, making their introduction to Lady Reach. "May I present Mister Edie Rent and Mister Finley Rent to the Lady Reach." The houseman then quickly excused himself from the room, leaving the two only a few yards away from Reach matron as well as four other Celebrants. Two appeared to be nobles, in clothing nearly as fine as Lady Reach's, while the others wore full combat gear, not unlike the gear Edie and Finley wore.

"Hello," A noble to the right said. "Lady Reach has head of the Rent band. She has asked me to inform you that she thinks the name is *very* clever." The noble paused to snicker for a moment. "Thank you for coming today, on such short notice. This contract is very dear to The Reach."

"Is it protection, or destruction?" Edie asked.

"No questions." The nobleman said. "Not yet. You know the rules, after all. Lady Reach would also like me to inform you, before we begin, that she was *very* impressed with your video CV. I must say I was as well. It is not often we find a band who is so…committed…to advertising. It was quite refreshing."

"Well, thank you very much, your lord and ladies." Edie and Finley bowed as one.

"Yes, thank you." Finley said. "We're really trying to redefine the mercenary experience. Bring it into the new age. Our goal is to give you more than just protection or the dastardly alternative. We want to give you an experience. A story."

"Yes, very nice." The nobleman said. "Now, let's begin. The bout will not last longer than five minutes. If our warriors sustain more damage than yourselves, as is the custom, you will be given the contract."

The two warriors at the side of the nobles stepped forward, quickly releasing long shards of bone from the inside of their forearms. They came at Edie and Finley with perfectly executed forward thrusts of their arms, the sharp bones shooting for eyes and other softer areas on the mercenaries' bodies. Edie and Finley bobbed right and left, dodging each of the thrusts deftly, so that the four of them appeared not unlike a synchronized dance number, so in tune were the two sets of warriors with each other.

Edie broke the dance first, now finished growing the weapon along his backside. The mercenary broke off a large, heavy bone from underneath his gear, nearly as long as his body. He swung it wide, forcing the warrior attacking him backwards. Edie quickly jabbed forward, meeting the blocking arms of the Reach warrior, the long bone chipping slightly from the hit. Edie quickly turned and swung the blade wide again, over himself, swiping low at his adversary's legs. The Reach warrior attempted to hop over the swing, a move which Edie had hoped for. As the Reach warrior's feet left the ground, Finley, who preferred to fight with much smaller weapons, forced his opponent backwards with a straight kick, turning immediately to throw the shard of bone in his right hand at Edie's opponent, who could not hope to dodge while airborne. The bone shard cut the Reach warrior on the cheek, revealing a long line of blood on the side of his face which quickly bled down onto his shoulder. Momentarily stunned from the maneuver, Edie pressed the advantage, jabbing forward again with his two-handed bone, forcing the warrior into a corner. Edie backed his opponent up until he was behind the other Reach warrior, who continued to fight to a stand-still with Finley.

The nobleman called out the two-minute mark.

Positioned then behind Finley's opponent, Edie forced his opponent back once more before the Reach warrior could regain his footing and engage in a counter attack. He swung wide again, taking one step forward, though he did not stop when he returned to his starting position, continuing the swing, letting the large bone fly at the back of the other Reach warrior's head. The bone hit the warrior hard, who then hit the marble flooring even harder, the skin on his forehead splitting on impact. Finley threw another small shard of bone at Edie's opponent, who managed to catch the missile with one hand and throw it back at the Rent mercenary. Finley ducked to avoid the missile, growing two more small bones from the center of his hands as he ran forward. Edie grew similarly sized bones along his forearms to the straight weapons the Reach warrior still had attached to himself, and the two mercenaries surrounded their prey.

Edie and Finley wasted no time in beating on their remaining opponent. To the Reach warrior's credit, many of the blows Edie and Finley landed were superficial. The point was not to kill their opponents, though. Simply to do more damage to them than they might receive.

When the nobleman called time, the Rent band had not only sustained less damage, they hadn't been harmed at all.

Both of the Reach warriors were escorted from the room, the warrior with the busted forehead practically carried away. The two nobles took either arm of Lady Reach, the three of them leading the way to a parlor just as luxurious as the library. Natural light fell into the room from a skylight, causing Lady Reach's dress to sparkle as she walked. She sat again on another couch of similar design to the previous, again crossing her legs as she did, a small smile on her face.

"You two work well together." Lady Reach said.

"Thank you, my lady." Edie replied. "Known each other since we were kids. Just kind of worked out that way."

"What made you form your own band? The money? The power? Or do you simply *love* the work?"

"Probably a combination of the three," Finley said, looking to Edie who shared the sentiment. "You do enough of this work, you get to knowing how much more of the upsides you don't see when you're just a member of the band, rather than a founder. Where we were before was great. Tough band to leave behind, no doubt. But the perks to having our own band…well…I'm sure you know how it is."

"Indeed. Wonderful, boys. *Splendid.* Please, have a seat." The houseman from before appeared as if from nowhere, pushing in front of him two oversized chairs, placing them both quickly behind the mercenaries. As big as the men were, the chairs were bigger, the backs two feet higher than either of the men's heads as they sat. "I would like to hire you for a destruction contract. Single target. Not much in the way of intel. We don't know much other than the city we believe her to be in." Each of the nobles handed one of the mercenaries a thin manila folder. Inside was the contract, a copy for each of them, and a single piece of paper with driving directions to their destination.

"Lady Reach would like this done as quickly as possible." The noble who had spoken before said.

"There's no picture," Edie said. "How will we know who we're after?"

"When you arrive at the city, you'll need to go...*ahem*...down. You'll be looking for Spice."

The Rent mercenaries' eyes lit up. They knew who Spice was. Everyone did. The Wretched were not known for having reputations. To their knowledge, Spice was the only one. They knew him as many things: A trader of information and secrets, an arms dealer and manufacturer; there were even stories of Spice's propensity for cooking, which was apparently how he had gotten his namesake.

"Spice is in...er...Spice is *under* this city?" Edie asked.

"He is. He'll be expecting you, as well. We believe he is offering refuge to your mark, at least occasionally. And if he is not, we have paid him handsomely to point you both in the right direction."

"Well, it isn't much to go on." Edie replied.

"But we'd certainly be remiss if we let this opportunity pass us by," Finley interjected. "We happily accept the contract."

Both of the mercenaries looked over the documents they had been given, half-heartedly examining the legal phrasing contained within. It was all the usual, standard jargon. Turning the pages was more a show of respect, both men knew, as well as part of their branding strategy. This was their third contract that year, having only recently coming off of a protection job for The Far, who wanted to ensure their prince would be safe on vacation. What the two men really cared about, though, was the number on the bottom of the final page. The line showing how much money they stood to gain from completing the contract. The number, they saw, was larger than the previous two contracts combined.

It was shaping up to be a great year for the Rent band.

Chapter V

Trajen dreamt fitfully. He was not one for remembering the things he dreamt, the fragments he woke with each morning often nothing more than a rapid blur of images. On this night, however, the images in his sleeping mind played more clearly.

He saw each of the races, gathered in a great hall. Though he could not remember having seen them before, he knew them now by name. Large pillars held up an impossibly high ceiling, beautiful carvings of stories long lost to time's embrace all along the walls. He felt that he was among others like him, other Peacebringers and Warmongers stood proudly by his side. His eyes scanned the bodies nearest to him, but their faces were blurred and unclear. A sense of dread and worry filled his body as the dream directed his gaze towards the front of the hall. He was not so used to being in control of his dreams. More than once, Bren had commented on how rare that is for some people. Lucid dreaming, she said, did not come naturally to most. Quickly Trajen realized he was not completely in control, but being directed on where to go and look. He felt a small bit of dread, though he was unsure why. His curiosity rapidly overriding his need to be the driver in what he saw, Trajen allowed himself to ride out the images. He was content to learn as much as he could.

His gaze turned to his right, where one face had become clear. A powerful Lyra stood tall above the rest, his hair impossibly black in contrast to the white stone behind him. A line of silver ran from the top of his head and down his back. The great wolf began to give a speech, though the words were lost to Trajen. While he could not hear what the giant werewolf was saying, his dream gave him the meaning behind the words. The wolf called for action, an answer the injustices his race had faced.

The great wolf called for war.

Though only a dream, Trajen could feel the power of the oversized werewolf. It reverberated clearly throughout his awareness. With passion fitting of a leader commanding a powerful force, the great wolf's speech had ended. Throughout the hall, the air stood still. Trajen looked around him, at the others of his kind. He realized they stood in pairs, one Peacebringer to one Warmonger. Trajen turned to his left to see the woman he knew to be tied to him. The bond felt natural, and the woman smiled as she looked at him. He could see that her teeth were pointed, but did not feel threatened from her presence. Without a doubt, she was his friend.

All eyes turned to the Peacebringers and the Warmongers, whose blessing is required to declare war. Transgressions committed against another race are often met with swift justice at the hands of Trajen and the others like him. He remembers this. In his dream, his eyes fill with tears, an effect he could feel spill over into his sleeping form. Though some of his race felt worse about it than others, they had already come to an agreement. As one, were people are unanimous in their decision.

A Great War it would be.

Trajen woke clutching to the dream he'd left, trying desperately to hold on to everything he'd seen. Rather than begin the ritual he'd come to work through each morning, he made his way towards Bren and Garrett's room. Pausing a moment to ensure they were awake, he knocked lightly on their bedroom door. He'd made the mistake of barging in only once, a few months ago. The position he had caught them in was…embarrassing. At least for Bren, as he understood it. He always knocked first now.

Garrett answered shirtless, his body below his neck revealing itself to be engulfed in hair. "What's up, Trajen?"
"Garrett, are you guys both awake? I had a dream. I think it was a memory. I don't know, it might be important."

Bren called from inside the room for Trajen. As they settled, Trajen relayed the night's events, recalling as many details of his dream as possible. He told them of the great hall, and the other races he had seen filling the space. He told them, too, of the giant wolf.

"Mordacity," Garrett said. "He's led the Lyra for over a thousand years. The rest of the world knows him now as Morgan Wolfstone, CEO of Lyracorp. You're right about the stripe, and his size. It's like I was saying last night. Lyra have as many variations in their DNA as other canines. Mordacity's bloodline, like Great Danes and Irish Wolfhounds, have always been much larger than other Lyra. The biggest of us normally live the shortest life-spans, but he has been alive for centuries."

"So where would you be, in comparison to dogs, dear?" Bren asked. Trajen noted a playful smile on her lips as she did so.

"Probably somewhere between Border Collie and Labrador. Maybe a little German Shepherd thrown in the mix; Schneider is a family name, after all." Garrett's answer was swift, and obviously somewhat practiced. Was this a common question for the Lyra who took on canine forms? "Anyway, you'd also be right about the power you felt, Trajen. Mordacity is different from other Lyra in more than his size. In combination with his incredibly long life, he's said to have other abilities, as well."

"Like what?" Trajen asked.

"I mean, I heard he can read minds. And phase through walls. Someone said once at a retreat that they had the honor of joining a hunting party, with Mordacity at the lead. The story goes that as they closed on this trio of deer, Mordacity instructed everyone to wait beyond the clearing, outside the range of the deer's senses. The man who told me the story said his curiosity got the better of him, so he climbed a nearby tree to watch our leader at work. He said Mordacity, as he approached the deer, went without his Lyra form and transformed back into the guise of a human. And as Mordacity got closer, he said, they stood perfectly still. Apparently, Mordacity was able to exert his will so strongly, with such force, that the deer all collapsed in the clearing."

"What, so he can *look* things to death?"

"It doesn't end there. The man told me what happened next was what really had him rattled. Mordacity's mouth opened wide, impossibly wide for his human form, and from his mouth released what the man described as bloody tendrils which shot towards each of the deer. Each tendril had some kind of sharp appendage at the end, which sliced the flesh of each deer, the marks appearing similar to what Mordacity's giant claws might have left. The man said he was so shocked by what he saw, he nearly feel from the tree he was in. Afraid Mordacity had heard him in his spying, he jumped down immediately. He said when Mordacity made his way back to them, he was again in his Lyra form. No one ever asked how their leader had killed the deer, I guess. It makes sense that they all assumed he did it as they might have. But my buddy knew the truth. We had been drinking all night, him especially. After everyone went to bed, we were the only two left by the fire in the seating near the bar, and he told me everything."

"Do you believe him? You think Mordacity can do all these things?"

"I don't know, Trajen. Right now, all I'm concerned with is keeping you safe and working towards removing Lyracorps strangle hold over everything. Something isn't right, with Mordacity especially, and I know in my heart things will only get worse from here." Garrett turned to his wife, aware that he was sharing more of his other side with her in this conversation than she might be ready for. "How you doin', Bren?"

"At this point, just starting to accept it I guess. Maybe still in shock a little bit. Mainly I'm trying to decide if I like the Border Collie assessment. Obviously the whole Mordacity thing is scary. You know, because this guy is sending people after Trajen, and was keeping him locked up in some secret underground facility. But I've got to be honest, I'm not sure what makes you think you're as clever as a Collie. I saw a video of what that knew the name of over a hundred of her toys. And she found all of them first try. You can hardly remember where you parked the car when we got to the market!" Bren finished her statement with a smile as she got up to get ready for her day, kissing her husband on the cheek. Step one was to start making the house breakfast, of course.

Garrett watched her leave, looking back at Trajen as she exited the room. "God," he said, "I love that woman."

Downstairs, Bren began the process of collecting the things she would be cooking and preparing. The ritual was something she realized she missed once it had begun again. That morning, like many mornings before, she wondered if she had forgone her true calling. If working in some kind of culinary profession hadn't been what she was meant for, rather than the nursing job she had now. She certainly liked being a nurse. It was fulfilling in all the ways she wanted a profession to be, and the paycheck was nice. But she *loved* cooking. She always had.

Either way, breakfast isn't going to make itself, she thought. As she did each morning, Bren first set a kettle of water on the stove to boil, and made her way to the porch to collect the day's newspaper. As she set it on the kitchen table, the headline gave her immediate pause.

CITY RESPONDS TO GRUESOME MURDER.

Bren scanned the story as the water began to boil. Though their time in town was short thus far, she had yet to even hear of something so vile happening here. The news story detailed, with vivid imagery, the grotesque nature of the killing. It said that the head of the body had hung slack, far removed from the neck and shoulders, a single strand of sinew its only remaining connective tissue. The reporter used the phrase "nearly decapitated," five times throughout the front page telling. The water now nearing its boil, Bren made her way to the laundry room, retrieving the day's scrubs from their dryer. As she reentered the kitchen, the kettle gave its familiar whistle, and Bren placed her scrubs on the counter without a second thought. The day's paper lay beneath, the imagery in the story doing an excellent job of keeping the way the crime scene looked fresh in her mind's eye.

As Bren cracked each egg into the pan, she mused at their sizzling. The sound was always one that made her feel happy, even hopeful. But the gruesome news story, coupled with the news of Trajen's uneasy dreaming, only served to muddy her mind with worry. Still, solitary worry never accomplished anything, she knew. If they were going to find success in each of their tasks, recovering Trajen's memory, halting the plans of Lyracorp, Bren knew she would have to keep the lines of communication open.

Although every part of her wanted all of the bad stuff to go away, although she desperately wanted to simply make breakfast for her husband and their guest, take a shower, and go to work, she knew that couldn't happen. As she placed the bacon on its skillet, she called upstairs to Garrett and Trajen.

They needed to read the paper.

Bren had her own business that day as well. It was the day she was going to be firm when she saw Kevin. She would tell him in no uncertain terms that they were over. And she had a plan to make sure that whatever happened afterwards she could handle. Kevin would probably scream, or cry. That didn't matter to her. Manipulative people will do that; go through the spectrum of emotions to get what they want. It was what might come after that she worried about.

If Kevin were to show up at her home, or confront her husband. Then, she might have a problem. But she realized that morning, she had already planned for such a thing. Bren and Kevin had only ever communicated via a messaging service. When he called her phone, it through an application on her phone, not the traditional route with her phone number. She had actually never given her number to the man. When she ended things, all she would need to do was break her phone. When she went to the store and got a new one, she would have to re-download all of her apps. Even if the messaging app was backed up and transferred over, it wouldn't transfer over with her chat logs saved. And it would be her last lie. A small pang of guilt touched her soul as she thought about lying to her husband at all, but then she thought of recent events.

Her husband wasn't human.

He'd hid that from her for a long time. She was sure there were other secrets the man was keeping. Like, who were these other people, or *Loren*, that he was working with in secret? Bren still hadn't met the older gentleman her husband talked about. There had to be others. It couldn't just be the two of them trying to "bring down" LyraCorps. And Bren didn't know *anything* about that. Really, as much truth as had come out recently, there was still a lot husband was asking her to be okay with doing behind the scenes. So she would keep her own secret, too. It would only be a lie until the end of the day, and when it was over she would never tell anyone about it. She planned on sending a text message to her husband when she was at the cellular store. It would say something about how she'd had managed to leave her phone on her trunk, rummaging through her purse or something. That she'd forgotten it was there, and wouldn't you know it, managed to run it over. She'd tell him this was her new phone she was texting him on. And then she would mention some creepy guy following her around the store. Knowing her husband, he would ask if she needed him there. She would say no, and that an associate was going to walk her to her car. That she was fine, and she'll call security before she gets back to work so they can escort her in if she still feels unsafe. Then Kevin could do whatever he wanted. He could show up at the house and cry and yell and threaten her livelihood, and all she would have to do is act surprised and say, "That's him. That's the man from the store. Oh my god, that man is *crazy. "* It would be far-fetched, sure. But the believability of a lie hinges on the details. Hers would all match up.

Bren's phone buzzed in her pocket as the boys sat down at the table, and she excused herself to go to the bathroom. She pulled her phone from her pocket and unlocked the screen, seeing there was a notification from Kevin on the app. Bren didn't like what she read. Kevin had to cancel. She would have to wait to break things off with him, knowing if she didn't do it in person she couldn't fully control the situation the way she wanted to. She thought maybe the man had been suspicious, that he had known she planned to end things with him. Perhaps that was why he canceled. She didn't like having to wait to end things, but he asked to reschedule for the next day. That would just have to do. She didn't want the man to be too suspicious.

She'd have to lie for another day.

∙∙

High above the Lyracorp compound, in an expansive corner office, another soul was also reading the news. A large flat screen television displayed the town's local morning anchors introducing the story on Channel six, as well. As Mordacity finished reading the written story, he watched the anchors relay the facts the paper presented.

As he listened, he grew angry.

This was his town. His territory. He *owned* it.

As the segment ended, the anchors continuing on with the morning news, a hand rapped on his office door. He could smell who it was before they'd knocked, pleased at least a portion of that which was meant to bend to his will was doing as it was told. Roper, his second in command and leader of his most elite hunting pack, entered his office. Roper was one of a handful of Lyra that Mordacity did not show open disdain for. Indeed, the two were companions and friends. Beyond any other Lyra alive, Mordacity trusted Roper implicitly. They would speak now in absolute confidence.

"I have bad news, Mordacity."

"Everyone does this morning, it seems. Continue, then." Mordacity's sat back in his office chair, his form huge even in its human guise. His eyes blinked slowly as an instinctual sign of calm. "We are still unable to locate the prisoners. A portion of the pack tracked the boy back into town, but he managed to escape with help from the old one." Roper named Russel with disdain prevalent in his tone, sitting into a chair opposite Mordacity. The lieutenant's blood was rushing, but not from fear, as any other Lyra's blood might rush when so close to their fearsome leader. Roper's blood rushed from anger. He was a Lyra who hated to lose, one who was used to finding his prey quickly. The men looking for the boy were his, after all. He had trained them well.

"The old one. I can't say I'm surprised. His line always has been particularly...clever. If a little self-serving. So stereotypical, that one. You know I watched his father bite his own foot off when caught under a rock? And now his son, making the attempt at being clever by masking the boy's scent. Annoying, really."

"He's managed to stay quite quick, as well. He and the boy put three of the pack down and ran off, presumably together."

"And what of the boy's abilities? Are you saying he left our hunters alive?"

"Just barely, yes. They said he acts as if he does not know what he is capable of. They nearly had him subdued, in spite of his rapid healing in the sunlight. The old one took them by surprise, and they said it was as if the boy suddenly realized he was much stronger than them all. He threw Thrask into the wall so hard one of his ribs shattered. He says it's *still* mending. If Hector wasn't a Lyra, the blow he took was so strong he'd probably be dead as well. The boy was either holding back or the poison still holds his memory at bay."

"I'd wager on the latter, Rope. I made that poison myself."

"Of course. So, what are our next steps? We lost the scent, but I swear to you I can find it again." Roper stood up quickly, expecting his leader to affirm the self-assigned directive.

"No....No." Mordacity said with a smile. Roper hadn't seen the man's smile in at least a decade. "Haven't you seen the news? This is no time to be hunting some escaped Loren. We captured the two of them once before. We can do so again."

"What would you have us do?"

"For now," Mordacity said, his form changing instantaneously, his voice deepening to match his newfound size, "We have a Vampyr to hunt." In spite of his leader's calm demeanor, Roper skulked backwards as Mordacity changed. He could feel his leader's anger, the rage seeping strongly from the air around them. Roper knew what caused the anger the same as any other Loren alive would know.

The Vampyr were supposed to be gone.

A short distance away from the Lyracorp compound, where multiple floors worth of Lyra felt the rage of their powerful leader, Trajen walked to class. Safe for now from Mordacity's hunters, he thought again about the fight from the day before, and how easily he'd beaten the Lyra he encountered. It made him wonder how strong he was. Garrett had said he had the abilities of all the other races. Could that be true? If he happened upon a decaying pigeon, or some unfortunate road-kill on his way back from class, would he be overtaken with the urge to *eat* it? Could he sprout wings from his back and fly across campus? If he thought about growing a shard of bone from the top of his wrist, perhaps in the shape of a spike, would it happen?

The idea was both exciting, and somewhat frightening. Certainly not something he wanted to test in a crowded campus setting. Bren told him once this city was rated as one of the "quietest" for its size, in one of the periodicals she liked to read every week. Trajen wasn't sure what was supposed to be so quiet about it, but to him it seemed there were always people walking around or nearby when it didn't benefit him. The street had been deserted when he was attacked, but he had to avoid dozens of people as he ran home, afraid they would see how quickly he was running. On this day, the campus was full of other college students. Perhaps some of them were Loren, and wouldn't think twice at seeing spikes of bone sprout from his forehead. But it wasn't worth the risk. He would wait until he was safe inside Bren and Garrett's home, tucked away in the silence of his room, before he tried to determine if he truly possessed any of the other races abilities. He was obviously strong, and had much more stamina than he felt. As desperately as he wanted to explore himself, it would need to wait until he could do so in private.

As he neared the door to his next class, he began to pull a textbook from his bag, a tingling sensation building behind his ears. For a moment, the tingling grew stronger, a high pitched noise playing just at the edge of his hearing. The sensations startled him, and he looked around to determine their source. Early for class, there was no one in the hallway, no one in the classroom. He was alone, as far as he could tell. The tingling quickly subsided, the noise fading along with it. After another moment of scanning, Trajen sat within the classroom, studying before the lesson began. The sound almost instantly forgotten.

Outside the building, walking across a small section of grass, a young woman made her way to the taco shop across the street. As she left campus, certain no one was looking at her, she focused her will, her left arm straight down her side. Before crossing the street, a small shard of bone shot itself free from her pointer finger, a muffled *'tink'* the only indication of the event as the bone struck the asphalt. A small smile graced her lips as she realized she had been successful.

Pulling open the door to the restaurant, her eyes flashed a myriad of colors.

From the pages of Hrath's Golemnic Tome. Vol 1. The Lyra.

When the Lyrans arrived, they were beautiful. I recall seeing my first specimen as I was bathing, a week-long event for any Golem born in the same era as me. Each morning before the sun rose, I would layer myself in the wonderful, cold earth, and wait for it to dry and crust in the midday sun. Each evening I would rinse off in the lake before me, then rest through the night. I had nearly finished the sixth day of the ritual, when I was greeted by a man from the woods. He was bold in his action, a trait I imagined was brought on by his size. He was the largest man I'd ever seen. He inspected me for a time and I allowed him to do so freely. Mine is a race for whom time would have little meaning, if we did not provide it with such. Each step I took was only a moment for me, though for this man it must have been an hour. Eventually, I realized he was waiting for me to move again, as he must have seen me applying the dirt to my body.

I made my way more quickly to the lake again, the dirt falling in clumps away from me to reveal my obsidian nature. In my mind, I was sure my speed had been the man's speed. But when I turned to him for conversation, wanting to learn of his origins, he was gone. Instead, a great bear had found its way into the area. I had not heard the animal arrive, though I was sure its presence had ultimately caused the man to leave. I have found the strength of men to be their creativity, though I know that is because naturally they are very vulnerable. The bear and I shared the clearing and the lake for a time. Perhaps a few minutes, or hours. With the man gone, I had stopped giving as much care to the passing of the sun ahead. My kind can live lifetimes moving nothing but their mind. Time, in its infinite relativity, does not treat us as it does others. But I had decided my cleaning was done, and would be moving on again.

Then, to my surprise, the bear turned into the man!

I had never seen such a thing before. The humans had only just arrived on the earth, learning rapidly how to rely on nature for sustenance.

Many of them followed the herds of their prey, and though I had seen some learn the value of seeds and rich soil, I had seen few who kept their lives in a static area. I know now that this man-bear was not the first Lyran, he was simply the first I had come to see. My mind came so quickly to the present as he released his animal form that I startled him with how quickly my questions came, causing him to revert back to his bear form immediately. I apologized profusely for the transgression, assuring him I meant no harm. I could not blame him for being startled, of course. There has not been a time where my kind have not made themselves scarce upon the world. Millions of each race live their entire lives without seeing one such as me. It stood to reason that a talking body made of black, shined stone would give the man a cause for concern.

When he was again in the form of a man, our dialogue began.

I kept myself in his present moments, taking in the world by the second, something I was unfamiliar with then but happy to explore. I was delighted to see that he spoke the common tongue of the humans. "I have never seen one such as you." I said.

"I would say the same of you." He replied.

"What is your name?" I asked.

"They call me Second Father. Though when I was young, I was known as Cathbad. Do you have a name?"

"I do," I replied. "Let me see if I can remember it. It has been so long since I have had use for such a thing." It took me a moment to recall the name my soul had been given. "I believe my name is Hrath."

"Hrath is a strong name." Second Father said.

"Thank you."

"Where do you come from, Hrath?"

"The earth, mostly. Deep below, where the ground is very, very hot. Where do you come from?"

"I too come from the earth, of course. All things do. My people live not far from here."

"Are they like you? May I see them?" I asked. Second Father thought for a moment. "Yes. Come with me."

We made our way through a copse of trees, eventually finding a trail that took us through the thick forest. The trail branched in two directions, and we chose the westernmost path, each step of mine done with care so not to disturb the creatures in the forest around me. Second Father, Cathbad, led me carefully, sensing my intention. I could hear his people, before I could see them. The sounds of laughter nearly assaulted us as we came closer to the Lyran camp.

There were many structures, made of wood and mud. Plenty of wheat, so they would not need to worry about a barren winter, though I recall a pen for sheep as well. It was a beautiful village of beautiful people. Though, they were not quite people, at least as I had come to know the term. As the children ran and played, a myriad of appendages from other animals came and went on their bodies. Some children's legs changed mid step, their stride unbroken as they hopped along as a rabbit. Others lost their balance, as children do, a tail sprouting from their behind to help right them. Even in their human guises, they climbed on everything. Men with great oxen forms pulled plows in their fields. Women with long feline tongues groomed the children in the brief moments they sat still. There had been a moment, as the people in the village viewed my presence, where the air seemed to hang still. The moment passed as soon as their eyes met with Second Father's, though. He had brought me to their home. For them, it seemed, that was enough.

"Your village is beautiful, Second Father."

"Thank you, Hrath. Have you never seen people like us before?" Cathbad beamed at the question. He was a proud man, of that there was no doubt. Proud of himself, and proud especially of his kind.

"I have not. Is this common? Are all people now gifted with aspects of other animals?"

"Not all, no. These children are the third generation. My father was the first of our kind. He was our First Father, as I am our Second."

"I see. How did this happen?"

"We are blessed by our Mother, the earth. Other people live in fear of animals. We do not. Our people respect nature, and know the balance of our world. Because of this, our Mother has allowed us to transcend, and become more than simple men and women. My thoughts are not always the thoughts of a man. Sometimes my thoughts are that of a great bear, as you have seen. My body is the bridge between both, connecting my soul, the human soul within me, to nature, the soul of the bear."

"Well, it is a beautiful thing. I would love to know more about your people, and your culture."

"Just as our Mother welcomes those who would know her, so do we welcome you, Hrath. You may stay as long as you like. Though, if you stay too long, my men in the fields may put you to work. Just because they can *pull a plow, that does not mean they* like *it!" Second Father laughed and patted his hand upon my obsidian arm. He would do so many, many more times over the years. He was a good spirited man until the end, laughing until the moment death came to take him.*

I often asked myself, living in the village of the Lyra, how could they have become as they were? If the earth were granting such things, my kind would have already known. It was not unheard of for magic to give a man the ability to change his shape, but the children? I saw many Lyran births as I lived among them. I knew many Lyran healers. Not a drop of magic to be found. If it was magic that allowed these people to shift their features, it was a very strong spell, and it had been cast long before I had ever arrived. Could it have been evolution? Some random combination of genes producing a specimen able to pass on their DNA? Was the first Lyran some sort of truly monstrous individual which had managed to copulate with enough of the opposite sex to produce a village's worth of offspring? Truthfully, I do not have the answer. I'm certain no one ever will. Whether or not the Lyrans were a natural occurrence, which did not change the fact that they had, indeed, occurred.

And they were not going anywhere.

Eventually I left the small village, which I knew would soon become a large city. Third Father, a man named Cohp, relinquished his title. He believed the earth wanted more for his people than their simple village. They had become experienced with nearby people, and traders who traveled between the many sects of people. Cohp believed his group was meant to rule all. I left before I saw him try.

It is often said that war has many advantages, though I cannot say whether or not I agree. Culture is shared just as often as it is taken. War was the road the early Lyra walked, though. Their soldiers, and the progeny of such individuals, spread far and wide in the ancient world. Far even for those who did not truly grasp how large, or small, the earth is.

In my last waking moments before a well-earned rest, I surveyed the parts of the earth I enjoyed, capturing the images I wished to take with me into my dreams. The village was a city, as I knew it would be. My favorite lake had lost depth, but still remained. And everywhere I looked, even amid the villages which had begun as human settlements, sometimes hidden away from prying eyes, were the Lyra. The race had gone beyond simple survival, becoming instead abundantly fruitful.

Chapter VII

"Can anyone tell me what implicit bias is?" The man at the front of the classroom walked calmly from his desk to the whiteboard. He removed the cap from a dry-erase marker, writing the words IMPLICIT BIAS large at the top of the board. He then turned back to the class, eyebrows raised, waiting for an answer.

Silence.

"No one?"

Trajen raised his hand.

"Yes, Trajen? Please."

"Implicit bias is when someone unconsciously holds either a positive or negative attitude towards a person, thing, or group."

"That's correct. Can you give us an example?"

"Well, the one in the book..." Trajen started.

He was quickly cut off by the professor. The man's dress shirt hung loose on his thin frame, his shoulders hunched. The glasses he wore nearly fell free of his face, he spoke so quickly. "Not an example from the book. There's one in particular I'm thinking of, relevant to right here in this city. Anyone?" The professor paused for a moment, though the man clearly had his own agenda when it came to the lecture.

Trajen was unsure for a moment if he was supposed to know the example the professor wanted, but now it was clear that anyone could have raised their hand and they, too, would have been wrong.

"Two years ago, LyraCorps was facing allegations of favoritism in the form of gender discrimination. Then, there was not a woman to be found in a single managerial role at LyraCorps. After failing to cover up what was on public record, they did what any corporation with that kind of money and power does: They hired some sociologists. They conducted a *study*. A study which *proved* that the hiring staff at LyraCorps were simply *suffering* from implicit bias. All of them. It wasn't the company that was at fault, simply the people they had trusted to ensure they were an equal opportunity employer. And in the end, their employees weren't at fault either, because they were suffering from biases they did not know they had. And now, their staff is exactly in line with Equal Opportunity guidelines and standards."

The young woman next to Trajen raised her hand. "So, does implicit bias actually exist?" She asked.

"Of course it does. Isn't a lie always better when it's wrapped up in the truth? But if you think that *every* hiring manager at LyraCorps was experiencing the same psychological phenomenon, you've got another thing coming."

"Well doesn't that…I don't know…make LyraCorps kind of *insidiuos?*" The girl asked the question unsure of herself, as if the phrase itself were ridiculous.

She slunk down in her chair as she finished the question, her physical embarrassment mirroring how unsure she was in that moment, but the professor only smiled. It was a broad smile, though it hardly reached his eyes.

"A conversation for another time, I think." The professor looked down to check the time on his watch. "Look at that. Class is dismissed." As Trajen gathered his things to leave class, he could feel the professor's eyes upon him, his peripheral vision revealing the continuing of the same broad, almost fearsome smile. Though he was not afraid of the man, he felt as though others ought to be, with a smile like that.

Walking out of class, Trajen passed by a woman carrying a sack lunch obviously meant for the professor, as she walked by the students still trying to exit the room as she entered. Before getting too far down the hallway, Trajen was stopped by the girl in class who had spoken. Seeing her now in front of him, he found her hair to be much curlier than hair he was used to. Parts of it frizzed and frayed, though she seemed not to be bothered by it. Her hair reminded Trajen of a documentary on the early 20th century, specifically the portion which discussed the popularity of the perm. Her hair was not like that, as it was obviously in its natural state, but he found the two styles similar. Her clothes hung on her well, though it was obvious she paid little to no mind to how she put together her outfit. Her shirt showed stripes while her pants showed polka-dots. She wore pink and purple on top with neon green on the bottom. The girls smile, unlike the professors, set Trajen immediately at ease. She seemed to smile even beyond the confines of her eyes.

"Hey, that was crazy, huh? You believe all that about LyraCorps?" If the girl had been unsure of herself in the classroom, she did not show it now.

Trajen wondered if she were simply afraid of speaking publicly, which he knew from a previous course in school to be the most common fear throughout the world. He still wondered why that was, if it were actually true. He had seen plenty of documentaries about things much scarier than talking in front of people. Unless the people had you lined up against a wall while you talked. That documentary, about types of executions, he had found particularly disturbing.

"I'm not sure," Trajen said. "It seems a little far-fetched, but I don't really know too much about corporations, I guess. What do you think?" A light breeze found its way inside the building, then, and Trajen caught the girl's scent for a moment. She smelled fresh, like sweet flowers. It was a different kind of sweet than Arnold, and made his mouth water.

"I don't know. I mean, my dad works there. Yours does too, doesn't he? I think I've seen him drop you off before. I think our dads work together. I don't think our dads would work somewhere that wasn't right, you know?"

"Oh, he's not...Uh, he's not my dad. He works there, though. And I'm sure you're right." Trajen's blood was rushing all around in his body. Why was he nervous? As the girl spoke to him, she would occasionally lean in, as if the emphasize her words. When she did, Trajen grabbed even more of her scent in his nose. She was making it so hard to focus.

The girl smiled again. The same, bright smile. Again it was boundless in its domain. The girl smiled with her whole body. "Sounds like you're in the right place, I guess. Plenty to learn on campus." She stopped for a moment to allow Trajen another opportunity to speak, but silence crept between them. Before it was awkward, she continued hastily, inquiring if Trajen was hungry. "I'm about to meet up with some friends to grab a sandwich. Do you want to come?"

"That sounds great!" Trajen replied. "I haven't really had the opportunity to meet many people here. Our family is pretty big on routines. Mine doesn't really come with very much interpersonal relations; I guess you could say."

Trajen had eaten in the school dining area only once before, when he was unemployed. Bren had made sure to send him off with lunches then, but had forgotten to one day. He'd had to use the little bit of money they gave him. Trajen still hadn't quite grasped the concept of currency at that point, and gave the cashier a large bill for a paltry order. When the cashier laughed, asking him if he were serious, his only response had been that he was. The food had been excellent. Not as good as Bren's cooking, but still good. The two began to walk briskly together towards where Trajen knew the food court to be. He could already smell the delicious sauces so many meats were being cooked in. He could practically taste the fried potatoes already.

"Yea, I've been there." The girl said, relating her own family to his. "We only moved here two years ago. Being new is tough. But you don't have to worry about that anymore. We're meeting up with some pretty nice people. I'll make sure you come away with at least a few friends, after today." The girl winked and bumped Trajen as she finished her sentence. She was so nice, like Bren. Trajen was so excited at the prospect of making friends, he forgot all about wanting to get home as soon as possible to explore his abilities. In that moment, if someone had asked him how long he could run, or how strong he was, he wouldn't have had an answer any different from the other normal people around him. Trajen had given up on the idea of socializing after his first few weeks on campus.

It had been a short, Summer semester, and not many people seemed particularly interested in making friends. In spite of his best efforts, after an entire week of no success, Trajen had decided it simply wasn't meant to be and kept to himself. He was happy at the prospect of that changing. Keeping to himself was, at times, very difficult. Sometimes it was hours before he had Garrett or Bren to talk to.

Back in the classroom, Professor Dalbrin greeted his wife Gracia warmly, with a tight hug. She had brought him his favorite lunch, though he would have greeted her just as warmly otherwise. He could smell it even before she'd entered the classroom, as he always could when she arrived with his favorite meal.

As Dalbrin looked at Gracia, he noticed large bags underneath her normally youthful, vibrant eyes. Opening his laptop, Dalbrin accessed the online platform for his remaining courses of the day. There were three left for him to teach, sixty students more to educate before he was off the clock. Rather than his carefully planned lectures, he opened the messaging system within the platform, looking again at his now seemingly exhausted wife.

Hello Students, his ninety emails began.

Class is cancelled.

Dalbrin had anticipated his wife feeling this way. He had seen on the news that parts of the country might become affected by solar flares. Where solar flares may normally mean the loss of cell phone connection, or the GPS in a car, for Dalbrin's family solar flares were more impactful. They made his wife feel ill, for one. Their arrangement was one built around love, but with Gracia sick, Dalbrin would be stuck having to feed himself. If that were the case, he certainly couldn't be stuck on campus teaching.

That just wasn't the way his life worked.

•••

Trajen was having a wonderful time with the other students. He found it hard to relate to many of the kids, feeling much older than some, and much younger than others. Some of them seemed to have themselves so figured out. They were absolutely sure who they were as individuals, it left Trajen feeling exactly the opposite way himself. He found that many of them often had adept knowledge of technological concepts or items which were well beyond hid breadth of knowledge, as well, though he rather liked listening them talk about things which he did not know about. As caught up as he was on life, there was still plenty that the many documentaries hadn't been able to teach him yet. The company was nice, he told himself many times over.

When he'd first ventured to that portion of the school for a sandwich with the young woman, he had tried desperately to recall her name. He feared it would become obvious he couldn't remember, but was saved as the introductions began. Thus far, he had met Billy, Robert, and Jeremy, three young men on the Junior Varsity Football Team. He'd also met Sally and Breanna, who both wanted to transfer to the same law school after they finished their first four years. Rounding out the group were Nick and Jones, the two he felt the most connection with, as they seemed to skirt on the outside of this mismatched group of companions. Nick introduced himself to Trajen with a statement, with Nick saying that he, "likes math." Jones hardly said anything at all, the slight smirk on his face the only greeting Trey received. Though Jones's smirk seemed to say enough, Trajen found, along with the other simple facial expressions he offered to the conversation. Trajen found that in spite of his lack of vocalization, he often could tell exactly how Jones felt about the topic at hand.

That left Kris, his ambassador and newfound friend. Kris was an unequivocal social butterfly, as far as Trajen could tell. She projected her intellect well, but was not overly boisterous as they all sat and talked. Quite the opposite, she encouraged others to speak their mind even as she offered her own opinions on the gadgets they all held in their hands or had resting on their heads. She reminded Trajen a lot of a CEO he had seen in a documentary, in a scene where the company executives have gone on a corporate retreat. The way the CEO spoke to her colleagues in the documentary was precisely the way that Kris spoke to the group. They even took the same pauses between some of their words. And like the CEO in the film, when Kris began to speak, Trajen saw that the rest of the group quickly quieted down to hear what she had to say. Try as he might his stomach got the best of him and Trajen began to eat. His sandwich was on rye bread. He thought rye bread was delicious.

After the group had finished eating, Trajen found himself walking towards his next destination, still at the side of Kris. He was joined as well by both Nick and Jones, which he found to be the most favorable outcome, as he tried occasionally throughout the conversation to learn more about Nick, or to convince Jones to speak at all. Alas, he never received more than mathematical related conversation from the one, and never more than the movement of facial muscles from the other. The four of them walked well into the evening, talking about everything and anything, Nick and Jones both breaking off one at a time towards their destinations, until only Trajen and Kris remained walking together once again.

As they approached a house much larger than the one Trajen called home, Kris stopped their journey.

"This is me. Thanks for walking me home, Trey. I'm glad you came to eat with us, you're a pretty cool guy." Trajen smiled at the compliment, and before he could react was met with a small kiss on the cheek.

Stunned, he wore the smile as Kris scurried her way inside. Then, he wore the smile all the way home.

Kris's father was there to greet her as she walked in the door, sitting on the couch in the front room.

"Hi honey," her father said. "Home a little later today. Where'd you go?"

Kris walked over to sit next to the man, immediately picking up the remote control to their television and changing the channel. "I was walking around with some friends. Nick and Jones, and this new boy Trey. You work with his uncle, Garrett."

"Oh, Garrett's boy? Is he nice?"

"He is. Really sweet, and he's always paying attention in class. Like, the whole time. Doesn't take notes but he's all over classroom discussions. I think he actually likes reading textbooks, too."

"You sure seem to know a lot about this boy," Kris's father said. "Is he cute?" The man smiled at his daughter. "Are we going to meet him soon? I can make his uncle bring his family over for dinner, you know. I *am* his boss."

"Oh my gosh, dad!" Kris threw a pillow on the couch at her father. "No. Please, don't even joke about that. We're just friends. I barely know him! Ugh, and there's nothing on TV. 1100 channels and nothing. Grrr…I'm going to run upstairs dad, guess I'm doing homehork."

"Okay honey." Her father said as Kris walked away. The man followed with, "If you call Trajen, tell him I said 'hello!'" though the girl was almost out of earshot as he finished his sentence.

Kris's room was extravagant and more than big enough to fit three additional beds, and her bed was the largest size they made. Her father was like that. He always bought things that were much bigger than they needed to be. It was only the two of them in her family; her mother had passed away years ago. Her father threw himself into his work of being a father as well as his work at LyraCorps, tasks he did not take lightly. People show their love in different ways. Some people are physically affectionate. Others verbalize their love. Kris's dad liked to give gifts. Her life was full of presents.

When she was a little girl, she was fine with her oversized teddy bears and battery-powered ponies that she could ride around their huge backyard. But lately, it was hard for her to see the value in those kinds of things. Her room, as large as it was, had become increasingly minimalist. Each of the items she kept in her personal space needed to have more than one function. If she had a bedside table, it needed to have storage space. Her shoe rack was also her coatrack and had cubbies for bottles of water if she came in thirsty. She saved so much space she could have rented it out at a premium. Her father, of course, continued to buy her lavish gifts to show his love, but she had become more adept at guiding his hand, and his wallet. Now she got first editions of her favorite books. She had all of her textbooks the first day of school, and when she found a new charity she thought could use a hand, her dad donated promptly.

She had one item of sentiment: Her diary. The pages were changed out regularly, the old writings mostly burned with a few pages saved here or there in a lockbox. It was the binding she really cared about. The moleskin was the last gift Kris received from her mother before the woman had passed, an inscription on the inside with loving words that she thought of often.

As a little girl, writing in the diary helped Kris deal with the loss of her mother. As a young woman, she thought it was a good habit to keep. Getting her thoughts down on paper helped to keep her feet on the ground and her head out of the clouds, where so many of her peers seemed to have theirs. Most days it wasn't anything exciting. She would write down what she was frustrated about, or even more simply where she had been. Today she wrote about Trajen.

In spite of herself, she realized her father had been right. She'd been paying attention to almost everything Trajen did. Didn't she always do that, though? She paid attention to plenty of people. She knew everything about Nick, and more than most people would take the time to learn about Jones.

Was Trajen really any different?

Chapter VIII

Trajen decided to walk home. He could have called Bren to pick him up, but even after so many months living together, he still felt like a bother when he pulled her away from anything. To Trajen, Bren always had something going on. At that point in the middle of the day, Trajen knew Bren was probably reading. Garrett described Bren as a "loud reader." Trajen didn't know what that meant until he had tried to get the woman's attention one day while she was in the middle of a particularly good book. It had taken him at least ten minutes to pull her away, as if the words she was hearing in her head were simply louder than the ones he had been saying. Considering the voracity with which Bren was constantly reading and finishing books, Trajen often couldn't bring himself to rouse her from the activity.

As Trajen reached the end of the first of thirteen blocks he'd be walking home, he came to his favorite park. There were quite a few parks in the city, but he found this one to be the best. Green Sleeve Park, as Garrett had once explained to him, was one of the oldest parks in the area. The trees at the park towered over many of the trees throughout the city, most of which were transplants from the areas they were meant to grow. Unlike other parks, the grass at Green Sleeve was natural, with the city having been built around it. It was an intensely large park as well, appearing not unlike a large sleeve of green space when one looked at a map of the city. It stretched across almost three miles in length, with almost two miles of width. Trajen could feel the difference between this park and the others. The ground at this park was much softer, almost pliable, as he walked on it on the days he found himself in the area. There was no sidewalk surrounding the park, the grass stretching right to the edge of the parking lots on either end and all the way to the roads it touched in the middle. The

only thing Trajen didn't like about the park was how strongly it smelled sometimes. There were days he had to walk around it completely, so heavy were the smells he would find himself walking into. But on that day, the park smelled just fine. The air was crisp and the sun felt nice on his skin. On most walks home, Trajen found himself thinking about things from earlier in his day. On this walk, his mind was almost completely clear. He had watched a documentary on meditation the previous month and found that he was very taken with the idea. There were spiritual aspects that he didn't particularly care for one way or the other, but the idea of clearing his mind for better focus and relaxation stuck with him. In most of the documentary, the people meditating found themselves sitting upright with their eyes closed. One person, though, said that they often meditated while hiking; moving physically helped them focus their mind down to a halt. It was easier for Trajen, as it was for the woman in the documentary, to clear his mind while he was on the move. As he placed one foot in front of the other, he allowed himself to become less and less focused on what was happening around him until he had only a few thoughts remaining. Then he focused only on his breathing, manually drawing and releasing each breath. This allowed the rest of his thoughts to fall away, until his mind was almost completely clear. It had only been a few weeks, but Trajen managed to gain quite a bit of skill when it came to walking meditation. It had quickly become a habit for him. Trajen was meditating, walking through the park, as another pack of hunters made their way into the area.

The men were all officially off duty, though their shift was starting soon. The four of them had planned on having a few drinks before they had to walk around all night looking for someone they'd never seen, who likely didn't exist. The Vampyr were gone.

They all knew that.

The man in the front, a Lyran with heritage not unlike that of a bloodhound, with his seemingly unnatural sagging jowls, perked up almost immediately as they entered the area. The men around him realized he had caught the scent of something important, their conversations dying off instantly. The other three Lyrans looked around in either direction, assessing their level of visibility. In spite of the daylight shining down on them all, the men found they were the only other individuals nearby, the boy they saw only a hundred yards away from them. The age looked right, according to the report they had been given. It was their lucky day, they'd gone out looking for one myth and accidentally found another. The four men quickened their pace towards Trajen, one of them briefly remarking how unaware the boy was of their presence. Roper would be pleased with them they knew, if they brought this boy in. The man leading their charge was almost frenzied, so sure he was that he'd caught the scent of the one they sought previously.

The men were only a few feet behind Trajen when he noticed how quickly they were coming up behind him. A combination of instinct or intuition kicked in at that moment, and he realized he was being pursued. The body has an automated response for such instances, and Trajen's flight reflex came on in full effect, his legs moving almost with a mind of their own. He didn't know where he was going to run to, but he found that the softness of the ground beneath him made it much easier for him to reach top speeds.

He looked back for only a moment to see that each of the men was wearing a LyraCorps vest, a sure sign to his rational mind that they indeed meant to do him harm. The five bodies neared the end of the park in just a few moments, Trajen coming up first to a small wall, the barrier between the park and a man-made wash designed to catch and deter the runoff from heavy rains. Trajen lifted one foot after the other, hurdling over the wall with ease, his front foot landing him in a slide as he sped down into the wash. Concrete surrounded him on either side, his feet continuing to pound with excessive force as he ran along as quickly as he could. He found himself running in parallel to a small stream of water which was still present in the wash since the last bout of rainfall.

Looking forward, trying to formulate a plan or identify the next place he would run to, Trajen could see that the wash led to an oversized grate, the water being led to a free-fall into the earth. Signaling the end of the journey was another wall, this one at least five times higher than the small two-footer he had just hurdled. He could feel the heavy books in his backpack dig into the small of his back with each swing from the momentum his moving body caused. Knowing he would soon be at the end of his run, he chanced another glance behind him to see if he had created enough distance to attempt either climbing the wall or removing the grate and venturing into the earth. Trajen swung his head only slightly in their direction, taking a prolonged look when he realized he needed to confirm what he saw.

There was one fewer body chasing him.

The girl was downwind, following along with the men chasing the young man. It seemed unlikely to her when the chase began that the lot of them would manage to avoid being seen by anyone else, but now after a few minutes into the event she briefly marveled at their collective ability to avoid any unwanted attention. There hadn't been a single car or person in sight since the men had gotten close enough to make him run. She had positioned herself downwind from the event to ensure she was following undetected, though she knew that at least one of them was so focused on having found the scent he was looking for that he likely didn't know up from down.

Slender bones began to grow down both of her forearms until each was double the length of her arm. She broke the first one off and took aim, firing her missile at the closest Lyran. The man had managed to lag behind the chase somewhat, and was closer to her than his comrades. The bone flew through the back of the man's head, its point protruding directly between his eyes. His form rag-dolled and tumbled onto the ground. Then the girl broke off the other bone and let the second missile fly at the next nearest Lyran. Her aim struck true, though the hit had not landed her a kill. The man fell to the ground like his comrade before him, and the girl turned towards his prone form as she made her way closer to the Lyrans still in pursuit. She kicked her foot out hard as she passed by the man, shattering his cheek without breaking her stride.

The remaining Lyrans grew closer to Trajen, who was only a few feet from the high wall. He decided he would climb, dropping his backpack before jumping as high as he could. His hands managed to dig directly into the concrete wall, though he found his shoes prevented him from allowing his feet to do the same. As roughly as he could with only the strength of his arms, Trajen flung himself upwards, his fingers barely grasping the top of the wall. Trajen pulled himself up quickly, dusting off his pants out of habit, wiping the sweat from his forehead. He peered back over the edge of the wall to see if his pursuers were still coming, surprised when he saw that he was alone. To him, it was just like his first run-in with a LyraCorps Strike Team. If he weren't sweating so profusely, standing on top of a twenty foot wall, he'd have thought he imagined the entire scenario. Trajen shook his head lightly, astounded at how quickly the situation had erupted, and how much quicker still it was suddenly over. A brief gust of wind seemed to signal to him that it was time to continue walking home, though he was feeling done with meditation for the day and would likely hurry through his journey.

Trajen turned around to see his backpack a few feet ahead of him, a curved bone hooked around the strap on the top.

Trajen walked in to an empty house, nearly exhausted and happy it was almost over. It was unlike Garrett not to be home so far into the evening, though he knew Bren was working a double that day at the hospital. Rather than worry about where Garrett was, Trajen was excited. He was alone.

Time, finally, for some discovery.

Trajen stood in the middle of his room, his eyes closed, his focus completely on his body. His breathing was controlled and deep. He thought of how quickly Garrett and Russel, each of the Lyra he'd encountered, really, were able to take on their canine features. He focused on his hands, picturing them as claws instead. He imagined he would need to visualize the transformation, and in his mind saw exactly the length his appendages would take on. The points his fingers would come to, and the sharpness they would have. He saw the long, brown fur that would cover his body.

Trajen opened his eyes and looked down at his arms, at his hands.

He saw that nothing had changed.

Trajen drew a labored sigh, somewhat frustrated with himself. Garrett was so sure that Trajen had a myriad of abilities at his disposal. If that were true, he'd only accessed a small fraction of what he was capable of. He was determined to figure out the rest of himself. His race was meant to bring balance. And it seemed everywhere he went lately, another person wanted to tell him how out of balance the world truly was right now. He knew if he spent enough time, he could do it. If he could figure out quadratic equations, and he was really only just beginning to do that, he could figure out his own body. He'd failed his first attempt, but he would try again and again until he got somewhere. Still, it had been a long day.

Trajen's gaze fell upon his bed. It was placed against the far wall, his sheet completely unmade and untidy. Making the bed each morning was the only part of his daily ritual he almost always refused to adhere to. Unmaking the bed as he entered each night felt like a waste of time to him. It didn't look messy to him as he stared at his bed. Only comfortable. So, so comfortable. Maybe, he thought, he would just take a little nap. And when he woke back up, he could try to discover some more abilities all over again. Taking his step, he simultaneously thought about how great it would be to already be lying in bed. Before his foot could hit the floor, his toe about to land at the edge of a stray beam of light coming in through his window as though to bar his path, his body jumped around the space, stepping through the shadows in the room instead.

In the blink of an eye, Trajen had traveled with less than one step a trip that should have taken four or five. It was not a great distance by any means, but that didn't stop Trajen from thinking, as he laid down on his bed, that it was the perfect way to end his day. As he drifted into his nap, he realized he was much more tired than he thought, the bed suddenly much more comfortable than it had ever felt before.

He fell asleep quickly, a small smile resting on his face.

Chapter IX

In spite of his need for secrecy as he lived his double life, Garrett occasionally found that manipulation was not enough. Sometimes, no amount of contacts or moles could accomplish the task he needed done. In these instances, it fell to him. He had planned one such evening for a night when Bren would be working late. As luck had it, security would be light. He could sneak in and out of the satellite facility with no trouble as long as he kept his wits about him.

Lyran Special Forces aren't like similar units for other races. The training they're given comes in two waves. They learn to fight in their human form *and* their Lyran form, eventually learning to merge the two styles completely. The Lyrans chosen for Special Forces training have the ability to halt their transformation at any stage, as well. The common Lyran has only their human form or their Lyran form. Many Lyrans' forms differ from others, with some taking on more the guise of an animal than a man, while others may only gain some sharper features. Garrett was chosen for the training because he had the innate ability to halt the transformation, so that he only took on some of his Lyran features. In his full Lyran form, he was a dog completely, although quite oversized in comparison to the average canine. Still, he walked on all fours and was without any human features. And he could naturally choose to take on as many or as few of these aspects as he wanted, sometimes fighting with sharp claws and teeth but upright as a man, or as a giant dog, rending his enemies with his ferocious bite.

The LyraCorps satellite facility was located two miles outside of the city, in an area that caught more starlight than the yellow glow of man-made streetlights. It was an area the corporation kept things during transport, the cover of darkness and remoteness of the facility making it easy for items to come and go with little issue. Garrett planned to use the darkness for himself.

Most Lyrans come equipped with the heightened senses of the animal they can change their shape into. Garrett's sense of smell was naturally amplified beyond that of a normal man, and when he focused he could allow it to take over. Garrett had parked his car a half mile from the facility, knowing it was unlikely for there to be a patrol which might venture that far out. He removed his shirt, pants, and shoes. He had swim jammers on under his pants with a hole cut through the back for his tail. His change into his Lyran form was almost instantaneous, his vision going from the full spectrum of color to only a few. His Lyran eyes saw better at night than his human ones. His other senses quickly caught up as well, his sense of smell amplifying even further than it already was, so that sense and sight mixed fluidly, Garrett's brain applying its own colors to the mingling smells he could now sense more fully. Where there had been only human skin before, Garrett was now covered in long, shaggy hairs. His nose and his jawline grew longer and more pronounced, as did his fingers and toes. The nails at the end of each appendage were stronger and hardier, with an edge that could rake skin with ease.

Garrett made his way into the forest, staying vigilant. Soon he was met with an abundance of scents, working to stay quiet as he filed away the smells which were important from those that were not. He began tracking the musk of two canines, finding quickly that one of the scents belonged to a small fox living in the area. Garrett found that he could always tell when a musk belonged to an actual dog versus one of his kind because animals had a tendency to spray the same areas over and over, while his kind fell more often into variety when choosing the location of their markings.

As he stalked his way through the trees, the scent of the Lyran musk grew stronger. Garrett began to choose his steps more carefully, as the Lyran musk quickly became the only scent in the area. It was likely he had found a common relief area for a guard or soldier who patrolled the area. Garrett's movements were almost completely silent, his feet shuffling more than stepping, the balls of his feet hardly leaving the ground at all. Garrett made his way up and over a small hill, the satellite facility quite suddenly in view, roughly two hundred yards away. The forest around the facility had been cleared, giant lights on top of guard towers in the distance telling Garrett that the people running the place were more concerned with *keeping* whatever was inside from getting out, rather than keeping people like him from entering. The man was a ghost as he walked the perimeter of the trees, searching for a portion of the open area which would still afford him some cover as he approached the building.

Garrett stepped around a small bend, realizing then exactly how quiet he was being, as he came suddenly upon two men having an almost silent conversation above him. Garrett ought to have smelled them before he heard them. He looked up, ducking quickly behind a large tree trunk, seeing that the men were not Lyrans of a canine persuasion. While incredibly uncommon, it was not the first time Garrett had seen members of his kind who did have dog-like attributes. He briefly scolded himself for focusing so intently on the musk he was tracking, as he hadn't smelled these other men at all. Now that he had a better look, he could see long, bushy tails and sharp, extended claws. They appeared to be not unlike chipmunks, or squirrels. Garrett didn't know the difference. As he focused more intently on their scents, he realized their smell was everywhere. These two men commonly made their way all over this portion of the surrounding forest – it was pure luck that he'd happened upon them and not the other way around, as he was sure they likely spent almost all of their time above the ground floor. Garrett listened closely to their conversation for a moment, attempting to decide if he needed to deal with them now, or risk sneaking by and possibly dealing with them later.

"Did you get out to Jimmy's game last night, Tim?"

"You know, I did Rog, thanks for asking."

"How'd the little slugger do? Hit any home runs?"

"Ah no. Kid still can't hit the ball to save his life. We're gonna get him some private lessons, I think. You know I don't care if he ever hits anything with that little metal bat, but Jimmy is pretty into the baseball thing. Figure if he's gonna put that much energy into caring about it, we're gonna try to get him to at least be good at it. Not great or anything, but good enough to hit the ball at least."

"I hear you on that. That's the way it was with Sally. Girl can climb like nobody's business – better than you or me, tell you the truth. But she couldn't score a goal to save her life. They'd pass her the ball and she would, I am not kidding you here, she would completely miss the thing entirely. I think she had the all-time high for possessions stolen in her age division of the soccer league. We got her some lessons recently. She's doing alright. Got them through the youth center. I can give you the information when we get back in later on if you want."

"Yea, that sounds great, man. If it isn't too hard on the pocketbook, maybe we'll just go for it. The kid can't get any worse, I'll tell you that much."

Garrett found the disposition of the squirrel men agreeable, in spite of himself. He was completely on the fence about wanting to engage them physically at all. Before he could decide, his question was answered for him.

"Better get to it." One of the men said, flinging himself backwards off of the branch he'd been sitting on, his legs flipping over his head as he landed directly in front of Garrett, who had chosen that moment to step out from behind the tree trunk he'd used for cover. The other Lyran sensed Garrett immediately, turning to meet him, seemingly unsure of what to do.

"Hey, you can't-" the man began, before Garrett shot his fist into the man's nose. Cartilage crunched from the direct hit and the squirrel man stumbled backwards, nearly falling to the ground. Garrett swiped his tail out to the side, attempting to swat the man even more off balance. His companion, the other guard, dropped quickly to the ground then, blocking Garrett's tail with his own. The Lyran guard leapt forward then, grabbing Garrett by the shoulders and wrestling him to the ground. Garrett saw then that the squirrel-man's arms were much shorter than they ought to be. Sharp claws dug into Garrett's shoulders and the two men rolled around on the forest floor. After a moment, Garrett worked his feet up, raking the sharp claws through the man's pant legs and deep into his skin. The guard screamed out in pain, releasing his grip, and Garrett was back up immediately.

The first man had gained his bearings, the blood still coming from his nose, though tears no longer filled his eyes. He grabbed a metal baton from a pocket in the vest he wore, throwing it outwards, the metal unfolding itself from the force. The man came at Garrett immediately, swinging wide but quickly. Garrett bobbed and weaved two consecutive swings, stepping inside of the third, his huge jaws clamping down onto the man's arm. The guard called out in pain in the moment before Garrett's hand shot up into the man's throat, flattening his windpipe. The man's other hand clutched his throat immediately, his feet instinctually stepping backwards. Garrett released the guard's arm from his mouth, spitting out the bit of skin and hair in his teeth, before turning to meet the other guard. To his surprise, the man was still on the forest floor, clutching his legs. Both men quickly changed back into their human forms, the quickest way for Lyrans to heal themselves from damage sustained while in their animal form. Garrett stepped forward, but was quickly stopped by the prone guard.

"Wait!" The man screamed. "Please. No more, please." Garrett could see that the men were much older than they had appeared in their Lyran forms. Too old, he thought, to have such young children. It took longer for Lyrans to look old, in comparison to humans, so these men easily had a hundred years or so on Garrett's lifespan.

"Give me your shirt, and your vest." Garrett said. He turned to the other man. "And you. Give me your pants." The men removed their clothing, somewhat begrudgingly, and Garrett put them on quickly. He found a keycard in the pocket of the vest, which he assumed would get him into the areas he would need to go.

"When were you due back?" He asked the men.

"Not for another twenty minutes," one of them said. That was fine with Garrett. It gave him time to survey the area a little more, decide which door he wanted to enter through, should there be more than one.

"Don't move," he told the men. "Heal up. I'll be back by the time your wounds close with your clothing. Just rest easy and everything will be fine."

Garrett took his time, then, finishing his perimeter search. He finished circling the building completely by the time his twenty minutes were finished. There was only one entrance he could see from that distance – the front door. As it was, there hadn't been much time to formulate the actual entry portion of his plan. At that point, it wasn't just good luck that he'd gotten the drop on the other Lyrans, but that he'd managed to land himself a guard uniform as well. In spite of the guard tower looming above the entryway, Garrett could see as he drew near that his initial suspicions were confirmed. The towers were only occupied when dealing with escape attempts. Otherwise, it was an automated security system barring any common soul from entering. He withdrew the keycard again from the pocket on the front of his new vest and swiped it across the sensor. The lock clicked and the door fell free from the magnetic lock. Garrett reverted his features fully back into those of a man before entering, keeping his eyes on the floor. He'd studied the floorplan of the building well before coming. If he didn't meet any resistance, he'd be in and out without issue. He had planned to worry about the keycard as the need arose, happy once more that issue had already worked itself out.

Garrett made his way down the first hallway, fluorescent lighting shining brightly to illuminate the gray walls around him. He walked carefully, but with intent. In the event someone was watching the cameras pointed at him, he didn't want to appear as though he was sneaking. Still, he made little noise as he moved. He turned right as soon as he could, knowing there was another thirteen steps before he would turn left, and two floors of stairs to make his way down after that. He'd found the first set of stairs quickly enough.

Unfortunately, it was not without guards.

The building plan had seemed odd to Garrett when he'd studied it. Now that he found himself inside the building, the oddness seemed to be only affirmed. The two guards at the end of yet another hallway leaned against the wall slightly, neither seeming to take their post very seriously. The guard on the left did nothing but talk, the man's hands expressing many of the words he was saying, moving through the air as if he were conducting his own conversation. The other man did almost nothing to engage in the one-sided conversation, and was literally holding a book up to his face. Garrett approached them cautiously, but continued to project an air of authority as he did so.

As he neared the two men, he could smell their scents. They were, like the men outside, not the common canine variety of their kind. Garrett found himself wrestling again with the difference between a chipmunk and a squirrel as the man on the left ceased his talking to look over. He briefly touched a hand to one of his shoulders, feeling that the scabs on the wounds had already become dry, the skin underneath new and nearly ready.

Garrett cleared his throat slightly. "'Evening fellas. Just making the rounds."

"You can't go down here," the man on the left said.

"Oh. What? They said to get to sub-level 2, room 1A." Garrett knew from the plans that was the armory.

"My vest doesn't fit right. Flops around when I run." The other man with the book closed the cover and brought it down from his face, looking up at Garrett.

"They? They who?" Garrett thought for a moment, realizing he didn't have too long before his thinking might land him in trouble.

"Home office. I got the call a few minutes ago out front. They said my vest had come in yesterday." The man with the book didn't look like he believed Garrett very much. Garrett could see him wrestling somewhat with the story, which Garrett was sure everyone knew was full of holes. The man's fingers brushed the edges of the pages in his hand then, though, and his disposition lightened somewhat.

"Fine," the man with the book said. "Hurry up. Get to the armory and come *right back.*"

"No problem, guys. In and out and back to my post." Garrett smiled as he went. He continued his careful walk as he descended the stairwell, doing his best to appear confident while making as little noise as possible.

Garrett made his way to the bottom floor and opened the door to a large, open space. There was less of a need for structural integrity in the underground area, the ceiling above him somewhat low and concrete, completing the grey theme the facility thus far had to offer. He could see three ways which he might venture, none of them labeled as to what the areas contained. He tried to call to mind which way he was meant to go, realizing that he had convinced himself after studying the plans that getting downstairs was the hardest part to remember. On the paper, it all looked so close. He assumed he would be able to simply see his destination at this point. Of course he had been wrong. Everything had gone too easily thus far for him to keep up the luck he had experienced. Four men exited the room farthest to the right, laughing riotously as they went. Garrett ducked his shoulder and worked not to meet their gaze as he walked by, hoping they'd pay him little to no mind. He almost made it.

"Hey, who's this guy?" One of the guards asked.

"Hey, guys." Garrett said. "Just here to...ah..."

"You don't smell right," another man said. The man's features grew angled, his teeth elongating, his fingernails turning to sharp points. Garrett kept his hands down, though he readied his own claws as well.

"Come on guys. Don't be like that."

"No, he's right," the man in front commented. "You *don't* smell right. Everyone down here, s'posed to smell like the rest of us. What are you doing?" The other three men's canine features began to show then. Garrett realized the pivotal moment had arrived. The one that acted as the calm before eruption, so common among actual dogs. Each of the four guards took an extremely slow step forward, each of their weights shifting to allow for explosive power. Garrett saw it coming, his own weight slowly shifting. When his eyes darted to the left, checking to see if the door the men had exited required key-card access, the scene erupted.

The four men lunged forward, their boots squeaking audibly on the linoleum flooring. Garrett literally turned tail, running towards the door the men had recently exited. He kept himself barely out of arm's length, widening the distance only as he reached the opening of the next room, the door of which swung outwards. As he entered the area, he grabbed the door behind him, slamming it shut. The men crashed into the door behind him, pounding on the barrier immediately. To Garrett's surprise, the door was made of wood. He managed to lock the deadbolt, buying himself a few moments at best. Something would give, he knew. The men would either break through the door or crack the jamb. Looking around, he saw that he wasn't where he needed to be, though he'd managed to complete the lie he'd recently told, and ended up in the armory. The men crashed into the door with unrelenting force and Garrett looked for tools he might be able to use. Lyrans were inclined to use their natural gifts when it came to combat, but when it came down to it even the best trained soldier is going to have a hard time dealing with more than one person with any kind of training. Garrett was Special Forces, but he wasn't invincible. Unfortunately, any projectile weaponry he might have used was stuck behind a gate at the far end of the room. There was an entire wall of pistols, rifles, and shotguns that he would never be able to get to in time. Luckily, to his right on a table were some metal batons. Garrett steeled himself mentally, knowing that even with weapons he was adeptly trained with, he still might not come out of the encounter alive.

But there was nowhere left to run.

Garrett grabbed two of the batons from the table to his right, swinging them briefly to test their balance and weight. The weapons were perfectly crafted, which gave him a tiny wave of relief. A moment later, the wood of the door jamb cracked. Another hard blow later, the four guards entered the room, the two in front somewhat stumbling, imbalanced on entry.

Garrett used this to his advantage, striking fast and hard at the first two guards. He hit the guard on his right squarely on the side of the head, bringing the weapon around quickly enough to hit the other side of the man's head as well. The guard fell quickly from the blow, as Garrett was lashing out with the other baton at the guard on his left. This man proved ready, dodging the swings of the baton, turning them into near-misses. The two guards in the back fully entered the room, and the three men still standing tried to surround Garrett, who swung the batons wide, outlining a perimeter. As one of the attacking Lyrans would attempt to step forward inside of Garrett's striking area, he would lash out viciously, each swing a near miss that the attempting guard would have to dodge as quickly as possible. One guard stepped in just after Garrett swung a baton, thinking to strike in between attacks. Garrett quickly shifted his feet and kicked out at the man, landing the blow squarely on the guard's chest. The man dug his claws into Garrett's leg as the blow connected, hanging on. Garrett hissed in pain, another of the guards stepping in to attack. Garrett swung a free baton at the advancing guard, who quickly stepped back out of reach. Garrett dropped his weight, then, and kicked up with his free leg, turning over in the air as he did, bringing his heel across the jaw of the guard holding his other foot. The man's head snapped to the right from Garrett's kick, and his claws released the leg immediately. As Garrett landed, he threw the baton in his left hand hard at the guard to his left, jumping at the man to his right. The missile hit the first guard in the cheek, effectively stunning him while Garrett tussled with the other man, who had been ready for Garrett's scramble.

The guard managed to wiggle his body out to the side, wrapping Garrett's arm into a hold. Garrett's elbow was pressed against the man's hips. If the guard raised his hips even a few inches, Garrett's elbow would be bent far in the wrong direction. With the baton still in his hand, Garrett swung rapidly at the man's legs, doing his best to hit his kneecaps as he did what he could to push against the man's hips and prevent his arm from bending in ways it should not. He took on his Lyran teeth and bit down into the man's thigh, barely breaking through the thick pants the guard was wearing, continuing to swing as hard and fast as he could. Finally, one hit landed where it was meant to, cracking the guard perfectly on one of his kneecaps, causing him to release Garrett's arm just a little. It was enough, and Garrett rolled slightly into the man, bringing the baton directly into the guard's face. The guard's nose cracked, spattering blood outward in nearly every direction.

Garrett tried to stand, but was met with the boot heel of the remaining guard, who landed a solid kick directly to the side of Garrett's head. The blow dazed him severely, and he found himself swinging the baton wildly to prevent any further hits. He was met with two more quick blows – a slash across his cheek, which split the skin, and then a knee to his forehead which he managed to avoid enough to only be grazed. The pain in his cheek had a sobering effect, and Garrett stood up with his wits renewed. The guard came in with a right cross and Garrett lifted his left arm to catch the blow, bringing the baton in his right hand down on the man's elbow. The guard's arm caved and Garrett punched him hard in the face, still holding onto the man, continuing to hit him until he crumpled to the floor.

Garrett surveyed the room, a mixture of pride and pure adrenaline coursing through his body. He almost couldn't believe he had survived the encounter, his head now beginning to pound again, the wound barely closing on his cheek. He kept the baton in his hands as he left the room, hoping beyond hope not to run into any more guards. Exiting the room, he made his way towards his destination, the farthest room from where he was. The coast was clear as he entered. The room was tangibly warmer as he entered, full wall to wall and floor to ceiling with electronics. Garrett could hear large fans running behind the units, pushing the hot air away from the electronic components, but it was like the water in an engine. Cooler than the electronics, but still too hot to touch comfortably.

Garrett removed a slivered jump drive from behind his right molar, wiping the spit off of the device before inserting it into the closest computer. He recalled from memory the password and access codes he'd been given, navigating until he found the documents he needed. As quickly as he could, he transferred building plans, quarterly reports, and the schedule of any executive he could find. Any information was useful, he knew. Especially after the chance discovery of Trajen and the off-the-books portion of LyraCorps headquarters that had been built underground. There were hundreds of Lyracorp buildings across the globe. Each set of schematics could be just as likely to show them something useful. There was simply no telling what else the company might be hiding.

The files finished transferring after only a few moments. Garrett grabbed the jump drive and placed it back behind his molar, making his way out of the room and towards the surface. He was relieved, his mission was nearly over.

His second time passing the two guards on the main level, the man with the book was no longer standing next to the door. The chatty man was standing silently against the wall, startled as Garrett made his way into the hallway. Garrett simply kept walking, saying nothing, waving once as turned the corner towards the front door.

Once he was out the door, he would be home free, he knew. As the door closed behind him, he embraced again his full Lyran form. He quickly came again upon the guards whose clothes he'd taken. They were still laying where he'd left them, though the man with the leg injuries appeared to have fully healed. Garrett said nothing as he approached the men, removing the vest and pants quickly. He placed them at the guards' feet and made his way back into the woods towards his car. He was anxious to get the jump drive out of his mouth for good and give it to Russell, who would know what to do with the information.

Until then, he'd settle for a hot bath and, when she came home from work, a few hours of closeness with his wife.

Trajen woke the next morning to the smell of chocolate chip pancakes. This would be his third time having such a breakfast, and he'd been anxiously awaiting its return since the last occasion. It was almost easy for him to believe the pancakes were in celebration of him honing one more of his abilities the evening before, though he recalled immediately that no one had been home. He found himself skipping his shower entirely, simply fixing the mess of hair his sleep had caused, and dressing himself as quickly as possible so that he might dine upon the delicious, chocolate filled breakfast waiting for him.

As he loaded his plate with cake after cake of chocolate delight, only beginning to lather his syrup on top of his stack, he noted the dourness with which Bren and Garrett were conversing. His focused shifted not fully away from his sugar-soaked breakfast, but it did move enough so that he might listen in on the topic at hand.

"It's just scary, you know?" Bren said. "This is the second death like this, now. And it was so close to the campus. I don't know. It's scary."

"I'm telling you, honey, there is *nothing* to be afraid of. These are random acts of violence. It's pure coincidence that both of the deaths were so gruesome in nature. Read the article, it says very clearly that the cause of death was a car accident. It was happenstance that the man ended up on the sidewalk like that."

Bren seemed unconvinced, but decided not to speak of it now that Trajen had arrived and slowed the voracity with which he was attacking his pancakes with his fork. She wore an expression as she spoke which was a mixture of surprise and mock shameful judgment, "That good, huh?"

His mouth full of gooey chocolate, Trajen managed an "Mmf-hmmf" before finishing chewing his food. "I think this is my favorite thing to eat!"

Garrett folded up his paper at that, revealing his empty plate before him. "Guess I'd better get in on this," he said. "Before you take the whole pile for yourself. How's everything going at school, Trey? We haven't talked about that for a while."

"Really well! I met some other students yesterday, and we had lunch. One of them, Kris, is *very* nice. She said she thinks her dad and my...er, that her dad and you work together."

Garrett dropped his fork. "What? Trajen, does she have curly, impossibly frizzy hair? She smells faintly of that soap that Mrs. Gartner across the street uses?"

"Why do you know what so many women smell like?" Bren interjected.

"Dear, I know what *everybody* smells like. Dog. Nose. It's a thing. Trajen, tell me, is it the same girl? Do you know where she lives?"

Trajen was taken aback by Garrett's feverish response to his new friend. The concern was evident across the man's face. But he felt no need to lie, never to lie, to Garrett. "Yes, I believe that's the same girl. Why? What's the matter?"

"Trajen, you must be *very* careful with what you say to this girl. Her father is my boss."

"Jesus, Gar. You're afraid Trajen will get you *fired?*" Bren said, her face now a mask of true judgment.

"Listen, both of you. What I'm doing when I'm at work, it may be fake, but it's *necessary.* Losing the job there would set everything I'm working for, everything necessary to keep the world safe, it would set it back years. Maybe more. I have the kind of clearance not given out lightly. But it's more than that. Trajen, you must be very careful who you allow yourself to be around at all. Remember, you were broken out of a compound underneath LyraCorps. The cover we've crafted for you, the dead ends we've led LyraCorps to in their search for you, all of that could be for nothing if the wrong person found out you aren't who we say you are. Do you understand? All it would take is some prolonged contact. A friendly hug versus a pat on the shoulder, and some innocent person would walk around with your scent on them. The hunters would pick it up in short order and it wouldn't just be you in danger, but possibly someone else, as well." In his feverish speak, Garrett's face became slightly hairier, more angled, as his emotions clearly began to take hold of his person. After a moment, he calmed and his features returned to normal, though the tension was still palpable in the air. Trajen decided in that moment not to tell them he had been chased by another group of hunters the day before, or the strange way in which they seemed to disappear.

"So, what do I smell like?" Bren said, to the ease of everyone present.

Garrett wore a smile. "Baby, you smell like love."

Trajen had never seen Garrett wink before that moment.

"There's some other news, too." Trajen said. Garrett turned back to Trajen, eyebrows raised, a slight nod of his chin beckoning the Peacebringer to continue. "Well, better if I just show you." Trajen took another bite of the pancakes and took a few paces back, so that he was resting on the shadow cast by the archway behind him, where the living room met the kitchen. He focused on the closest shadow, six steps ahead of him, and took a small step forward into the light. Within an instant, as he set his foot fully down, he was across the room.

"Trajen, that was amazing!" Bren shouted. Any tension still lingering had now passed completely. Trajen took a step back towards his chair, realizing he was still just as hungry as when he'd sat down only a few minutes ago.

"Takes a bit out of me, though." Trajen said.

"Oh?" Garrett replied.

"Yehmf," Trajen continued to chew more pancakes, the disregard for how full his mouth was of food continuing as well. "I took a much smaller step last night when I came home and it totally knocked me out.

I slept all the way until this morning. And just now, it's like I never ate any pancakes at all."

A Shadone. It was true, Garrett thought to himself. They have all the powers of the Loren or at least many of them. What else was Trajen capable of? Could he walk out into the sun and heal himself? Could he remove the light from the room like some of the elder Shadones were rumored to be able to do? This was a startling revelation. He had to contact Russel and tell him the time table was moving up.

"Hmm. I could be wrong, but I don't believe that's common. I've only ever met a few Shadone, the race who can shadow walk as you just did, but I've never heard of one saying that stepping around the light made them weak."

"You think it's different for my kind?"

"Could be...could be. Then again, maybe you just need some practice." Garrett smiled at that statement. "Why don't you have some more pancakes and give it another go." As Garrett finished speaking, both men heard Bren inhale sharply, Garrett and Trajen turning their attention towards the woman simultaneously.

"I mean," Bren said, "I don't have *nearly* enough chocolate chips for that!"

From the pages of Hrath's Golemnic Tome. Vol 8.
The Morkhavians.

The dung beetle is a wonderful invention of nature. This is, of course, an insect whose entire existence revolves around the refuse of everything that lives around it. Many a dung beetle are the companion of Golems, who often live for years inside the deepest, darkest parts of the caves they can find. Would that we could fly, we might have found commune with bats, as well. Alas, we are confined to live only along, or below, the earth. As a result, Golems become very familiar with many different types of insects. I find dung beetles to be especially delightful.

Caves develop extremely efficient ecosystems which are often completely removed from the outside world. There are many insects and animals which feed on dead and decomposing flesh, but so few who feed on feces. It is often not until I observe a lone dung-handler, rolling their ball along the floor of the dark cave, finally attracting a mate with their gathering of excrement, that I am reminded to ask myself what it is I enjoy as much as a dung beetle enjoys dung. These beetles' entire lives revolve around what the rest of the world would view as waste. It is their sustenance, their prize, and even their home for a short time, as the female dung beetles will lay their eggs inside of large balls of dung. If you allow them to be, dung beetles can become the most inspirational insect you ever take the time to observe. They certainly are for me, during the periods of time where I have not the willpower to travel the earth, and decide that I would rather relax in the darkness of the earth.

Dung beetles, as with many species of insect, are also wonderful in terms of their adaptive capabilities. I think of them not just when I think of being insidiously passionate about something, to the extent that it may become my entire existence, but also when I think about how quickly life can change from one form to another.

The Morkhavians did not always live for death. Their branch of The Tree of Loren was once filled with life, and light. As with other instances of sparked adaptation, the Morkavians eventually ceased to be fully human, becoming the fungus which they had come to worship. A rational mind can be dangerous if left to ignorance. Unable to explain the heart rot in their trees, the first Morkhavian village thought their dying trees to be more gift than curse. Many in their village died from consumption of the fungus-filled wood. Those who did not passed on the tradition, giving the tree-killing fungus an environment in which it could prosper, and itself evolve into something new. It was six generations before the Morkhavian race was fully established, another offshoot from the strong branch of the Humans. I had been calling them Fungus People, until a colleague had come to visit, something which no longer occurs between Golems. During a bout of what can only be described as 'Naming Clarity,' he managed to give them a title which, when translated, meant 'Death but Life.' It was a Golemnic word, which sounded in the common tongue like the title which the race now has as their own, Morkhavian.

I loved watching the race develop almost as much as I love watching dung beetles, so committed were they to the fungus that they allowed it to worm its way into every facet of their lives. Eventually, babes fresh from birth would come to spend their first few months of life wrapped in the decrepit protection of a fungus-ridden tree, allowing them to become not only immune, but enhanced by the fungus's properties. These are hardy people, immune to the elements, poisons, and venoms. The only thing they cannot consume, I had come to learn, was anything which had recently died. Indeed, even the wounds of battle fall away from them if they are able to feast upon anything which has begun to rot after receiving the damage. I watched an elder man regrow a lost limb after only two days of digesting ash and rotten meat, his form reassembling itself as the he worshipped might, if it is not all cut or burnt away from that which it infects. Whether this race of the Loren is truly alive, I cannot say, though the most recent generations have become less and less human, by my account.

Morkhavians of the modern world seem more driven than their ancestors. I have noticed this. There are many who choose not the life of their race, and do not worship the fungus which sparked the growth of their race. These individuals find a life for themselves somewhere else, able to withstand any climate, no matter how harmful it is to humans. They go wherever the wind takes them, it seems. But a vast collection of Morkhavians continues the traditions of their ancestors. They worship the fungus that takes the lives of trees. Their entire existence revolves around reverence of something which, by any standard definition, cannot, does not, have sentience. These traditional Morkhavians are so driven, so compelled to worship the fungus, that their wars are never civil. The Morkhavian race is one which is forever united, bound together in fungus, and has never warred with their own race. They seem to share what I can only describe as a hive mind, and are capable of silent communication, no matter the distance. My personal hypothesis is that their bodies have found a way to send messages along the spores of any fungus, not just the type which they revere. There are spores of fungus everywhere, all over the earth. Many simply bide their time, waiting for the proper environment to grow. I think, somehow, the Morkhavians use these spores to send messages to one another. Long before the advent of technology which allowed for communication with far-away peoples, the Morkhavians participated in huge, collaborative efforts of previously incalculable size and complexity.

Of course, there are plenty of other answers for why that might have been. My colleague offered his own opinion before the end of our visit. His thought was that, not unlike another type of fungus, which is known to target a species of ants, perhaps the majority of Morkhavians were being controlled as well. Perhaps their biological directives and ability to reason or properly function was gone, and many of them were simply a shell playing host to something else. I do not pretend to know which is true.
Whatever the case may be, of this I am certain: Morkhavians are both fascinating, and terrible. They are both beautiful, and dangerous.

Morkhavians are life.

Morkhavians are death.

Chapter X

Garrett liked his job. Sometimes he felt bad he was trying to destroy the company. Not bad that the company would go up in flames, but that when he resumed his semblance of normalcy, his workplace wouldn't be as fun. That was assuming, of course, that he made it out of the whole thing alive.

So far he was doing alright.

When Garrett needed a break from trying to sabotage the largest corporation on earth, he would do his job and test products. Garrett was one of twenty people whose job it was to try and find something wrong with whatever the company put in front of him. Most days, it was some kind of software. He was new to the position, having received the promotion that caused he and Bren to move to the city that was home to the LyraCorps headquarters, but he had already tested hundreds of products. Everything from skin and haircare products to tax software had landed on his desk at some point. Sometimes the entire team was looking for structural defects in children's toys, and was paid to shoot foam darts at each other for a few hours. Other days they clicked buttons and navigated user menus. Every day was a new product, and Garrett had found early on that it didn't take the entire day to test something to the parameters his position called for. Multiple breaks were actually mandatory at the corporate office, as a way of increasing productivity. For Garrett, he wasn't really working until he was on break. Garrett had had to work hard to get this position. It was highly coveted. But he knew that if you wanted to bring something unimaginably huge to the ground, you needed to find its structural weak points.

Skyscrapers are built to withstand all kinds of things. But if you know which beams to hit, you can bring the whole thing down without too much effort. When Garrett was on break, that's what he looked for. It was a lonely security guard who walked into a high-security area for Garrett and made a duplicate key-card. It was a poor architect who had made a copy of the original plans of the corporate office for him, showing him the areas that weren't released to the public as having been built. And it would be somebody else, just like them, who helped him find another weak spot.

He didn't know yet which beams to target, so to speak. But he was learning fast that there were plenty of good places to look. The only drawback of his position was that his wage was hourly. If his team tested a product too quickly, he might not have the chance to take all of his breaks and be sent home for the day. Early on, when he'd first arrived in the city with Bren, he would have nothing to do if he were sent home. Now he had some resources, and a few contacts, he could spend time on while he wasn't on break from testing products. Sometimes, he would spend time with Russell. The two men couldn't be seen together, though. Couldn't even be in the same room for too long. Russell was an old dog – a veteran from the final years of the Great War. Men like him weren't supposed to roam free. The man was constantly in hiding, constantly being pursued by LyraCorps agents. Too much time around him and his scent would rub off onto Garrett. If the wrong person got even an inkling of Russell's scent on Garrett, everything was over. Garrett and Russell only communicated in person when it was absolutely crucial that they do so, their work divided up so that Russell did what he could outside of LyraCorps headquarters, while Garrett continued to work as the inside man.

Garrett was taking his first break of the day, which he had decided to spend at least partially on a treadmill. His team was testing the user interface on some kind of software being brought into schools all across the continent. It was going to be boring during the times he was actually doing his job that day, so he wanted to make sure he got in some physical activity to counteract the slow pace his work was going to take. LyraCorps headquarters had three floors throughout the hundred and twenty in their building dedicated to physical activity. Garrett, like every other non-executive level employee, had access to two of the gyms. Each gym was a flood of treadmills, stair-steppers, stationary bikes, and elliptical machines – areas obviously designed to ensure that the numerous canine shapeshifters in the building had a chance to take themselves for a walk at least once a day, something Garrett often found himself appreciating and snickering about in private. The outlying areas of each gym were composed of machines designed to isolate muscle groups, with no other weightlifting equipment in the building. Then, circling the entire floor was a track, for those who didn't want to spend their time running or walking on an automated device. The track was occasionally the better place to have a conversation, Garrett had realized, as you could more easily keep your conversation private there. The view was nice, as well. Like so many large buildings in the modern era, LyraCorps headquarters had almost no windows which were not set with a limo-style tint. This was a common security measure taken by big corporations to protect their data from probing eyes or radio signals, as the tint kept those out as well. The only clear windows were those on the gym levels. This created a somewhat unique design on the outside of the building, which might look unfinished to the casual observer, three of the floors appearing out of place as one took in its design visually. The clear windows were how Garrett knew there was a third gym in the building. It hadn't taken him long to learn that the area was only for executive level employees. He had also deduced early on that a pair of ears in such an area would likely prove inherently useful.

Presently, Garrett was trying to find a way to get a few microphones into the area.

Garrett had all but exhausted his security contacts. There weren't many weak links among the men tasked with guarding the building. He had found the only one, he was sure. Their dealings had left the man so paranoid, Garrett knew he couldn't call on the man again unless he absolutely had to. Paranoia, mixed with the false sense of loyalty so many Lyrans had, might make the guard do something stupid, like tell his boss what he did. But security guards weren't the only people with access to high security areas.

Someone had to clean the place.

There were fifty employees tasked with cleaning LyraCorps headquarters. Most of them worked overnight, which made the daytime employees especially hungry for friendship. Sometimes Garrett felt guilty about pretending to be people's friend. The pangs of guilt would come, often in the moments just before he had to ask them for a dangerous answer, or an even more dangerous favor. This was the way things were, though. He was doing what needed to be done.

Garrett was running on a treadmill, keeping pace at a comfortable twelve miles an hour. He was waiting for his newest friend, Tran.

Tran was going to help him put some very tiny microphones throughout the executive's gym.

The cleaner was just entering the area, Tran's first break of the day having just started. The man was thin for his size, his clothing hiding the features on his person that were unusually elongated or otherwise noticeable as being out of place. There were no humans in the building, but some of the Loren were less accepting of The Wretched than others. Plenty of the Lyrans in the gym would give Tran a harder time than he needed if they were reminded too openly that he was not like them, and was not one of the other races who worked closely with the Lyran Empire, the Shadone or Morkhavians. Even the Celebrants, a race composed primarily of for-hire individuals, received preferential treatment over The Wretched, who are known universally for their neutrality. Tran's arms are noticeably long for his body, his form hunched over to draw less attention to himself. His kind are tall and slender, with bodies designed for easy flight. From the front, Tran would appear somewhat frail to the casual observer. If the man took his shirt off and turned around, the muscles on his back would be on par with a professional bodybuilder, so large and powerful was his back, similar to the breast meat on a bird. All Wretched had wings to be called upon when they chose – parts of themselves that simultaneously existed and did not. The history of their race was somewhat mysterious, their personal origin story naming them to be beings from outside the normal scope of reality. Garrett wasn't sure he believed any of the origin stories each race of the Loren had for themselves, but he often found himself wondering where the wings *went*. Tran didn't have wings right now. But Garrett knew that if the thin man wanted to, he could call upon them, and fly around the gym with a fourteen foot wingspan of leathery, clawed appendages. Many of The Wretched lived outside of society, though some, like Tran, searched for integration and a life of what many deemed as normalcy.

Tran made a beeline for Garrett immediately. The two had never discussed it openly, but Garrett could tell that Tran felt safe when they talked. As if Garrett were keeping away any of the Lyrans who might want to give the cleaner a hard time.

"Hey Garrett." Tran said.

"Ran, what's goin' on?"

"Not too much. Six miles already? Man, I wish I had the stamina." This was part of their routine. Tran pretended like he couldn't fly faster and farther than Garrett could ever run, and Garrett took the compliments as gracefully as he could while running in place.

"So Tran, did you get that thing I sent you?" Garrett had already sent a package of tiny microphones to a pickup point downtown. Tran hadn't been able to confirm yet whether or not he'd made the pickup.

"I did, thanks. My wife is going to *love* the new dinner-wear, Garrett. I really appreciate it." The two hadn't established any kind of code beforehand. Garrett had planned on simply being ambiguous when they talked about it, and was a little surprised with how fluidly Tran came up with the false details. "She's already cleaned them, and they're ready to go. When did you want to come by for dinner with your family?"

"I was thinking as soon as possible." Garrett replied. "You guys up for tomorrow, or even tonight?"

"Ah, tonight is no good. But I like the idea of as soon as possible. We need to clean up a little. You know how it is."

"Awesome, Tran. We can't wait. Just let me know when you're free. Hey, good talking with you. Break time is almost over, got to make sure I hit the showers before I get back up there. I'm drenched!"

Garrett left the gym with a smile on his face. Getting intel on what the executives talked about behind closed doors was important. He needed to know as much as possible. Thanks to Tran, he'd know more very soon.

Garrett thought then about the implications of the game he was playing, and the stakes involved if the powers that be ever found out he was trying to bring them down. It wasn't just dangerous for him. He had a wife; a family, now. It would be the end of all of that if he were found out. But he had to try.

Once upon a time, he'd been a soldier. That was when he'd met Russell. They were just two men, then, in the same place around the same time. As their paths continued to cross, Garrett saw something in the old dog, and Russell saw the same in Garrett as well. They became fast friends. Garrett remembered the time Russell had saved him from an improvised explosive device. Sometimes, even the best trained solider can make a mistake. But Russell had been there. After that, Garrett was Russell's man. Garrett's loyalty was unquestionable.

Even when it came to fighting their own.

Few and far between are the Lyrans who would strike out against another of their kind. For the most part, the Lyran Empire is a united entity. Each shapeshifter pledges their fealty to their patron, Mordacity.

There are ranks and lords and plenty of people whose title landed them above Garrett, in spite of his status in the Special Forces, but ultimately each solider like him only cared about their standing with their true leader. When they obeyed the command of another who was not Mordacity, it was out of fear, respect, or both for the oversized Lyran. Garrett had been this way until Russell had saved him. After that, his loyalty lay with Russell completely. And when Russell eventually told Garrett of his plans to bring down the Lyran Empire, brick by brick if need be, Garrett didn't bat an eye. He would do whatever he needed to. He had already done so much.

It had been a long road to the position he held now. There had been one particularly nasty fight with a few guards at an alternate facility, before Garrett had met Bren. Even with his training, Garrett had barely made it out alive. He and Russell had been a real dynamic duo that day, too.

Garrett went on many missions for the Lyran Empire. Even after the Vampyr were gone, the Great War didn't seem to find its end. There was always someone more for the soldiers to fight. For a time, many of them fought the wars the humans had given themselves, the petty, pretend politics of their faux society providing the outlet so many Lyran soldiers needed. Garrett couldn't deny that without something to fight, someone to kill, many Lyrans would rampage and frenzy. He often wondered what kept him from feeling the same, seemingly insane bloodlust so many others seemed to be born with. Perhaps he would never know. More to the point, he had grown sick of the missions even before he'd found himself pledging loyalty to Russell, and to what Garrett had found to be the greater cause of bringing down LyraCorps.

The man finished his shower, retrieving his work clothes from his locker.
They were closer than ever to their goal. Garrett had done so much just to secure his position inside the building.

Though, there was still so much more to do.

Chapter XI

Spice was many things as he sat upon his throne, a reconstituted lounge chair with a base made of green plastic. He was a Wretched, a tall, gaunt individual, with arms longer than they ought to be and large, leathery wings that could sprout and disappear upon command. He was an informant, with a mouth full of secrets for hire. Wealthy, and not unlike a vizier among his people, he was the deadliest, most fearsome Wretched there was. To the contrary it was once noted that he cooked some of the best food this side of the underground; unless he was standing on the other side, but more than those things, Spice was something else, too.

He was *known.*

Spice was surrounded on all sides by reinforced rock. It was a secret his people carried within them, how to reconstitute earth into something more than it was. It allowed them to carve out their places underground without having to worry about their space collapsing. His space was warm, carved out underneath a solar energy plant.

In a race with thousands of nameless faces to those who live along the surface of the earth, many are the Loren who know Spice. He had transcended the bonds which would serve to crush his spirit, like so many of the Wretcheds' spirits that came before, and after, his. Spice had spent his entire life cooking, clawing, flapping, and even biting his way to the top of his race. He was a revolutionary among his kind. Not the first to want for than a subterranean lifestyle, but the first to keep the *style* in his life as he sought for something more.

His throne was uncomfortable, at times. To his surprise, he often found himself safer above ground, where his kind had no place, than below in the darkness that was his true home. Many were The Wretched who sought to preserve the essence of their race's neutrality. There were those who believed that the more Spice stepped outside of the boundaries they had agreed upon with the other Loren, namely the Lyra, the more likely the Lyra were to bring war to their homes. The Wretched were everywhere. They were under every city, and every town. They suckled from deep aquifers in places where no life can survive on the surface. Thought for each Wretched, they knew, was also a Lyran. The Lyra were organized. They had lifetimes worth of soldiers, entire strains of their kind who had been bred for battle and little else. The Wretched were not a race of warriors. So afraid of backlash from the Lyra were many of The Wretched that attacks upon Spice, even as he sat upon his throne, were frequent. He found he spent less and less time underground, venturing back only when it was absolutely necessary. Being known also meant a modicum of wealth. He was not without the means to ensure he was well protected when he came back to the underground cities his people called home. Sometimes, it was what he needed to do to perpetuate his wealth, and more importantly, his namesake.

Today was one such day.

It was not often Spice was contacted by Celebrant nobles. He found the lot of them so snuck up and self-absorbed, the lack of contact was preferable to dealing with them at all. Unless they wanted something. Spice had plenty to say about the stupid, inbred imbeciles the *royal* Celebrant families had allowed themselves to become, but the thing he loved to say the most was that they were, in a word, loaded. Celebrant money was the definition of old. When they wanted information, which was not often, he could ask for anything he wanted. There were no limits when it came to the bone-growers. He had only heard the whisperings a day before the nobles had. Still, they came to him.

They wanted the girl.

It was a curious task, finding her. Not difficult. Not for Spice. For each Wretched he knew despised him, there were plenty who lived a partial life on the surface, desperately searching for the secret to the ascension he had achieved. Many Wretched yearned to be accepted, truly accepted, by the other Loren. Spice knew it would never happen. He imagined often that was the true difference between him and the other Wretched who lived upon the surface. Where they sought acceptance, Spice sought only to make a name for himself. He didn't need to be loved. He needed to be known. And he was. When he wanted to find someone, he simply asked where they were. Those looking for love or respect would help him every time. Finding the girl had ultimately proven curious because, he came to realize as he closed in on her location only days ago, she was the real deal. He had seen it himself.

She was a Warbringer.

Spice knew as well as anyone that there were no more Warbringers. As far as he was concerned, there never were. But he watched the girl run with Vampyric speed and grace, only to see her grow bone an instant later to use it as a weapon. Her aim was exemplary as she shot the grown missile at her unsuspecting foe. He did not need to see more to know what she was, though he would be lying if he did not admit to delighting somewhat when he watched her feed. She did not just move as a Vampyr, she fed as one, as well. As he thought about it, Spice realized that was likely not something he should tell anyone else he enjoyed watching.

He didn't want to kill the wholesome aspect of his reputation.

So Spice found himself sitting across from two Celebrant mercenaries. A new band, named Rent. Celebrants who are not of noble birth are without a family name. These men were named Edie and Finley Rent, though there was no relation by blood. Spice could tell, however, that the men had come up together. They might even have been lovers. Spice watched the way the bone-growers kept their eyes on the others' 'six.' He observed how easily and adeptly the men watched out for one another. Spice knew that even the biggest paydays did not often convince two Celebrant mercenaries to be so concerned for each other. The only answer was that the two had been close for a long time.

They certainly did business as if they were. Spice was used to negotiations. They were a part of his namesake. He had no problem pitting one member of a group against another to get the leverage or price he desired, even if everyone was sat in the same room. Spice was currently being stonewalled, though. The two-man Rent band refused to budge in their offer. They came with the money that the nobles had provided to them, in exchange for the location of their target. Spice was certain the two men had more to offer. If they were being contracted by the first family of Celebrant nobles, their skills must be formidable indeed. Spice would do well to have a favor from two such men he could call in. He had offered them many things already, resorting again to attempting to play them against the other.

"I think your friend ought to reconsider my offer," Spice said, turning to Finley as he spoke. "You seem to be a more reasonable man. My reach is far, as I'm sure you know. There must be something you believe I could assist you both with. For the glory of your band!"

"For the glory of Spice, you mean." Finley replied. "And for a favor that we might need to deliver on, when it suits you."

"Ah, you two are too smart for me, it seems. Fine, fine. Hand over the payment."

"Hold a moment," Edie said. "We would prefer to pay you half now, and the other half when you have led us to the woman. We trust The Reach would not send us to you if you could not deliver. Certainly, your reputation speaks volumes. There is no reason we should not trust you. But…"

Spice mused to himself, "The Reach." That noble house would be the death of him yet. Their plotting and scheming within the celebrant hierarchy were fair enough, but as of late was going to be the death of him yet. If The Reach had sought these two out then their time on this

111

earth was not guaranteed or they were just that good. Spice would bet on the latter. These thoughts quickly passed however sensing the patience level of his guests in front of him getting the best of them.

"But you would prefer I lead you to the girl myself." Spice said.

"I mean, most of the way, at least." Edie said.

"A little past halfway, perhaps." Finley added.

"I cannot." Said Spice with an heir of finality.

"I'm not sure we can pay you, then." Said Edie.

"Gentleman, please. I cannot lead you to her *myself*. But I can ensure it is she whom you find. Don't worry about paying me now, if it makes you more comfortable. You can pay my courier. They will lead you to where the girl is." Spice could see that the Rent mercenaries were unsettled by his reluctance to lead them to the girl. That was the way it had to be, though. Spice had chanced nearing her once already. The only way he would go near her again, willingly, would be if he were absolutely certain he would not draw her ire. Spice had no idea how quickly the mercenaries would try to attack the girl when they found her, nor did he know how quickly she would respond. What if he were too nearby when the battle began? It would be foolish to be less than a hundred feet away. The men could follow, and pay, his courier. He didn't need the trouble.

To his delight, the Rent band accepted Spice's offer.

Spice watched as the two mercenaries made their way from his throne room, a space carved out underneath another. The two seemed so confident, so sure. In that moment, out of habit more than conscious thought, Spice also began to lament that he was not able to squeeze the two men for any more than they had offered him. Then he recalled again the precision with which the Warbringer had fought. Spice recalled her speed, and her absolute skill of battle. Watching the two men leave, Spice, for the first time in years, was satisfied with the deal he had made. His courier would lead the men where they wished to go. And Celebrant mercenaries always paid their way, as was their custom. He would ultimately receive the money he had been promised. It was alright with him that he would not be owed an additional favor from the Rent band.

Spice was sure they would not be alive long enough to return it.

••

Dalbrin had some catching up to do after cancelling his classes to care for his wife. In spite of how trivial he felt his job as a professor was, he had come to like the house he lived in very much. Modern architecture did little to satisfy his artistic side, but damn if technology didn't make living in the modern day downright *better*. His fridge talked to him each morning, to tell him what things he was running low on, and he liked it that way. His wife liked it, too, and there was not much he wouldn't do to make her happy. So the teaching had to stay. Even if it was, to him, literally more boring that sitting in a ditch and waiting. Dalbrin had sat in many ditches. In his mind, if someone had never dug a ditch before, they hadn't yet become an adult.

He'd prepared his lesson plans for the week already, of course, but cancelling his evening classes the day before had put him behind. He needed to make sure he could cover everything he planned to that day so he wasn't behind for the rest of the semester. As he unlocked the door to his office, removing the bag from his shoulder to set it on his desk, he grabbed instinctually for his laptop bag on his other shoulder.
It was not there.

With a great sigh, Dalbrin realized he'd left his laptop at home. Without it, he could not get his work done. He came in early to revise his lesson plans for the day and grade papers before his morning classes. Without the laptop, he could do none of those things. Luckily, he could be home and return with enough time, if he hurried. He'd skip his morning meal fixing his mistake, but that was nothing new. The myriad of police cars and television crews, whom he had expected to be on campus this morning after reading about the mutilated body in the paper, had caused him to park closer to his office than normal. Most days he enjoyed the long walk from his car. This city had a way of keeping its freshest air for the newest hours of the sun, a time his wife was always awake for. As he locked the door on his way out, he let himself slip deeper into his thoughts, ensuring with a mental checklist that he was aware of everything he needed to do.

He started to formulate a concrete plan, imagining which tasks he would complete first and in what order. His pace quickened as he recanted how many papers he needed to finish grading that morning, briefly considering grading them at home before returning. *But no,* he thought, *that's not fair to the students. They may need to come by during office hours.* Per each of his syllabi, students were welcome to come by as early as 8am, when morning classes on campus began. As an educator, he couldn't swallow the idea of not being there for one of his students with good conscience. Even if he didn't care for the job, he was never one to go halfway. The hallway lifestyle of the current generation bothered him to no end. So many of them were quitters. He had met student after student who, upon being unable to do something the first time, never tried again. It was like, if they couldn't run a mile in six minutes, or dunk a basketball their first time on the court, 'what was the point?' If they had trouble remembering dates, they gave up on learning about their own history. If they had trouble with math, they didn't bother with a single formula. There was no conviction anymore. No passion. Dalbrin knew he couldn't make up for the whole world, but he wasn't going to let them bring him down to their ridiculous level.

So engrossed in thought was he as he walked that he didn't notice the men in thick vests as he bumped into the back of one.

He began to apologize, then stopped himself as he eyed the LyraCorps logo on the man's vest. Noticing as well that the armored man's face showed anger. The two stood in silence for a moment.

"Something you want to say to me?" The LyraCorps man asked.

Dalbrin thought again about his commitment to his life, to the duty he accepted so long ago. He gave his reply in spite of himself, "Yea. Get a new job." The scoff exited from the professor's mouth without so much as a second thought, his disdain for LyraCorps not only open, but almost overly expressive as well.

Dalbrin began to walk away, but the man grabbed his arm before he could.

"Hey! You bumped into me, you know. Don't you think you should apologize for that? Now I guess you owe me two, once for your stupid feet and one for your *smart* mouth." The man in the vest smiled a wide smile. The other men in vests walked over, now privy to the commotion. Dalbrin looked at the five of them.

"Take your apologies," he said, "And put 'em someplace they can rot, so they'll match your souls." His arm still in the clutches of the other man, Dalbrin gathered as much spit as quickly as he could and released it into the man's face. It landed with a spray, more foam and wet air than actual saliva. Still, the damage was done.

The mens' collective smiles quickly turned to more serious looks. One of them turned his head to peer at the scene around them. Dalrbin noticed what the man did; what they were doing. Looking for witnesses. There were no students around. In fact, they were alone for at least a hundred yards in any direction. Far enough, Dalbrin knew, that even if he screamed as loud as he could…

The first fist struck him hard to the stomach. As it did, he reeled and doubled over in pain. The blow came from someone much stronger than any average man. The next came to the side of his face, causing his head to cock to the side. He could feel the intense pressure the second hit placed on his neck, the bones in his face threatening to break. A great ringing played out in his ears immediately, and he bit his tongue with enough force that he spat blood when the next fist hit his other cheek. As the kicks began, the man he had bumped began to scream at him. He told him to respect LyraCorps. He told him they were the law. Didn't he know? The man continued to ask questions as he screamed, soon joined by his comrades. It was almost as if they were expecting a reply. Dalbrin could not have given one if he wanted to.

He was already unconscious.

Chapter XII

Kris was running late for class. It had been somewhat of a late night for her, but she had desperately needed to cram for a quiz. Her hair had managed to reach a maximum level of frizz and dishevelment. Physics in high school had been so easy for her, but in college none of it seemed to make sense. She grabbed her bag from the trunk of her car, trotting briskly away as she checked the time again on her phone. Seven minutes. She would just make it.

As she looked up, she saw Dalbrin lying on the concrete, covered in layers of blood. Some of it had already begun to dry.

"Oh my god. Professor Dalbrin! Professor Dalbrin, are you ok?!" Tears formed quickly in Kris's eyes, but she would not let her fear conquer her in this moment. As she reached for her phone, Dalbrin's hand shot up to stop her, his eyes now open, showing only red veins where the white of his eyes were meant to be.

Kris screamed as he grabbed her, the sheer quickness of it enough to pull the noise from the deepest part of herself. The fear she was feeling in the situation had become even more real. The longer she shared her gaze with Dalbrin, the more frightened she became. After only a moment, she could hardly move.

Trajen heard the scream, though he was well beyond the range the noise would have normally carried. As he looked in the direction of the sound's source, he realized he was looking at Kris. For a moment, his heart beat at twice its speed. As his foot fell in the shadow of a tree, his next step took him many yard forward, out of the shadow of another tree only a few feet away from Kris. This was the farthest he had stepped so far. When he emerged from the other side, he realized the distance might wear him down too greatly. It was possible he might collapse right next to his professor. But there was no time to reflect, as he could see the full extent of the scene before him. As he walked up, Kris screamed again, her fear now beginning to snake its way to the forefront of her thoughts. Trajen was thankful he wasn't panicking as Kris was. Keeping a clear head, he grabbed Kris lightly by her arm, pulling her away from the broken teacher. As she took a step backward, her screaming stopped instantly. Trajen smiled before turning towards Dalbrin, taking a deep breath as he tried to figure out what he was supposed to do in this situation.

Kris and Trajen watched Dalbrin lift his leg, part of which fell back down at the shin, his bone clearly broken underneath the skin so that it was two smaller shins instead of a singular bone. One piece pointed directly outward, the other perfectly towards the ground so that they created a ninety-degree angle. Trajen began to tell Dalbrin not to move, for surely the man was in no condition to do anything other than lie still and wait for real help to arrive. But the professor silenced his students, grabbing his foot with his left hand and holding it up until the bone in his shin seemed to match up with the rest of itself. After he was sure he had lined the pieces up correctly, he pushed them towards each other, an action which gave way to a powerful *pop* as the bones seemed to snap back in place. Trajen thought it sounded like when he pushed his pen back together after removing the back from the base. He was sure that bones didn't work that way. So was Kris, who whimpered when she heard the sound.

Kris then swooned a moment later, nearly falling backwards to the ground. Trajen caught her just before she lost her balance. She steadied herself and looked the other way, afraid she may throw up. Dalbrin wore a small smile as he looked over the rest of himself for additional broken bones, as if he might simply push himself back together entirely. Finding nothing else which was in need of apparent mending, the man simply dusted himself off and stood up, his leg somehow already able to carry his full weight.

"There," he said. "See? I'm totally fine. Nothing but a few scrapes. Trey, is she alright? Make sure she doesn't faint and hit her head. We don't want to have to call an ambulance."

Trajen turned to regard Kris, who sat with her eyes closed, her body still turned away from the professor. As he turned back to reply to Dalbrin, he was met with nothing more than a wisp of smoke where his professor had been. The smoke was so light it might have gone unnoticed only a moment later.

The color quickly returned to Kris's cheeks, her eyes now open again. Realizing Dalbrin was gone, she turned to Trajen. "Where...where did he go?"

Trajen was honest in his reply. "I've no idea, frankly. Are you ok?"

"Yea, I'm ok now. The noise his bone made. It set me back a little. And all that *blood.* I can't even get shots at the doctor. Did you see him? He was *covered!"* Kris seemed frantic as she spoke, though Trajen was glad to see the restraint had made its way back into her. She seemed now to simply be a little shaken up by the whole thing.

"I saw, yes. But he said it wasn't that bad. Must have been right, eh? Figure he'd still be here otherwise." Trajen smiled has he helped Kris to her feet, being sure to watch her in case she fell.

"I mean..." Kris wore a look of pure confusion, as she considered the possibility. "I....I guess so. Man, what a weird morning. I was rushing because I-" Kris's face quickly changed to one of realization. "Oh my god. The quiz! I have to go."

Trajen smiled as Kris ran off, in full agreement to her assessment. It had been a crazy morning indeed.

Far off, even farther away than before Trajen had stepped through the shadows, a hooded figure, inexplicably drawn to Trajen, watched Kris hurry away as well. The girl pulled her hood on tighter as she perceived Trajen to also continue on with his day, knowing full well how professor Dalbrin was able to be gone so quickly, as if he had disappeared in a puff of smoke.

She could do the same thing.

The hooded woman smiled, continuing on the way she was headed before all the commotion, musing for what felt like the thousandth time at how insane the city was. She had never been anywhere like it. As often as she saw events like the one she just saw unfold, she figured that of the fifty thousand or so residents living there, maybe a little over a tenth were actually human. It couldn't be any other way. It used to be, she knew, that you had to go looking when you wanted to find somebody who could turn into a wolf. Stories about people able to throw men a hundred feet, or run full speed for miles; those used to by myths. Legends people told to their children. Events such as those were once considered to be miraculous. Here, it was all over the place. She couldn't decide what was crazier: that this place had such a strong concentration of non-humans, or that nobody was talking about it. She had only recently learned about the news. The idea was certainly brilliant, though it didn't seem to her as though what was discussed on the news was always newsworthy, even in her extremely short time as a viewer. Still, it seemed to her that, eventually, someone on television might mention that their city was full of people who weren't humans. And yet, the human news anchor hadn't brought it up once.

The woman turned down an alleyway to see two homeless men rummaging through a dumpster. They were so deep inside the large receptacle, both of their figures were nearly hidden from view. She saw them only when they poked their heads up and pushed against the lid, presumably, reasonably, for a breath of fresh air. *Probably just hungry,* she thought to herself. As if in response to the mention of the word, her own stomach began to growl.

She was hungry too.

As she neared the dumpster, she locked eyes with one of the men, filling him with a fear as intense as the fear Kris had felt when Dalbrin had looked at her. The man could not have moved if he wanted to. The woman held the gaze with the man, whose friend poked his own head up to see why his companion had ceased his looting. The homeless man tapped his frozen friend on the shoulder, calling his name to get his attention, still unaware of the woman approaching them. As she grew even closer, a long, sharp shard of bone fell from the underside of her forearm, resting in her hand not unlike a javelin when it finished growing.

As the man perceived the approaching woman, he became startled, turning to get a good look. Before his feet finished their pivot, his chest had an extra bone, a bloody point freshly emerging from his back. As he fell down, no longer possessed of life, his friend continued to stand frozen with fear. The woman had finally reached her destination, climbing into the dumpster with ease, her gaze never broken from the first man. She pulled him down with incredible force, plunging her fangs into his neck, ripping chunks of fresh and muscle away before the man had time to scream.

Soon, she was no longer hungry.

•••

The test was over. Kris was walking from class with Nick and Jones. Nick was the only person Kris knew who would ever walk away from a Trig exam talking about how *fun* it had been. She was still reeling from her crazy morning, but in spite of seeing her professor in a bloody heap on her way to class, she had managed to do pretty well on her exam. Not as good as Nick or, surprisingly, Jones, but it was good enough for her standards.

The boys were trying to engage her in conversation about the weekend. Well, Nick was asking her what she had planned. Jones raised his eyebrows in anticipation. Kris found it difficult to get into talking with them. The three of them were great friends. She didn't feel uncomfortable talking with them about *anything*. Something as casual as what she was going to do with her weekend – eating pumpkin pie and streaming shows both days while lying in bed – should have been easy to talk about. But the more she tried to get herself into the conversation, the more she found herself thinking back to how she had felt when she'd seen Professor Dalbrin lying on the ground. Kris had been beyond scared. She was terrified.

That was weird for her.

Kris's father moved them around quite a bit. He had been with the company since nearly the beginning. The man wasn't a founding member of LyraCorps, but he was a shareholder in the company, which was not publicly traded. The company's history went back surprisingly far, if you knew how to look at the trail of parent and grandparent corporations. LyraCorps had ended up being the last subsidiary that its umbrella Alaskan Native Corporation had ever needed to create, they'd managed to work themselves into the right commercial and government contracts. The other companies fell to the wayside, as Kris understood it, and LyraCorps took on all of the current employees. That was one of those lessons that was so often skipped over when children are taught about the Nixon administration in high school. Say what you want about his scandalous ending, Nixon helped a lot of native Alaskans make sure their people were taken care of. They got land and *corporations.* Kris had shares in LyraCorps, too. Her dad had gifted some to her when she was a little girl, and made sure that she went to every shareholder's meeting. He kept her apprised of how important the things she voted on were, and always let her make her own decisions.

Part of being a young shareholder was having access to a program that helped the younger natives, or children of natives who were born growing up somewhere else, take the time each year to explore their heritage. For three weeks out of every year since she was ten, Kris had flown down to Alaska during the summer to learn all kinds of things about her people. She learned about their history and their language, she learned about their folklore and their traditional dishes. Most of the things she knew how to cook weren't even sold in supermarkets where they lived. Even though the fish in her region was one of their biggest commercial exports, you still couldn't find it in the majority of the lower forty-eight. The product really didn't make it past Washington. She learned to love messing with textiles, too. The intricate patterns she saw in her history books came naturally to her. She even took requests from the other kids, sometimes.

It was during a summer stay in Alaska that she'd felt terror for the first time. The event that solidified in Kris's mind what terror really felt like – something she knew not many people experienced. Her region isn't particularly known for housing many bears, but then again, there aren't many bears that you can tell what to do. She'd seen one in a circus, once, that seemed to be trained pretty well. But that had to be, like, the *only* one. Regular bears went wherever they wanted.

One time a bear wanted to be where Kris was.

You can learn a lot about yourself when you stare down an animal that weighs upwards of eight hundred pounds. There's a kind of clarity that washes over a person when they can smell the musty scent of death. For Kris, she realized the full truth of why the best thing you can do when you are face-to-face with a grizzly is play dead. She saw the claws on the thing close enough that she could have grabbed one. She could feel the weight behind each of the bear's steps as it reverberated through the earth, a few feet away from the beast. She knew in that moment that if she did anything other than try to remain uninteresting, if she didn't play dead, even a curious nibble or half-hearted swipe of the bear's paw would likely leave her cleaved in two. But that wasn't what Kris had learned. What she really took away from those moments with the bear, was that when she was truly scared, she didn't *look* like she was. She sweat more coming down the hill on the way back to her campsite than she did when she was standing next to a grizzly bear, terrified out of her mind.

But when she'd seen Professor Dalbrin on the pavement, she felt the same terror, and she could hardly breathe. When she got to class to take her exam, she realized sweat had been pouring down her backside. Her shirt was completely damp when she pressed her back against her seat. Even stranger was how quickly and intensely she had become terrified in the situation. In her mind, even though she was surprised to come upon the bloody scenario, she wasn't scared when she walked up to her professor. She wanted to help, see what she could do. Her first thought wasn't about being afraid, it was about calling an ambulance and getting him patched up. Then it was like a switch had been thrown, and she was standing next to the grizzly all over again. Her professor was no bear of a man, but she'd felt in those moments like he could have clawed her open just the same. Even though she could see that he was a battered, broken form of a person, all she had wanted to do was run for her life.

That just wasn't like her.

When she parted ways with her friends, she thought for a moment about Trajen. Had he been as scared as she'd been? Maybe it was just a different kind of thing, seeing that much blood. Maybe it was the kind of thing that could make anybody scared. Either way, now that she'd had time to reflect, she realized she was still pretty concerned about Professor Dalbrin. There was *no way* he got very far, even if he had managed to get up and go pretty quickly. The memory was a little hazy from the adrenaline, but Kris was pretty sure she'd seen some bone poking where it wasn't supposed to be. She could still remember the crunching noise her professor's leg made when she pushed it back into itself. Like the sound of cracking your knuckles, but louder, and with a distinct aspect of rough metal grinding on itself.

Kris might never be able to figure out why she'd acted the way she had, or why she'd been so suddenly terrified in the first place, but feeling weird didn't mean she was allowed to sacrifice her morals. That was another thing, maybe the biggest thing, she took away from her trips back to Alaska. It takes a village to raise a child, and it takes a whole lot of give-a-crap to keep a village going. She was going to start calling around to the hospitals when she got home to see which one professor Dalbrin was checked in to. The man had been beaten half to death, the least she could do was visit him to wish him well.

That most definitely *was* like her.

■■

Dalbrin hobbled into his front door, unsure how he ended up on his porch rather than in his den, where he'd intended to wind up. *Those wolves really did a number on me*, he thought. *I should have just fought back. Look at me! My brain is so scrambled I couldn't even make it all the way home.* He entered his house and took off his shoes, his arm clutching a broken rib out of instinct. He could feel it beginning to mend, but it would be some time before he was fully healed. The idea of waiting made him angry. It seemed no matter how old he got, he was unable to master the art of patience.

Alerted to the sound of the front door, Dalbrin's wife exited the kitchen. Any sickness she'd been possessed of before was completely gone now. Her skin was vibrant and alive with color, her cheeks full and plump. Her hair hung down around her, swaying slightly as she walked to her husband. Her face turned to a mask of worry as she saw her husband was hurt.

"Hi hon," Dalbrin said through blood-stained teeth. His smile was genuine, even through the pain. God help him, he couldn't help but smile when he saw his wife.

"Oh my goodness. Dalbrin, what happened?!"

"Ah, it's alright, Gracia. I'm fine. Just a little…misunderstanding. I asked for it, if you want to know the truth. Couldn't keep my mouth shut. And the wolves were so close to me this morning. That smell! You know how that putrid musk makes me crazy."

Gracia's expression agreed loudly with her husband's statement. As long as she had known him, he had absolutely *hated* the Lyra. Even if she didn't share the sentiment, she knew long before they had met that a life with Dalbrin meant a life spent against the Lyra. That was just the way it was going to be. Gracia thought briefly about the first time she saw her husband, adorned in Vampyrian armor, defending other, weaker members of his kind from a horde of bloodthirsty Lyrans. It seemed to be a running theme that the moments she felt she loved her husband the most were those he was half beaten to death. Or undeath. Half beaten to one of those, anyway.

She grabbed her husband's hand and led him towards the back door, where she let go and stepped outside. As she stood in the sunlight, each of the rays around her seemed to curve towards her cheeks, until her skin took on a sheen. The sheen quickly turned to fluorescence, and her skin began to glow outwardly. Her eyes took on a golden hue, and her husband stepped back inside. He loved seeing his wife like this, basking in the rays of the sun. There was nothing more beautiful to him than when she looked what he considered to be her truest self to look. As he felt the heat of her body fall onto his, he couldn't help himself. Just as she had her moments, Dalrbin had his own that served as invigorating reminders of the incredible love he had for his wife.

Gently, raising his hand from the clutching of his side, he cupped his wife's glowing face, touching his lips to her own. As he did, the blood about him turned to dust and seemed to dissolve away. The cuts and bruises on his skin quickly faded, his broken ribs now itching as they

126

healed and set themselves. Even his leg tingled a little, evidence he had not fully found its proper place under the skin. No surprise there, considering how haphazardly he shoved the bone together. The glow began to fade from his wife, though their kiss only grew more passionate as the vitality given to her by the sun transferred fully into Dalbrin. He pulled back a moment later to regard the woman he loved so dearly, who now wore as true a smile as he'd worn as he watched her bathe in the daylight a moment ago. This was the definition of their relationship. He protected them, and bore the weight of their lives, whatever that meant. He took care of the finances, took care of the fighting. Her kind were wistful. Most days, Gracia found it hard to concentrate on any one thing. That was just how her people were. But when the weight of the world became too much, when Dalbrin's cuts ran too deep, his wife was always there to lick his wounds. The arrangement may have been lopsided, but for the pair of them it worked perfectly. The love they shared was real.

"I have to go, love. I'm behind at work as it is." Dalbrin always found it was hardest to let go from moments like this. Walking away was the opposite of what he wanted to do.

"I know. Feeling better though, I hope?" Gracia smiled even brighter than before, proud of the healing she had accomplished.

"Oh, much." Gracia kissed Dalbrin on his nose. Dalbrin knew he'd better stay true to his word, but just he couldn't help himself.

He was already late.

What was another few moments?

Chapter XIII

The men in vests were still combing the campus. They'd been instructed to seek out and identify the cause of the most recent body, authorities unaware that less than two football fields away, two more bodies lay in pieces in the dumpster behind Sally's Hair Supply. Police were sure there were no clues left to find at the college, but the LyraCorps soldiers knew better. They could smell better.

And the campus stunk.

But as much as their preternatural senses told them there were clues to be had around the school, they continued to come up with nothing. In spite of their best efforts, each scent trail led nowhere. Soon, their leader in the field, Bando, commanded that they walk around with their eyes closed, to better track the things they smelled, bumping into students with utter disregard to how foolish or dangerous the exercise was. Knowing better than to return empty-handed to their superiors, each of their members soon grew restless. Casual bumps into students became full-on charges, each of the soldiers ready to fully transform if given something even somewhat resembling the proper reason. Their leader in the field, the man who'd caused the commotion with Dalbrin by stepping in front of the professor, causing their collision, was the most agitated at their lack of findings. He knew if he had to return to Roper, the second in command to Mordacity and overseer of all Lyran warriors, empty handed, it'd be his hide.

Most of their morning had been spent waiting for more people to show up. There was only one scent they'd been unable to properly identify, prevalent enough around the campus that they knew whoever it belonged to would eventually return. It took until midday, but after the soldiers had managed to manhandle just about every student attending classes that day, they found the scent had finally returned. A young man strode by as the Strike Team leader inhaled, and he reached out to grab the student. He pulled the young man to him, lifting the boy's feet from the ground completely. The young man's hair was dreaded and down to his shoulders, his clothes as loose fitting as they could possibly be. He wore thong sandals on his feet, one of which fell off as he was lifted from the concrete.

"Whoa dude, what did I do?" The student asked, a look of shock on his face

Most Lyrans don't hate humans. Many don't hate any other race at all. But the Strike Team leader was a purist. A true Wolf among the Lyra. He believed the Lyra to be the most *pure* race among them all. He could smell the scent on this human, could smell the puny boy's fear grow and release itself from his pores as the leader continued to manhandle him. He leveled his gaze as he held the boy steady, allowing himself a moment to emphasize his words with his actions before he spoke them. "Tell me about the body this morning," the leader said.

"What? I just got here, man. And I was partying all last night. I don't know anything about a body." The boy's legs began to shake. He was sure if he'd had to stand on them, they would not have held his weight.

Just as he could smell the boy's fear, so too could he discern he was telling him the truth. He knew questioning him further would lead them only further away from the information they were seeking. Still, his anger at the situation would not allow him to simply walk away. He now held the boy up against a tree, his right arm pinning the boy's form to the tree's trunk. As if the boy weighed nothing, the leader flung his right arm upward, taking the boy's body with it, causing the student to land high up in the tree after a brief moment of screaming.

In spite of the outburst, the Lyran soldier quickly realized he did not feel any better. The boy had been the only inclination so far that the scent they sought which had clung to the body torn to pieces that morning would return to campus. The man was beginning to think combing the campus might be the wrong way to go. He turned to his comrades, who looked to him eagerly for their orders. Deliberating for a moment, the soldier realized he had no idea what to do. The man slumped his soldiers, his head pointing slightly towards the floor. Raising his eyes again, he shrugged, beckoning his team to leave with him. They wouldn't return to Roper. Not yet. Perhaps the police were right, and there were other places that were worth looking into.

Moments later, a young woman spotted the boy in the tree. She knew his name to be Jeremy. They met at a party just the night before. She can see even from there that he is in peril, and obviously afraid of heights. As she made her way under the tree, Jeremy's foot just barely within her grasp, she swiped deftly at his low-hanging fruit, causing him to fall backwards off of the branch which he sat. Jeremy screamed again as he rolled down of the tree trunk, flipping once over himself, only to land in the arms of the woman. She smiled and said nothing as she held him in her arms. She was hoping never to see the boy again after the delightful sunrise they had only recently shared. Better to leave things how they were, she decided, and not say anything. She placed him gently down and walked away, neither speaking a word to the other. The girl flipped up her hood as the continued on.

Jeremy wanted to be embarrassed. Standing there, he was certainly feeling something.

He was pretty sure it was love.

The girl in the hood was growing somewhat tired of only following Trajen around. Unlike him, the girl remembered *everything*. She knew what she was, and she knew who Trajen was. It was insane, in her mind, that Trajen was able to continue on for so long pretending to be human. When she'd gained her freedom, her wits about her, her first thought had been to find a temporary place to squat and gain some strength. The morning after the breakout, she'd felt the pull. That singular, all-encompassing feeling that she knew would only lead to pain if she let herself stray too far from Trajen. He seemed completely unaffected by any such instinctual bindings, which only served to fuel the rage she naturally greeted each day with. Now she'd taken a few haunts around the city. Places where other Loren who chose not to embrace the society around them made their home. Recently she learned that humans often thought the wood in their homes needed to "settle" sometimes. That buildings just made noise. But she knew first-hand that there are more Wretched living in people's walls than there are people living inside their homes. The bigger the house, the more Wretched that lay claim to the spaces in between someone's stucco. Most of the world spent their time above ground.

If a person isn't a miner or a maintenance individual, they may never walk around underneath their city. If other cities were at all like this one, the girl thought the world might be interested to know that there were entire civilizations that carved their history into expanses of tunnels that expanded as the city above did. Most people didn't, but the girl laughed when she spotted news of sinkholes on the television. As if there were some sort of natural reason for large plots of earth to fall in on themselves. One day the world would learn the truth. The Wretched lived below, the eternal neutral party, preferring to keep to themselves than deal with anyone else. And they didn't just live underground. There were often too many. So they dug their tunnels around the pipes and power-lines. Through cement foundations. All it took were a few city planners in their pockets, she'd heard. And they didn't even need to be high-level individuals. In the modern era, you could really find most of the information you needed to know online, the city was often so afraid of the public digging somewhere and making a mess. She still didn't understand the internet. Not the way she could understand television; but she was trying, when the mood struck her. So it was that so many Wretched lived in the walls of people's homes, crawling and climbing up stories of apartment buildings, feeding on and cohabitating with the vermin that lived in the darkest spaces on earth. Rats weren't so bad with a little salt, once you got past the parasites.

The community did well to keep her conversational needs satisfied. Some of the elder Wretched knew her for what she was, as they should.

She gained the status she needed quickly among their ranks, which made it easier to keep tabs on Trajen. Wherever the boy went, she could be nearby; even as he slept in his bed, she was only a few feet away, resting on a beam in the wall. She often went without any sleep at all, of course. The first few months, she actually managed to find contentment in her routine. She would spend her day tracking Trajen, keeping an eye on where he went. And overnight, if she felt the urge, she ventured into the Wretched city while the boy slept for some conversation or lively company. Lately she found she was jealous of their wings, which they could sprout at a moment's notice. She liked the sharp, clawed tips the wings of each Wretched seemed to possess. That kind of reach would make tough situations much easier for her, she knew.

Situations like the one she had just walked into.

It was amazing so little trouble seemed to find Trajen in the months they had both spent living in the city thus far. It seemed to follow her wherever she went. She had only come to the surface to feed. Rat was fine most of the time, roaches were great if you toasted them a little or fried them in oil. But nobody likes to eat the same thing every day. And she could go a week or more without eating when she fed on human blood for a day. She kept a low profile, but plenty of Wretched talked with Loren outside of their own race. Plenty of other Loren still ascribed to an older code of conduct, as well. There were all kinds of power struggles constantly in play beyond the scope of the surface world. The Lyrans were concerned with running the world the humans lived in. That was an issue, obviously. She really didn't appreciate their efforts. But there were plenty of other Loren who grasped at more power than they were supposed to have in any of the numerous political or racial circles that lay outside the scope of human consideration. Societies and houses of nobles that had been around thousands of years. And many of them still believed that power was measured in what you killed. This was the seventh or eighth time one such band of mercenary Loren had decided to take a contract for one such political entity, believing that if they killed her they could add to their considerable scope of influence. She couldn't say she disagreed. Anyone bringing back her dead body would have quite a prize on their hands. But of course, she didn't want to die.

And right then, it was her or the two Celebrants that thought they had her cornered. Well, technically, she *was* cornered. That is, she was standing against the corner of two walls, in an alleyway with a sewer grate at is end. She had planned to go spend some time in the undercity while Trajen spent his day at school. That was the thing about plans, though. All it took was to make one plan befor the world decided to change it for you. This afternoon, she was going to play chess, even.

Now her plan was to win the fight, which likely meant killing the two Loren who had found her. The Celebrants hadn't made their move yet, so the girl decided to take the fight underground. She wouldn't need to be so quiet, that way. Plus, just one Celebrant would make for a messy fight. Two would surely cause all kinds of attention on the surface, something she didn't think the mercenaries would mind at all, but she wanted to avoid. The two Loren were following her so closely, she wondered if they thought she didn't see them, or simply didn't care that she did. It wasn't like this was a common entrance to the undercity. That's why she was taking it. Either way, she had just eaten. She was ready.

There are many types of fighting styles a skillful Celebrant may choose, she knew. They were a race of warriors, their abilities and enhanced stamina allowing them to be highly offensive or defensive in battle. The girl wouldn't know how the Celebrants following her would open the battle, but she knew she needed to be ready for anything. Her skill with Celebrant abilities was as honed as ever. If these were young Loren, she might even be better at growing bone than they were.

She led them down the first tunnel, turning to her right. At the end of the walkway was an opening. She would fight them there. She grew a layer of bone around her face, neck, and vital openings to prepare. Her shins grew another layer on top of themselves; her heels became covered to protect her Achilles tendon, and she grew a half an inch in height. Two long, thin shards of bone sprouted from under her armpits, slicing small holes through her shirt. As she made her way into the clearing, she broke the long bones off from underneath her arms, holding them as batons out in front of her as she turned to greet the Celebrants.

The mercenaries stood their ground. The silence before battle upon them.

"Impressive," one of the Celebrants said.

"I'd have to agree." Said the other.

"Come on then," the girl replied. "I have things I wanted to do today."

"Before we get started, would it be alright if we talked for a moment?" Both Celebrants began to grow bone around their faces and exposed areas. "We're going for something new."

"Something new? What do you mean?"

"A bit of rebranding, you know? Everyone looks for mercenaries to hire, and all they see are prices."

"Been like that forever." The other Celebrant said.

"Right. Forever. We're trying to change that. Give people a reason to choose us over so many other killers wielding sharp parts of themselves. Part of our marketing strategy for this fiscal year is to try and get some of our customers to give testimonials talking about how we come back with *more* than just proof of services rendered. We want to tell our clients a story. Make them feel like they really got their money's worth."

"I don't..." the girl started. "That doesn't even make sense."

"What do you mean?" The other Celebrant said. "Which part?"

"Stop. Just stop it. Are you here to try to kill me, or what?"

"Of course we are! *Of course*. And we'll get started in *just* a moment. But before we do, just do us a favor. Can you tell us what you did earlier today? 'Round six in the morning, if you were up then? We didn't find you until about nine. We'd just like to fil in those gaps, and then, yes, *absolutely,* we'll get going with our attempt to run you through with these pointy bits of ourselves."

"Okay. What if I just get us started? What if I just come at you, right now, with these batons I grew?" The girl asked.

"Well, that would just be rude, wouldn't it? This is just business; you know? No need to be *rude* about the whole thing." One Celebrant said.

"Yea. I mean, what is this? What are we doing here, on this earth, if you can't have a little civility between predator and prey? Don't be like that. Help us out." The other Celebrant asked.

The girl thought for a moment. She had certainly missed much during captivity. Her last few run-ins with mercenaries weren't anything like this. They were what she had expected them to be. Some quick blows, a few scrapes. This was more talking than she'd done with anyone all week, and these two individuals came to end her life! Things were so out of balance now. This had gone on long enough.

She sighed.

"Well, I woke up pretty hungry. It took me some time to try and track down some- "

The Celebrants came at her ferociously, the three Loren a mess of flying limbs and shattering bones as the two attackers batted at the girl,

135

growing more bones with which to strike her as their weapons broke with the blows. This type of fight could last almost indefinitely, so full of natural vigor were the Celebrants and the girl. But she was more than sick of the mercenaries.

The girl stepped back, slowly growing a large, thick bone down her side. She reinforced her forearms, shattering one of the bones the Celebrant to her right carried with her own baton, which also broke, while she blocked the oncoming strike of the other. That Celebrant's weapon broke as well. As it did, she seized her opportunity, tearing the piece of bone she'd grown which appeared not unlike a sickle. It took real skill to grow a curved bone in the heat of battle. She was hoping it might be enough to gain her a mental advantage over the two men, but they seemed unimpressed, if they gave the feat any thought at all. The sides of it weren't nearly as sharp as the metal of a blade might be, but she focused her will to ensure it was serrated. It would chop through the meat of her assailants easily enough.

She swung the curved piece of bone quickly, swiping twice to force her assailants backwards. She knew they'd quickly be growing bones to protect themselves, hoping the piece she swung at them was enough to force them to worry about their front. Within a moment, she had her answer.

Most individuals don't realize how heavy their bones are. Even a freshly grown Celebrant bone has substantial weight. Not like bird bones, which can be full of space. A regular humanoid bone is filled with things. It's got stuff inside of it. And so it was that her opponents gave such little thought to how balanced their bodies were. It was a gamble on her part, but when everything is on the line and victory isn't ensured, there is no better time to take a risk. She knew if either of her Celebrant assailants hadn't bothered to grow the same amount of bone on their backside, they wouldn't be able to pivot turn as effectively as if they were free of the weight. She swung her hooked instrument in an overhead chop, releasing it from her grip as a missile at the opponent on her left. The

Celebrant steeled his footing, prepared to take the blow head on, growing even more bone on the front of himself. The other Celebrant attempted to come at her, but as the man made the move, she called on one of her Vampyric abilities, her speed heightening intensely, her body appearing as nothing more than mist. She grew a tiny shard of bone as she did, the sliver sliding out from her forefinger. Reappearing behind the oncoming assailant, she shoved the tiny bone into the Celebrant's corroded artery, placing a small piece of herself inside one of her opponent's most important vital areas. An uncovered neck was a bad idea for any warrior, though bone shielding around your neck would mean limited head mobility. She was lucky this one had decided he wanted to be able to turn his head, as he fell to his knees clutching at his neck.

She swiped with her left hand at her other assailant, grabbing the Celebrant by the right shoulder as the bone she had thrown shattered against her opponent's chest, so deft had her movements been that she'd beaten her own projectile to its destination. She stepped into the blow as she swung her elbow into the man's cheek, her own bone fortified as it struck the Celebrant's outer casing. The Celebrant grabbed the girl around the waist and tackled her to the floor, quickly growing a hard casing of bone on his forehead. When they landed, he began to pound on her face with his, head-butting the girl repeatedly. She grew layers of bone to keep up, though they quickly began to shatter or fracture with each drop of the man's face into hers.

The girl writhed and wiggled, trying to get her legs into a better position. After a moment, she managed to work her right foot under her opponent's left hip, managing to kick outwards after a blow to her eye socket did the kind of damage that might take a lesser warrior out of the fight completely. These two men were good. Someone had finally paid real money to take her out. Overall, these mercenaries were much better than any of the previous individuals she'd dealt with. She almost felt bad she'd killed the first one so easily, as the Celebrant on top of her spun over himself from her kick. Her opponent landed on top of her again, and she had to move her head to the side to avoid the continuing onslaught of head-butts. She grew serrated bone on the inside of her forearms, wrapping them around her opponent's throat as she did as if to entangle him in a chokehold. Instead, she let the bones keep growing until the man ceased his movement, and even for another moment beyond that to be sure. She pushed him off of her, covered in faintly orange Celebrant blood, to see the other mercenary still breathing, clutching the shard of bone the girl had forced into his neck. She kicked him as she walked over, and the grunt that escaped the man was one she could tell had been nearly muffled by the fluid in his lungs. They both knew it had been a deathblow that she'd dealt, though it seemed the Celebrant was clutching to his last minutes of life as he bled out internally. He might have saved himself if the insertion she'd made had been clean. He could have tried to grow some bone internally, around the wound. But the shard she had jabbed him with was pronged to prevent just such a thing. Try as he might, and he most certainly was, she knew the man wouldn't be able to stop his internal bleeding. And it seemed some of the excess was making its way into his lungs, as indeed, the Celebrant coughed up some of the same orange looking liquid the girl was nearly covered in.

"Tell me," she said. "Who sent you?"

"Contract is, *huagh,* pretty big. Old…old family."

"How old?"

"The…oldest."

The Reach.

The girl knew who the Celebrant was talking about. The Reach were still as brazen as ever, it seemed. She wondered if every mercenary thus far had been sent by them. The thought amused her. She must be costing them a small fortune! She kicked the man's arm, forcing his hand clutching the bone in his neck away from himself. The move came on so suddenly, the Celebrant hadn't let go of the shard. Blood spurt from the artery in his neck in rapid, quick-firing bursts. She watched for a moment as the man finished bleeding out.

Then, she decided, she needed to find a particular Wretched. Someone who could get a message out. Set up a meeting. It was time to see some old friends. Take care of this mercenary business. She had heard the name a few times already. It seemed to be the only one people knew when it came to The Wretched.

It was time to see Spice.

Chapter XIV

Tran the cleaner made his way through the executive gym. The man occasionally scratched at places on his person, casually dislodging the tiny microphones he'd secured to himself. It was a careful dance, but Tran had practiced all night at home, moving the microphones to the parts of his hand he didn't use as he cleaned, swiping and placing them in carefully plotted points with ease. The executive gym was set up in much the same way as the other two gyms for employees, with an added area containing a sauna next to the showers. Tran had seen that the executives often used the area, so he made sure to place extra microphones in there.

Tran was alone in the gym, but he was not without eyes on him. The cleaner made sure to hide his movements as much as possible from the cameras in the ceilings and corners of the area. In spite of his efforts, he was watched intently by one of the highest ranking men in the building. Roper received word immediately that one of the cleaning staff had set off an alarm designed to scan for recording equipment. The man watched as Tran shuffled around the room from area to area, dusting and wiping, almost unnoticeably placing the microphones all around the room. Roper thought momentarily about confronting Tran, but decided against the move. Controlling the flow of information was part of Roper's job description on, and off, the books. He knew it was better to know where the leak was and control what information found its way into that area than it was to try to plug every leak he found. They sailed a big ship, after all. He would never catch every leak.

Plus, this way Roper could feed disinformation. It didn't really matter whether or not he ever found out who was having the microphones planted. He would make sure they left with the kind of misinformation that would benefit his own cause. Roper wouldn't even have the cleaner disciplined. Aside from the casual placement of the miniature listening devices, the man was doing an exceptional job at making the area spotless. Say what you will about The Wretched, and Roper could say quite a bit about the *neutral* Loren, but the ones that came to try their hand at a normal life didn't slack off at all.

As it was, less and less of the people who had access to this area even bothered to come here. There were so many things in motion, especially now, anybody with power at LyraCorps was hardly allowed enough free time to get a run in. Roper would have to speak with the few who could still find time to come down here. Make sure they knew what not to say.

Everything else could be memorized quickly enough.

The victory, even though it had not yet been fully realized, left Roper feeling hungry. He was already on one of the executive levels of the building. Might as well enjoy one of the other perks that many of the higher ranking LyraCorps members often left untouched: The executive dining area. The chef on duty today knew just how to sear a steak, something Roper found many people often thought was as simple as throwing the meat down onto a hot surface. Sure, you might get something that looked the same, but a truly well executed piece of meat cooked raw was a thing of beauty in Roper's eyes. There were so few pleasures left in the world for people like him. Food was quickly becoming the only thing, other than the cause which he served unwaveringly, which he truly cared about. Hundreds of men and thousands more all over the world knew his face. They would jump as high as he told them. He could have nearly any Lyran woman he wished. If he wanted a nice car, one was brought to him. Every creature comfort imaginable was only a snap of his fingers away, even at the status of second in command of the Lyran Empire. While he took furthering their cause extremely seriously, and would happily lay down his life to do accomplish their goals, there was simply no passion left in it for him. For many years, his kind fought hard to gain the upper hand. It was an even harder battle to fight to keep it.

But keep it they did.

And now… well, with so little left for him to do, with his kind so near to the ultimate victory, he found the only thing that seemed to truly matter to him anymore was a good steak.

Antonio, the chef on duty, knew just how to cook them the way that made Roper's taste buds dance along his tongue. Antonio could sear a steak that would leave the average diner breathless, even if they did not prefer their meat to be so raw. The man could make a believer out of anyone, Roper was sure. If it had been a courthouse where Antonio did his work, rather than a kitchen, Roper was certain the chef would have become one of the most respect, and possibly feared, judges in the country.

Roper was near to the dining area as he was approached by a disheveled soldier.

"Sir, excuse me. I need to speak with you." The soldier asked.

"Not now. Come back in about forty five minutes. Possibly an hour." Roper repled. He was even closer to his goal. The waitress in the room had already seen him, grabbing the place settings for his personal table by his favorite window in the building. It had the best view of over half the city. He loved to look out it as he ate and imagine how different it would all look soon. The world thought they had already gone green, but Roper knew that before long, they'd really get to know what going green was all about.

"Sorry sir. Strict orders. Your presence is requested at once."

Roper stopped in his tracks, turning slowly towards the solider, who then had begun to visibly sweat. Drops of the salty liquid poured down along the solder's face, a few falling so heavily that they fell to the linoleum flooring.

"If this order hasn't come from Mordacity himself, son, I'm going to-"

"It has!" The solider pleaded. He quickly averted his gaze from the second in command of the Lyra. "Straight from the top, sir. I can assure you."

Roper looked at the soldier for a moment, his gaze then falling to back inside the dining area. His heart sank as he directed the soldier away from him, his feet pivoting and turning his body towards the elevators.

Lunch would have to wait.

••

The excitement long gone, the day had passed by for Trajen in a typical fashion. He'd gone to his classes, then helped out at Arnold's store for a late shift. In spite of the morning's excitement, and the group of creepy men that people seemed to be seeing on campus from LyraCorps, Trajen's day had been pretty boring after he saw his professor in a bloody heap on the sidewalk. One of his classmates, Jeremy, a boy he felt lacked substance on purpose, complained loudly in one of his classes about some "super scary dudes" going around, "seriously messing stuff up, man". He'd regaled the class momentarily with his story of some angel of a girl who'd saved him from a tree. Everyone had laughed at Jeremy, but after what Trajen had seen that morning, he wasn't sure what he was going to believe. An angel on campus didn't make any less sense to him than his being able to step from one shadow to the next, or his professor being able to disappear in a puff of smoke. Though the more he thought about anyone having powers, the more he began to wonder if people with power had an obligation to share it with others.

Arnold's alarm sounded. The sleepy man made his way out from the back of his store to greet Trajen at the front.

"Ah, Trajen. Sounded busy earlier." Arnold said.

"It was." Trajen replied with a smile. "I'm glad you're up. I actually wanted to ask you about something."

143

"Oh? What's up?"

"Well, I like to watch documentaries, you know? They've really helped me learn about a lot of stuff. In one of them, there's a drug lord who they show as being very totalitarian. The man basically runs an entire country. The politicians defer to him, the police look the other way. He can basically do whatever he wants. I guess I was just wondering what you thought about when someone has that much power. What should they do? The drug lord kept the power for himself. Many people in his country starved to death every day, while he had food brought in on trucks from neighboring countries for nightly banquets on his estate. I was just thinking about it. Meant to bring it up earlier, in class. Sorry if this is, uh, weird or anything."

"And you want to know what *I* think?" Arnold's inflection attempted to relay to Trajen that he was surprised, but the man's face told a much different story. Trajen realized in that moment that he knew next to nothing about his employer. Other than that Arnold owned a shop, had a pleasant disposition, and smelled *wonderful*, Trajen couldn't recall anything else about the man. Trajen could clearly see that Arnold was excited for the chance to chat.

"If you don't mind." Trajen replied.

"Hmm..." Arnold looked pensive for a moment. Trajen could tell the frail man wasn't thinking of what he wanted to say, so much as he was thinking about whether or not he wanted to say it to his employee. Perhaps he pondered the way in which to deliver the message, as well. After a moment, the shopkeeper began to speak. "You know, history is full of dictators and empires. There are plenty of examples throughout the course of humanity of people who kept power for themselves. I'd say if you were looking for a decision to make based upon the actions and outcome of other peoples' lives, harboring as much power as possible to yourself and not relinquishing any control is a bad idea. For one, history

144

tells us that power is incredibly addicting, especially after the benefits become apparent. But even beyond that, when you keep power to yourself, it can look like you've got the only green lawn in the neighborhood. You ever been in a neighborhood with only one green lawn?"

"I don't think so, no. What's your point?"

"My point is, when more than one person has a green lawn, walking outside to some brown doesn't seem like anyone's fault. The person with the brown spot might even blame themselves for their misfortunes. But imagine you're a homeowner with a brown lawn, and you look around to see that everyone else on your block has brown grass too. Except one guy. Maybe he's your neighbor, maybe he lives down the block; it'll only take you a second to find out where he is because he's the *only guy* with green grass. And you know, for a lot of people, that's more than enough reason to think that if everyone has brown grass but one person, the person with the green grass is probably to blame. Even if the person with the green grass earned it. If they haven't shared their water, you can be sure trouble is coming their way."

"Oh. Yea...that actually makes sense. So do you think that applies to people with power who wouldn't necessarily be able to use it in a traditional sense? Like, say you have a woman, and she's the best doctor in the world. She knows more about medicine than anyone, and she lives in the same remote country as the drug lord, so she has very little contact with the outside world. Does she have an ethical responsibility to share her power with the rest of the world? Even if she can't teach anyone how to be as good of a doctor as she is, is it her responsibility to save the world?"

"Whoa, Trajen. Slow down, slow down. Saving the world is a pretty tall order for anybody. Just because you might have the ability to do something, that doesn't mean you need to risk yourself in trying. There would be all kinds of danger for that doctor. I doubt the drug lord would ever let her go. And the logistics involved with saving the world are, really, pretty ridiculous. There are a lot of people all across the planet. How could you possibly save all of them yourself? Just a tall, tall order."

"But do you think she should try?"

"My honest opinion? Only if she wants to. If the woman never decided to try and be a benefit to humanity, sure, we'd be a little worse off than we were. But it's not like a lie through omission, where you still do damage by doing nothing. If the woman chooses not to help, the world doesn't become any worse, it just doesn't become any better. And preserving herself in light of the drug lord's high likelihood of ending her life for trying to leave the country is completely understandable...Man, I haven't had a good brain game like this one in a while. What else you got for me?" Trajen could see that Arnold had really gotten going. He couldn't help himself, at this point. Of course he had something else to ask Arnold.

"Okay," Trajen said. "Let's expand on that same topic, just a little. We'll throw the alternative country and make-believe woman out the window. Let's say it's this city and the person with the power is me. Now, if we follow your logic – even though I can probably save this city, and maybe the world, from the powers that would see it under their totalitarian rule, you think I don't necessarily have an obligation to? Because if I try, I might get hurt, and beyond that, if I don't I'm not making things any worse, I would just be trying to make them better. Is that right?"

"That's right. If you do nothing, things happen as they were always going to. If you try to help, maybe you fix them. Better chance you get hurt, though. Or worse."

"I understand. But it just seems like there's a flaw to the logic. It's almost like you're presenting a scenario where time exists all at once, or at least in...I don't know...larger bursts? We don't live a year at a time, you know? Our lives are down to the second. We can change the course

146

of our own lives in the expanse of a single breath, if you think about it. Like when a girl asks a boy on television if her dress makes her look fat. His life can go so many ways from that moment on. He could say yes, and have a terrible evening. He could say no, and risk her not believing him – there's a chance she's asking because she honestly wants to know, but also a chance she has low self-esteem; then he would have to deal with trying to convince her he was being honest. Or he could say nothing, and take a chance on that. He could scream until his face turned red and he passed out from lack of oxygen. Our lives can change so quickly, Arnold. It just doesn't seem realistic to say to someone that they don't have a responsibility to help if they have the ability to do so. The smallest action of their part could have a huge impact on the outcome."

Arnold held his tongue for a moment, a smile slowly creeping across his face. "It sounds to me like you've got your answer, then." He said after a moment.

"Yea. I guess I do, Arnold. Thanks for the insight. You need anything before I go?"

Trajen matched the man's smile. He hadn't expected to have the conversation he'd just had with Arnold when it had gotten started, but he certainly felt better now that he had. It was weird, he could have talked about a million other things. He almost wanted to ask the shopkeeper about how his professor had been able to push the bones in his legs back together. But instead, he'd had a conversation about something he hadn't really even realized was on his mind.

"I sure don't. You are good to go. Here's your money for the day. Go ahead and take off."

"Alright. See you tomorrow!"

Trajen decided to walk home from work. He felt like he needed some time to think. All day he felt like he just needed a moment to process things. It seemed like every time he took a minute to let whatever had just happened settle down, something else was there to happen to him anew. He had walked to school that morning so that he could have some time to think and meditate, instead happening upon his friend screaming and his professor broken. He had hoped he would be able to stock the fridges and shelves at Arnold's shop, and take some time to zone out with the manual labor. Instead he had almost non-stop customers the entire evening. The flow of business there as the day progressed was, for lack of a better term, night and day.

Trajen thought about his powers; about the responsibility he was meant to have. The only glimpse he had been given into who, or what, he really was had been from the single dream he'd had. He tried to remember what the room looked like. To see the faces of those he knew to be his kind, who had stood around him in the dream. He could recall next to nothing. Garrett believed Trajen could be a great tool in bringing balance back to the world. Trajen had tried to bring it up once already, but to his surprise, Garrett brushed the conversation off. He told Trajen that Russel finding him was an accident. He wasn't part of their current plans, and until they knew how to use him, Trajen just needed to keep a low profile. If they, as Garrett put it, "played their hand too early," then they might waste the opportunity finding Trajen had presented. In a weird way, it had actually made Trajen glad to hear Garrett say that. He wasn't sure he was meant to have so much responsibility. Weren't there supposed to be others like him? He wasn't meant to do this alone! Arnold had just said that one person can't really change the world; that it's basically impossible for them to create change on that grand of a scale. Though, he thought, perhaps it wasn't. Garrett and Russel had some plan they were working through. They'd been trying to do what they could even before they knew Trajen existed. That made him feel better as he remembered it. He didn't have to do anything alone. Garrett and Russel already had a plan. Perhaps, when his time came, he wouldn't really *be* alone. Perhaps it was simply that he would be there to help. Maybe, he mused, helping would mean not doing anything at all. That would certainly be something, considering how sure Arnold had been that doing nothing was the same as allowing the things to happen as they were meant to. Life could truly go a million different ways. Trajen had believed that when he said it.

For instance, Garrett said Mordacity had some kind of mind powers. What if he was able to control Trajen? What if Mordacity knew how to make Trajen access the abilities he had yet to uncover access to on his own? Trajen could already do untold amounts of damage with the powers he had currently. The boy had lumbered his way through the last fight he'd been in, against *trained* men, and come out basically unscathed!

Trajen neared his home not knowing what to think, even though he'd managed to think about just about everything. He recalled a presentation he had watched about having too many options, and how paralyzing variety can actually be. *This must be what they were talking about,* he thought to himself. *I haven't even been asked to do anything yet, and already things could go so many ways that I don't know what to do.*

As Trajen stepped inside, Garrett too was just coming home from work. Bren had had the day off, and Trajen could see the house was much tidier than before he'd left. Other than his room, of course, which was his responsibility to keep clean. It was a task he did not take lightly, often spending each of his evenings searching the room for any dust which might have settled, even on surfaces where a little dust might have gone unnoticed for anyone who entered his space. He was given a job, and he'd make sure he did it to the best of his ability. He realized then that his conviction when it came to tidiness was likely the level of conviction he ought to feel when it came to doing the job he was supposed to be born to do. Did it really matter that no one had asked him to do anything yet? Garrett had already told him what he was born for. Should that be what he was doing, instead of pretending to be human and going to school? Should he have already traded the documentaries for self-defense classes, his comfortable clothing for steel-plated armor?

Garrett greeted Trajen first as he came in from the garage. They exchanged pleasantries, and each of them could smell that Bren was cooking something delicious. He knew immediately what was cooking, the worries he'd managed to cook up in his own brain suddenly on hold. Trajen found himself salivating, even though the food smelled much different than his favorite meal of chocolate chip pancakes. The aroma was, quite simply, intoxicating – the spices in the food dancing wildly around his nostrils with each inhale.

"Oh yes, coconut curry!" Garrett exclaimed, as he ran up the stairs on nearly all fours, presumably to change out of his work clothes. Trajen laughed in spite of the foul mood he had walked into the door with.

Trajen too liked Bren's curry. He enjoyed the way the spices seemed to dance on his tongue as they did in his nose, and the way they cooled themselves as they mixed with the coconut milk. The chicken in the curry was always very tender. Bren had remarked to Trajen once that in other parts of the world, texture was often just as important, or even more important, than taste. She had told him that in other countries, many textures were considered unfavorable in popular cuisine. Trajen finally figured out what she was talking about when watching one of his documentaries. In other places, people ate all kinds of things. Here, though, it looked like cartilage and skin were not often found in food, even when they were traditional aspects of the meal they were eating. Every part of chicken he bit into as he ate his curry was either a large piece of muscle or a small piece of muscle. There was no tendon, no skin, and absolutely no bones in his meal. He didn't mind, of course. But it seemed weird that one country would be so radically different in the way they preferred their meals.

As the three of them sat down for dinner, Trajen inquired about his professor.

"It wouldn't surprise me if that's really what happened," Bren said, "Nine months ago, I had no idea I'd married a puppy or that my pretend-adopted nephew was some kind of super-charged badass."

Garrett smiled at the comment, but otherwise seemed perturbed.

"You're *sure* he simply vanished, as if literally into thin air? Could you smell the smoke at all? Did it smell like ash or like something was burning?"

"You know," Trajen said, "I think it did, now that you mention it. There was a lot of blood, but I do recall the smoke smelling somewhat like burnt hair."

"Eyebrows." Garrett interjected. "They move so fast the hair on their face is burnt from the friction against the air."

"Honestly, I was pretty caught up in trying to calm Kris down, and keep myself calm as well. I was worried she would faint, or that someone *else* would see and that I might get in trouble. Plenty of documentaries about people who are sent to jail for being in the wrong place at the wrong time. I'd rather *not* be in prison for a couple of decades, you know?"

Garrett seemed truly put off, muttering to himself as he went back to his dinner. "No..no, they can't be real..." he said as he fed himself. He seemed to become almost completely drawn into his own thoughts. Bren, of course, had tuned out of the conversation midway through, trying to make sure the naan bread she was cooking would be as fresh as possible for their dinner. Trajen realized Bren hardly ever stayed sitting once they sat down for a meal. He knew that no one ate until everyone was sitting, but he didn't realize until that moment that Bren would often sit down, presumably so everyone would dig in, and that she would always get back up to do something. Sometimes she continued cooking, other times she began to wash the multitude of pots, pans, and dishes she always seemed to create whenever she prepared a meal.

Things were quickly becoming awkward. The silence was palpable. If Trajen reached out his hand and squeezed, he might very well wind up with some kind of awkward-air-juice. What did Garrett mean?

"Garrett, you're mumbling. Come on, what are you talking about? Who can't be real?" Trajen asked.

"There's only one race that can 'disappear' in a puff of smoke," Garrett replied.

Bren managed to hear that part of the conversation, still perpetuating the nonchalant attitude she seemed to have about the Loren. "Vampires." The woman said with certainty. "And they can turn into stuff too, right? Bats, wolves. And what else...Oh! Silver, right? Yea. Silver. Crosses...garlic...?"

Garrett chuckled. "Not quite, honey. The proper term is *Vampyr,* though most historians will get on you unless you say it with a long 'H,' like *'Vahm-peer.'* The bat thing and the wolf thing is some kind of mix-up. None of them could ever do that. The only shapechangers are the Lyra, and to be honest, you're hard pressed to find one that doesn't turn in to some kind of dog. Used to be there were plenty of other animals Lyra turned into. Lions, bears, rabbits. Pretty sure my race is where that whole dragon thing came from. Makes sense, you know? Every culture has their own kind of dragon and all that, continents apart. Now we're all just a bunch of mutts. The silver thing was all Hollywood. Some of the races heal faster than others. Vampyr and Lyra heal pretty fast, respectively. Most wounds aren't fatal to us the way they are to humans. But it doesn't matter if it's a wooden stake, a silver bullet, or a neon crucifix. You put something through somebodie's heart, there's a good chance they ain't getting back up."

"Alright," Trajen said. "Sounds like Vampyr are pretty common. So what's the deal?"

"The deal is," Garrett said, his tone serious once again, "That the Vampyr are all gone. Nobody has seen a Vampyr in a *long* time, Trey. There's a bit of history there, which we won't get into, but if your professor is really a Vampyr, I doubt he's the only one. This could be...I mean...this is *huge*. This breaks the mold. Even a couple Vampyr could change *everything*. And we've got you, too. A Peacebringer. It'll take some time for me to get the information into the right people's hands. Got to be extra careful about that." Garrett's features softened a little, as he came to believe his own words. "I was really worried. But now that I've had the chance to think about it, this is kind of great news. We should celebrate!"

Trajen wanted to share the excitement with Garrett and Bren, who had stopped doing dishes to finish eating. She was smiling because her husband was smiling, Trajen knew, but the excitement they shared was real. Bren trusted Garrett. If he said things were looking up, she was sure they were. Trajen trusted Garrett too. He trusted them both more than he trusted anyone else. More than he trusted himself.

Garrett had said it again. That they had him. The expectation he'd been so recently worrying about was all but openly confirmed over a steaming plate of coconut curry, a dish which seemed to emulate now how Trajen was feeling his own insides must look like. Trajen smiled along with Bren and Garrett, but beneath the smile he wasn't happy.

Beneath the smile, deep down - Trajen was yellow. He was scared.

Chapter XV

"Yes, that's correct…*my liege,*" Dalbrin said into the mouthpiece of his home phone. Gracia was nowhere to be seen, asleep with the sun as she usually was. It would take more than his hushed conversation to wake his wife, he knew. As was his own nightly custom, he was lurking their downstairs, his own brain even more active with the loss of the sun. His kind did not need to sleep daily, or even weekly, in Dalbrin's case. His age allowed the moon to replenish his daily energies, entering into sleep only when he chose. It made catching up on paperwork easier, he supposed. More than anything, it gave him time to live both of the lives he had. The life of a professor and doting husband, and his first life, that of a Vampyr general. Though, for the second one, perhaps *living* wasn't quite the right word. More than once he wondered how the human teachers got any of their grading done, especially at the collegiate level. There was no way they read every single essay, he was sure.

The voice on the other end of the phone asked how discreet he'd been in his getaway. Had anyone seen? Was he still hurt? More than that, the voice in his phone was angry. It kept asking if he deliberately provoked the Lyrans. Dalbrin wanted to scream into the phone at the question. So what if he had? Did they forget who he was? He kept himself calm, instead.

"No, sir, of course not. And I'm fine now. All healed, Gracia saw to my wounds. The campus was completely empty, and I remain uncompromised. Though, I would like to request permission to pursue the band and possibly engage if the opportunity presents itself. In my opinion, having so many of them roaming so openly does not bode well for keeping us hidden."

The answer on the other end of the line was not quick to come, though he expected nothing less. Dalbrin knew his kind were the slowest to do anything. The slowest to make decisions, the slowest to procreate. They were even, much to the disbelief of the many other Loren in the world when the time was right, the slowest to die out. In spite of the best efforts of those who would have seen, who would *still* see the Vampyr wiped from the face of the earth, Dalbrin remained. So did others of his kind, of course. There were still a few other Vampyr even someone as powerful as him had to answer to. Or pretend to answer to, anyway.

He was going to kill the Lyrans who attacked him no matter what the voice on the other end of the phone said.

He wondered if they knew that.

Perhaps that was why their answer was so slow to come. Perhaps they were trying to figure out how to beg him not to make waves, or break character. He had a role to play, of course. If his kind were ever to be revitalized, the ranks of the Vampyr replenished, he needed to be sure no one knew there were any Vampyr left in the world. But nothing would stop him from killing the soldiers who had beaten him earlier that day.

No matter what his *superiors* told him.

Then, somewhat to his surprise, the voice inside the phone said yes.

Dalbrin liked that answer. Once again he began to wear the smile he'd put on in class. It was impossibly wide, and threatening. In class he'd been happy, and he was happy now. It always made him feel good to badmouth LyraCorps, to anyone who would listen. Though the difference this evening was simple.

Tonight, he smiled for blood.

His duties done for the darker life he lived, Dalbrin was resigned to his paperwork. He didn't need to wear the glasses he grabbed from the table. Even Vampyr with bad eyesight did not need their vision corrected. Their kind could see like eagles. The feel of the metal on the bridge of his nose always made him feel more like a teacher, though. He even managed to walk with a bit of slumped shoulders as he went to collect his things.

The guise came on just in time, as Dalbrin heard a knock at his door. He glanced quickly at the watch on his wrist, glowing green numbers reading ten minutes after eight. He had thought it to be much later. His wife's inability to stay awake as the sun went down always seemed to distort his sense of time, especially when the earth was tilted this way or that on its axis.

Dalrbin answered the door carefully, prepared for a full-on assault. Things would go differently this time, though. He wouldn't simply take the beating. *I hope you brought at least* ten *friends,* he thought. They would need more than just the four of them from before to do any real damage to him, should the Lyrans have been dumb enough to find him in his home. He had thought he went faster than his scent could follow, but perhaps he hadn't.

Though, he supposed it didn't make much sense for them to knock, either. His door fully opened, he found he was more surprised by who *had* arrived, than who *hadn't.*

Standing outside was Kris. Her hair was remarkably free of frizzling, neatly tied back behind her head. She looked to be sweating a bit, her forehead glistening as the light of Dalbrin's porch shined onto her. She stood in front of the door anxiously. Dalbrin was completely surprised Kris had appeared at his home.

And she was holding...a bundt cake? "Hello Kris," Dalbrin said. "What are you doing here? And why do you have cake?" Dalbrin put on his professor voice instantly, sounding unamused at the likely delicious treat she had brought.

"I came to make sure you were okay, Professor Dalbrin. I hope that's alright. I've been really worried. I went by two of the hospitals earlier before calling around to the others. I bought the cake to bring to you there. Help stave off the food you get in those places, you know? Something about hospital cuisine has always given me the creeps...Anyway. What happened earlier? Wasn't your leg *broken?*"

Kris handed Dalbrin the cake, who placed it on the table next to his door.

"Right," the mock professor said. "Well, thanks, I suppose. That was...nice...of you. I'm sure this cake will be delicious. I'll make sure I tell you all about how much my wife liked it in our next class. Now-"

"Professor Dalbrin, stop." Kris interrupted. "Stop pretending like nothing happened earlier. When I was looking at you on the ground, I was *so scared.* More scared than I've *ever* been. You know I've seen someone in worse shape before? You know I've seen *dead bodies?* Why was I so scared? I'm not an idiot, Professor Dalbrin. I know there was no way you should have been able to get up and walk away from the way you were earlier. Be straight with me."

Kris crossed her arms as she stood in the doorway, a cool breeze making its way inside the house from behind the girl. She knew she was taking a chance coming to Dalbrin's house like she was. If she was honest with herself, she knew she was going to say these things to him the moment she realized he wasn't in any of the hospitals. No one could get up and walk away, let alone vanish, as Dalbrin had, from the wounds he'd suffered. He had needed serious medical attention earlier in the day. When she saw him standing there as he answered his door, all of the things she'd thought on the way over found their way to the surface. A part of her was sorry she'd said them. It was rude to have done so, she was sure. But it was done. Dalbrin could fail her at this point, for all she cared. Someone needed to tell him he was being ridiculous.

Kris's professor began to speak, her mind already made up on what she'd say to him next, regardless of what he was saying to her now. She was going to tell him that people would find out about what happened that morning. That she was *sure* there'd be a video online. And when she finally found the video, she was going to tell him that she'd make sure to show all of her friends. If it was the last thing she did, Kris was going to make sure what happened went viral. Even if Dalbrin told her she was right. To Kris, they were past the point of reconciliation. Maybe if her professor had answered the door in a wheelchair, or at least with some crutches. He didn't even have any bandages on.

Was it supposed to be a joke?

Kris realized then she hadn't been listening to Dalbrin at all. She was so caught up in envisioning the next thing she'd say, she hadn't caught a word of her professor's reply. As she began to tune in, she also realized something strange. No matter how hard she tried, and she was now trying exceedingly hard, she *couldn't* understand what Dalbrin said. His words sounded like gibberish. Was that English?

The girl suddenly felt very dizzy.

She tried again to decipher what it was Dalbrin was saying to her. Her head swayed, and she had to catch herself on the doorjamb, bumping her head as she did. Kris knew she should have felt the impact against the hard wooden surface, but her whole body began to feel numb. When she finally collapsed, Dalbrin caught her.

A few moments later, she was tucked into bed, her father oblivious to her arrival. Though, he'd had no idea she was gone, either. The man had only just returned home himself.

Dalbrin patted himself on the back as he returned to his own home. Fear was always what he'd been best at. The trait ran in his family. But fear wasn't the only thing the Vampyr could make their prey feel. Others of his kind had been incredibly adept at all kinds of emotions and beguilement. It had taken him longer than he thought it should have to subdue the girl's mind. Though, he was quite out of practice. Still, the girl had fallen asleep soon enough. He could tell from the way she swayed that he'd done as good a job as he needed to. Normally, he would have to follow up to be sure, but he'd only been given the go-ahead for the retaliation against the Lyrans. Asking for permission to dispatch of the girl would likely be too much. His superiors might pull the movement completely, which he could not have.

The wolves who'd hit him needed to die for their indiscretion. He was confident in his abilities otherwise. The fear he'd put in her that morning was strong. Asking her brain to forget the trauma, as he'd asked it to be traumatized in the first place, was well within his skillset. For a moment he worried about what might happen if someone, Trajen perhaps, mentioned the event to her. The trauma might hit her all over again. Without him there to regulate the way she experienced it, there was a good chance she would go into shock. *The things people put in their bodies now,* he thought, *she might have a heart attack if she's forced to remember. If she'd had even half a cup of coffee beforehand, she'll most definitely die.* He knew *he* wouldn't say anything, but he simply could not speak for the rest of the population.

When the girl awoke the next day, he was confident she wouldn't remember seeing him that morning, or coming to his house that night. Anything else that happened, he would just have to live with.
Or was it un-live? Whatever. She might die.

Kids.

From the pages of Hrath's Golemnic Tome. Vol 14.
The Shadone.

There are people living in the shadows.

I have seen them.

The Shadone first drew my curiosity when, as I was napping among the roots of a slow growing cedar tree, a fierce months-long battle roused me from my slumber. I raised myself to the surface, careful not to break the tender roots which had grown around my form over the passing months. As I broke free of the earth around me, my obsidian form marred only in appearance by the dirt which clung to it, I came face to face with a gathering of lithe, willowy forms. These people were as light as the air around them, inspecting me with equally unpracticed and unparalleled grace. I had read of their existence, of course. My kind know all who would choose to walk, or fly above, this earth. Though I would be lying if I said that I was not delighted to finally see some of them for myself. The Shadone were impressive, even to a Golem.

So playful and curious were these people that I could not help but wonder how they ever managed to find the time to hurt each other. I had sat in the same place for months without seeing one so much as lift a hand to harm another. I was happy for the pleasant company, though I grew more and more curious each day, as I had only come towards the surface at the sound of battle. To arrive and find not even the pettiest of squabbles seemed, as terrible as it is to say, unbelievable.

Then the night began to creep in.

The Shadone had built their lives in a part of the world that does not see night for many days on end. As the night returned to their homes, so too did the darker parts of their race. I had become entranced with how quickly a Shadone guard could walk the perimeter of the town. I had simply thought them quick. My people had never catalogued them properly. The Shadone were not simply light on their feet, they could ride beams of light. If the light covered their whole body, an adult Shadone could step incalculable distances away, traverse entire fields in an instant, as long as the area from which they emerged possessed ample light for their return. Those who returned as the earth tilted on its axis were Shadone as well, but unlike the people I had come to know. These Shadone traveled in shadow. Where one Shadone's abilities worked only in the light, the others worked in the dark. I found it a curious situation. This knowledge was nowhere to be found. My urge to study the phenomenon grew stronger as I held my place, never moving from the spot where I had emerged from the earth. Then the seasons evened out, and I was again faced with the war which had stirred me from my slumber.

What else could two groups of people, so inherently, despicably different, do to each other. The mornings would begin with a hunting party, the day-time warriors riding waves of light great distances to find their foes. Sometimes they were lucky, and came back with a head or two for their troubles. Most days, they found nothing. Each evening was met with fortification. The women and children steeled themselves inside of their huts made of mud and stone, many even further hidden inside of basements dug during the summer. Each of the town's daytime warriors took a brief rest at midday, preparing for the night to come. And as every morning and evening were the same, so too did each night occur exactly as the one before it. The Shadone who traveled within the shadows appeared quickly. Their prey, of course, was stationary. There was no noise as they materialized under the moonlight, and silence again as they disappeared. These warriors of shadow were not as brazen as the warriors of light. They preferred to take those they killed in utter silence, never engaging the men who stood guard if they did not need to.

The warriors of light knew this, never moving as a unit smaller than three at a time. Many nights, I was thankful to see, ended as the days

161

had, with no blood to be spilled. This continued for weeks, either side having only lost a handful of their kin. I began to grow hopeful, thinking I had simply awoken at a high time of the war, and that it was already on its wane. Wars, as all things, eventually die. I could not fathom how both sides would not grow old of the fighting in due time. It is, after all, difficult to continue to fight a battle which you are not winning, even if you are not losing, either.

Unfortunately, the Shadone had other ideas.

So despicable were the warriors of shadow that I watched as, on an evening which lasted much longer than it should, the women and children were no longer safe tucked away in their huts of stone and mud. I sat idly by, bound by a ridiculous code of conduct; an oath I had taken in a language no longer spoken. I watched the warriors of shadow slaughter the children of the light. I watched their petty tactics, as one or two would step in and out of the shadows, taunting the guards of the city, the rest of their hunting party making their way from hut to hut. The warriors of shadow were nearly done before the warriors of light were aware of the underhanded tactics. The real fear of losing their loved ones broke their resolve. They traveled that evening not as a unit, and each of them died swiftly, alone, a knife in their back.

I will forever live with the hands I carry. Hands that stayed when they should have acted. I wish I could say I'd been certain there were more Shadone in the world who could travel upon the light of the day throughout the world when I watched an entire village be slaughtered in the night. But that would be a lie. I knew in my heart of stone they were the only ones. I knew, when I finally mustered the will to move, that each warrior of shadow I killed would not bring the village of light back to life.
I was there when the people of the light left the world.

Their existence was short-lived.

They were beautiful.

Chapter XVI

Trajen stepped out from the shadows, a box held between his hands.

The box he carried with him was not heavy. He was used to lifting them. He knew it had to be this way, or he couldn't make the journey through the shadows. He'd learned this the hard way, cracking the wood of a pallet he had tried to take with him earlier in the day. It was only wood, but it wasn't his. Arnold was nice about it, in between naps. Trajen was sure nobody slept as much as Arnold did. But that was alright. It gave him more time to test out what few abilities he could call upon on command. It gave him time to think, too.

In spite of the welcome distraction his day of self-discovery had made, he found his mind drifted on more than one occasion back to seeing Professor Dalbrin lying on the ground only days before. He thought, too, about the way Kris had screamed. He asked Bren about that, describing to the woman the expression Kris had worn as best he could. Trajen had asked Bren for advice, but the she had hardly any to give. He'd been glad he didn't have to go back to school until tomorrow. Maybe by then, he wouldn't have to say anything at all. Maybe the three of them could sweep the whole thing under the proverbial rug. That'd certainly be easier, he thought, than any of them having to try and rationalize what had happened. Trajen hadn't had many chances to feel awkward in the nine months he'd been living in the city, pretending to be some nice couple's live-in nephew, but he figured if there was going to be a time for a conversation to feel that way, talking about what happened the day before with either Kris or his professor was as good a candidate as any.

He set the box down where it went, ducking his head around the corner to make sure no one had snuck into the store without him hearing the bell. The trips through the shadows certainly felt instantaneous. They seemed immediate. But who knew if the sound would carry. Luckily, he was still alone. He tried once again to focus on growing bone. Trajen envisioned it, the same as he did when he shadow-stepped, allowing his mind to play out the action for him before he attempted it with his body. But as with all of his previous attempts, nothing happened. No sudden growth of any kind.

It was a let-down, but at that moment he was satisfied with the powers he knew he *could* call upon. His form did not change when he attempted to use his Lyran abilities, but he could feel his senses heighten, the things he could smell bridging the gap and making what he could see more vibrant. Each of the spices along the walls of Arnold's shop would become a richer, darker shade of green when he accessed his Lyran abilities. He could taste them from where he stood, if he smelled hard enough. Earlier that morning, he had gone as far as to salivate so rapidly, a long steam had fallen from his mouth onto the floor. There were customers when it happened. He'd been embarrassed.

Sometimes he thought he could see the outlines of the scents he caught, but every time he realized it was happening, it went away. He knew now that when he took on his Lyran powers, he could run far, and fast. And maybe forever. He could feel himself become strong. But no matter what he tried, the bone would not grow. He recalled the other races Garrett had told him about, as he considered the sun landing on his back.
Light travels in straight lines, he knew. Tearing open a package of water bottles, he felt the coolness of the fridge on his face. The cold seemed to mesh perfectly with warmth of sun as the light fell upon him through the windows of the store. Before the shiver from the cold on his face worked itself through his muscles, he thought even harder about the sun, and his skin seemed then as if it were drinking in the rays around him. The light nearly bent as he silently beckoned it towards his body. His skin began to glow faintly, which he perceived in the glass. Surprised, he dropped a water bottle from his grip. As he lost focus, so too did he lose the glow. Though its effect had already arrived, and Trajen understood that he had literally soaked in the sun.

It had filled him with energy, invigorating his muscles in a way that, if he were to call upon his Lyran strength, he knew would make him a very dangerous person. He made a mental note as well that the little hunger he had managed to develop from shadow-stepping, as the action made him hardly tired at all now, was gone. Trajen couldn't imagine he could actually live off of sunlight. He was certain he'd need to eat at some point. But it seemed to him that at least minor hunger could be staved off through what he could only understand to be photosynthesis. Was the race from which this ability came more plant than person? He'd watched a lot of documentaries about animals, so he knew that a handful of animals experienced photosynthesis in minute ways, but not a single one could photosynthesize sunlight like a plant does. Or like he just had.

He continued to stock the water bottles, now delighting in how little he felt the cold on his face, his skin dull in color but still warm. An alarm from the back told him that Arnold was awake, and that his shift was now over. The sun was just above the mountains outside, strong rays still coming down but definitely soon to be leaving. Garrett would be on his way to take Trajen home. Trajen removed the phone from his pocket, pulling up Garrett's contact onto the screen. Even though Trajen had managed to spend almost an entire day working through his self-discovery, he realized he wasn't ready for it to end. When Garrett answered, he told Trajen it was alright. Garrett hadn't even left work yet. Today, Trajen would find his own way home. He'd be careful, of course. He didn't want anyone to see him using his powers. But then, if he didn't run too fast, who could even know? Plenty of people ran for fun. He only had one more thing to do before his day at the shop was done.

On that day, Arnold had been specific in that he wanted Trajen to perform some deep cleaning and get the dust out of the parts of the shop that were not frequently visited. This meant that whenever Trajen was able, if there were no customers to mind, he needed to be working in the storage area. Trajen realized at the start of the project that in order to clean as efficiently as possible, he would have to work on the area in sections, moving boxes out of the area completely so that he could clean the floor and shelving which was normally covered.

Throughout the course of his shift, Trajen had managed to clean a great deal of the area. He had been working left to right, and just after placing the freshly dusted boxes back into their area in the middle of the storage room, he began working on the final third to his right. Most of the boxes were stacked on top of each other in this portion of the tiny room, so Trajen grabbed a dolly to make the work easier on himself. Trajen shoved the bottom of the dolly underneath the first tower of boxes, balancing them carefully as he moved them out of the room. He managed to perform this action successfully another two times before the fourth and final tower of boxes swayed when he moved it, the top box crashing down to the ground. Trajen braced himself before impact hoping there were no glass objects, and was relieved at the sound of metal hitting the concrete. He checked momentarily to make sure that Arnold had not been wakened by the crash before continuing with the boxes on the dolly and placing them to the side.

Trajen bent down to beging the process of cleaning his mess, placing each of the items he could find back into the box. They were a mix of metal cylinders of differing width and length, appearing as what Trajen perceived to be as spare parts to the various types of shelving around the store. In the corner of the room was a single item which did not appear to belong in the same box as the metal rods, a metal cup. The cup was marked around its base and down its spine with a mix of circles, squares, and jagged lines. To Trajen it looked not unlike one of the early runic languages he had seen in a documentary on the history of the English language, though he didn't recognize any of the markings. Trajen reached over to place the cup back into the box. Instead of being met with the cold feeling of metal, the cup felt incredibly warm in his hands, like a thermos after it soaked up the heat of the soup placed inside.

Then, Trajen could smell berries.

As he looked around, he realized he was no longer in the back room of Arnold's shop. The feeling of displacement came and went, and Trajen's sense of touch was suddenly diminished, his senses of smell and sight taking over almost completely. Trajen noted that he could still hear, and perceived a brief gust of wind as it blew by his face, the wind itself rattling along the edges of his ear canal. Trajen had suddenly been placed in the middle of a flowering field, hues of purple and red as far as his eyes could see. He tried to stand, only to realize that his actions were not his own to take, as if he were dreaming.

Before long, Trajen's body stood up from its crouched position and began walking languidly among the innumerable wildflowers surrounding him. He could still smell, somewhere in the distance, ripe berries begging to be plucked and eaten as they let their sweet scents travel with the continually blowing breeze.

Trajen's body traveled great distances with each step it took. Soon, he was no longer surrounded by flowers, but instead came to the side of a great lake. The warm summer sun and light breeze were replaced with a gray, overcast sky. Trajen could tell the temperature was much lower than before, and that the lake had frozen over on its surface, though he could not feel the change in temperature and thus was not cold. Trajen's body reached its left hand out to show it clutching something. As the hand opened, Trajen could see red dirt and clay as it fell onto the surface of the lake. Trajen's body reached down, drawing a symbol similar to the runes he had seen on the metal cup with its finger in the dirt it had poured. The ice of the lake quickly cracked outwards from the rune until the entire surface had shattered, leaving only the area the dirt and clay had been poured intact. A school of fish in the middle of the lake began to fuss and fight, causing turbulence all throughout the surface of the water. Within a few moments, the turbulent water cleared away any remaining remnants of ice on the lake's surface, leaving the stationary circle of ice with the rune on top to be surrounded by a now calming lake. Trajen's body bent down and carved a pocket into the ice next to the rune, forming a straight line only a few centimeters deep. Trajen's right hand scooped some of the water from the lake and allowed it to fill the pocket it had created on the surface of the ice before using both hands to remove the ice from the lake altogether.

Trajen's body stepped three more times, traveling again in impossibly large distances, until it stopped and arrived at the base of a volcano. Trajen's hands set down the disc of ice and water with the rune of dirt and clay on top beside the warm mountain. Trajen's hands shot into the rock face, dust and large chunks of rock flying all around him. His hands pulled with impossible strength, a hiss of sulfuric air filling the space around him as his hands exited the rock. A slow stream of lava began to flow onto the disc of ice, water and clay, the liquid earth pouring down and over its shape. Trajen watched the lava cover the disc completely, surprised that the ice didn't melt.

The ground underneath the disc began to bubble, the lava melting everything else it touched. Trajen's body stepped back, watching at the disc sunk into the ground. Soon the lava cooled, sealing the hole in the mountain, leaving a trail of black earth. The ground shook lightly for a moment and cracked, and Trajen's body took another tiny step back. The cracks in the dirt grew larger, and an immense form raised itself from under the surface.

Trajen was unsure of what he was looking at. To him, it appeared to be the form of a man, though he was made entirely from stone. The stone figure stood solemn, appearing to draw no breath or movement. Then it took one great step forward, followed by another, the ground shaking lightly as it walked from its massive weight. The stone man placed its hand onto Trajen's left shoulder, nodding its head slightly, before walking off in the opposite direction. Trajen watched the man of stone depart, his vision growing cloudy as he did.

When the man of stone was completely out of sight, Trajen's vision went dark.

He blinked, and was back in Arnold's shop, the sound of the shop's bell alerting him to the entry of a customer.

The prospect of what he'd just seen being a vision of the past, or perhaps an implanted memory within the metal cup, left Trajen both intrigued as well as saddened. He was only just beginning to feel like he understood how some of his powers worked. Throwing another into the mix almost felt like too much. Fortunately, there was no time to worry about it then.

Trajen gathered his things as Arnold rustled some more in the back room. He felt rude without a proper goodbye, but Trajen knew if he stayed that Arnold would take so long talking, the boy would probably miss the little bit of sun thee city had left before the ball of fire made its way over the mountains in the west. Since their first time chatting at length days before, Trajen found that Arnold grasped at every opportunity he could to speak with him. Sometimes the conversations were short. Directives to the boy about what he should be doing at work, in between yawns and snored breathing. Many of them were much longer, though.

The boy desperately wanted to see if he could call upon more than one ability at a time, and try to use his Lyran stamina to make it home while he soaked in what remained of the sun for the day.

....

Arnold woke to his beloved alarm. It was his oldest companion. It had been in his life longer than even Garrett, whom he'd known for a decade or more. The alarm had always been there. Even *before* it was given a home in his clock. Before it was given the identity of the screech it now called its own. Without the clock, the alarm would still be there. Arnold would always wake as the sun was setting.

But he *loved* technology. So he embraced the clock and its screech. Embraced the things a vendor enjoys in the current century. Cash registers. Fridges.

Video cameras.

Arnold saw the men coming. His cameras saw *much* farther than the feeds on the monitors in his back room would have a casual observer believe. Arnold could see all over the city. He saw them coming, and he was not afraid. Trajen had gone. For a moment, Arnold wondered if the young soul might have saved him. Even in his slumber, he could hear the rustling of power as it was being honed. Soon, the boy who was not a boy, the Loren who was beyond the Loren, would be close to his destiny. Not ready for it, Arnold was certain no one was ever truly ready to face their destiny, let alone a Peacemaker without their memory. But soon, Trajen would have to face it anyway. Trajen might have saved Arnold this day, but it was not worth the cost.

The shopkeeper stood behind the counter, counting the seconds until the men entered the store. They had managed to track Trajen's scent again, he knew. Though, his own innate abilities would work well to mask Trajen's recent departure. There are some things about a man you just can't change. A dogs got to smell like a Golems got to smell sweet. It was the way of things, Arnold knew. Even in his body made of flesh and blood.

It was times like this, Arnold thought of his childhood. For many, the memories of their earliest years are fleeting images. Wisps of emotion wrapped in a notion that once, when they were young, things were different. A Golem's memory is different, so much so that Arnold knows things are almost always the same. When a Golem is born, there is nothing left to do. They arrive to life in their only physical age. Their progression is mental. And a Golem does not forget. When Arnold remembers his childhood, it is a celebration of a time when he knew haste. When he was impatient. Arnold used to be known for his youthful spirit, and his zest. Now, like the rest of his kind, Arnold was old. He was older most things a person could readily point to. Sometimes someone will say something is, "older than dirt." *I was there when stuff was becoming dirt,* Arnold would think. You could ask him, if you really wanted to know. A great many things, of course, were *not* older than dirt. Except Arnold.

But Arnold didn't feel old. He never had. One of the many gifts of his race, he often mused. Arnold hardly felt the passage of time, even now, as he was acutely aware of how long the strike team coming his way was taking. This was why he slept all day. Sleeping was a wonderful thing. There are many theories on why the body *needs* to sleep, the most popular being, "because it gets sleepy." For Arnold, the only reason a person needed to do something was because they wanted to do it. Sleeping was fantastic, and Arnold wanted to do as much of it as he could. He understood that the other races, who did not live nearly as long as Golems, could not afford to sleep as much as he did. They would miss their entire lives that way. But Arnold was no fool. He knew, if they could, sleep away their lives was exactly what they would do.

Arnold also loved magic. With the rapid advancement of the humans' machines, the separation of magic and technology had never been thinner. The old Golem knew if he spent a moment on the phone in his pocket, he could probably find a hundred ways to alert the rest of his order that he was about to die. Arnold thought mass-texting was marvelous. But the sigil by the door did it just as well. More than that, it did it the way he wished. For all of the uses technology gave him in the modern era, magic still had its place. Arnold didn't have to worry about losing signal during an emergency. Magical sigils worked the way you told them to no matter the situation at hand.

The strike team crossed the threshold of the shop, throwing wide the glass-paned doors. Arnold's sigil enacted its purpose, alerting the other Golems of the danger he was about to face. So too did it alert them of his intention. He would not fight these men. They had come to kill him, no matter the answers he gave. So he would give them nothing. The Lyrans clawed and raked at the Golem's fleshy body, in spite of his cries and pleading. He told them he knew nothing. Perhaps they could smell his lies. In the end, he was right.

The final blow was swift. Angry.

His next breath was labored, but familiar. It was always that way.

Great eyelids composed of stone flickered upward as Arnold's truest form began to move for the first time in nearly a century. This was the way of all Golems. Their natural forms were the sturdiest of all, their souls the lightest of all. A swath of roaches and rats, his unknown roommates in the chamber where he left his stone form, gathered quickly to investigate the sweet smell which now pervaded the room. He tried to smile as he saw their intent, but his stone face would allow no such movement. He thought to brush them away, to save the rats' tiny teeth from the agony of his impenetrable stone skin. But time was short.

The strike team had found Trajen's scent. It would be a long journey back to the city.

But he was compelled to help.

Arnold set about calling upon the magic in many of the stones around him. His great, powerful legs brought him carefully up the stairs, his mind desperately searching for more stimulus than his sense of sight would give him, so fresh he was from the human form he had taken. The mind was finicky that way. Once it had grown used to perceiving the world with more, it did not do well with less. Soon his eyesight would become more expansive, when his mind realized it was the only sense available to him in this body. But for now, the dark quarters in which he'd left his Golemnic form did well to keep him somewhat fumbling about.

In spite of their size, Arnold could use his hands with precision and care. He carefully searched for the stone on the wall that would light his chamber in a comforting blue hue. When the chamber was lit, he made his way to his table, pulling out a chair that weighed more than a thousand pounds.

Numerous one-of-a-kind tomes written in the language of the Golems sat on the right side of the table. On the left was a panel, with smaller stones. Arnold thought for a moment that he would do well to keep a telephone down here, now that he knew enough about running phone lines to have one put in. There was only so many sentences you could say with magic in one message. He pushed the first tiny stone, a yellow light illuminating the sigil carved into it. He pushed two more one after another, each taking on their own yellow glow as well. As he pushed the fourth tile, the light on the stones turned green, signaling that his message was sent. It didn't matter where they were, or what forms they had taken, the other Golems would know it was time for the Parliament of History to gather. It would take some time, but they would all come. When they did, Arnold would relay to them what he had been practicing saying in his head for at least a decade.

It was time the Golems came back.

....

The soldiers in Arnold's shop were nearly frenzied. It was always this way after a kill. Each of them had gone their separate ways. If they stayed together, there would be even more blood. One of them remained in the shop.

Bando, who led the strike team in the field, liked to *feast* upon his kills.

The shopkeeper tasted sweet upon his lips. Almost as sweet as he had smelled. The man's blood had formed a pool, which Bando used now as a sauce for the limbs he was eating. He remained fully embracing his Lyran guise, his lineage giving him a form barely humanoid. His was a breed unable to transform fully into a large wolf, though he looked more animal than man when the human parts of himself fell away. His limbs were long, their joints reversed. He could run on all fours if he wished, though he was just as fast when running upright. He dipped the shopkeeper's dismembered limbs into the pools anew after each bite,

174

savoring the uncanny sweetness which seemed to completely invade all of his senses. It wasn't enough to simply eat this man for Bando. The taste incorporated into each delicious bite called to him in a way no meal ever had before. He didn't want to keep eating, he *needed* to. Soon it was all he could do to keep from rolling around in the mess of muscle, bone, and blood on the floor.

So engulfed in enjoying his meal was he that he never heard the displacement of air behind him.

That was all the sound Dalbrin made.

Dalbrin came upon the Lyran with the precision only an elder Vampyrian combatant could possess. He threw three strikes, designed to stun his opponent, to Bando's neck, and both underarms. Had Bando been any other breed of Lyra, he surely would have been left incapacitated and ready for questioning. Instead, the dog-like humanoid howled in agony as he spun his body to meet the threat, arms extended so that his razor-sharp claws slashed through the air ferociously, the claws on his feet digging into the tile so that he would not fall. Dalbrin easily dodged the attack, stepping back only as much as was required for the miss.

As Bando glimpsed his opponent, his blood boiled over in rage, and his frenzy came on in full. He came at the vampire with his arms raking through the air, prepared to rend Dalbrin as viciously as he could the moment he made contact. Each swipe of his claws was met with an open-handed slap from the Vampyr, whose demeanor remained calm. If Dalbrin was exerting much energy keeping the frenzied Lyra at bay, his opponent, had he had the wits to do so, would not have been able to tell. The two were utter opposites in combat, as if Dalbrin were fencing an untrained man with a broadsword.

The pair continued their dance, Dalbrin deflecting the harrowing blows of the dog-man, Bando doing everything he could to use his natural weaponry to kill the Dalbrin's wispy form, until they came upon the fridges, in the back of the shop.

Dalbrin reached for the door handle as Bando came forward, opening the door so that Bando shattered the glass with his strike, the Lyran cutting his arm deeply as he retracted. Dalbrin was excited at the sight of blood, though he knew this particular sample was no use to him. Lyran blood, as was well known to his kind, was poisonous to vampires. In spite of this, however, Dalbrin was more than happy to delight simply at the sight of the Lyran's life force, enjoying deeply the patterns it drew as it spurted from his arm upon the checkered tile flooring. Dalbrin knew in a moment more, the Lyran would bleed out and collapse.

But Bando grew sluggish in his next movement. Dalbrin, as skilled as he was, would not let the opening go free.

The vampire reached forward with all of his might, shoving his hand fully into Bando's chest. Dalbrin squeezed, feeling the Lyran's leathery heart in his ancient hands, smiling as the now pitiful organ attempted futilely to continue to beat. Dalbrin held his grin, the same impossibly wide smile he was so accustomed to as of late, as he watched the life fade from Bando's eyes, and felt the Lyran's heart give its last effort before stopping its movement completely.

The ancient vampire had known many joys in his long, long life. Some of them he liked more than others.

But he *loved* killing Lyra.

He threw his right arm out to his side, slicing the air with his fingernails. The heart he was holding flew and shattered against the far wall, the force of his movement causing nearly all the Lyran blood to release itself from his skin. The movement was not unlike the thrust one takes before they clean their sword and place it back into its sheath. He couldn't bite his fingernails any time soon, but it was enough to ensure

176

that if he picked his nose, he would not go into shock from the poisonous dog's blood.

Dalbrin stepped out onto the sidewalk, briskly stepping his feet away from the crime scene of a corner store. As he reached the end of the block and stopped, searching for what he needed to track down his next victim. He hoped he would find all of the other soldiers in the same place, though he knew their kind. It was likely they had scattered. Although he had been given the go-ahead to pursue the Lyrans, he was pressed for time. He had an evening class to teach in two hours. Hunting during the day was risky, as well. It was only a few minutes when he spotted what he needed. It made him think again of how impatient the world had become. Nobody stood still anymore and just *waited*. If they did, as he was, they might realize that old adages become old for a reason. People miss things when they never stop walking.

But he saw the rat.

Dalbrin could not talk to the rodent. Nor could he command it to do his bidding, or manipulate its mind the same way he could the mind of one of the other races. Dalbrin knew animals, though. He could see that the animal was skittish. The casual observer might have thought the rat was simply cautious in the daylight, but Dalbrin knew better. It could smell the musk of the Lyrans nearby. Rats do not have a traditional prey mindset. It is often that a rat might become a predator themselves. That was how Dalbrin knew the rat was afraid, and not simply skittish. It was cautious, its tiny rat nose alerting it to the presence of something much bigger nearby. Dalbrin felt the wind on his face as it blew directly at him. The same wind was likely carrying the scent of the Lyrans he sought. It was a long shot, but he had no other discernable leads.

The Vampyr continued on across the street, walking directly in line for the rat, who scurried back into the sewer opening under the sidewalk as he came too close. He looked quickly inside of every shop he passed, and down each alleyway as well. Dalbrin had been excited he was able to catch up to the Lyran thugs, and knew he could eventually find them again, though his excitement waned as shop after shop proved devoid of those he sought. He caught sight of a beautiful sunstone necklace in one of the store windows, silently making a note to himself to go back to purchase the item for his wife Gracia. Her collection of the orange stones was already quite vast, but he knew there was almost no better surprise gift for his Dayrunner lover.

He had almost given up his search when, as he walked past one alleyway, he nearly missed seeing two of the Lyrans he sought conversing against a far wall. Truth be told, it was the blood on one of their vests which caught his eye. He had hardly been paying attention, he was so suddenly caught up thinking about his wife's favorable reaction when he presented the gift to her later. His excitement soared anew as he stopped himself, pivoted immediately in place, and began to walk down the alleyway. He was halfway there before the two Lyrans spotted him. The nearest dog cocked up his face, a look like he knew he recognized Dalbrin, but could not remember where.

"Hey," the Lyran said to his companion. "Isn't that-"

Dalbrin was there in an instant, one hand clasped around each of the Lyran's throats. He began to squeeze gleefully, applying the pressure slowly so he could feel the exact moment each of their tracheas collapsed.

His hands occupied clutching the Lyran's necks, Dalbrin did not see the third man standing in his blind spot. The hit came hard, to the side of his head, the man's follow-through exceptional as he hit the old Vampyr. Dalbrin spun with the blow, ready to be tackled and pummeled more, as was common custom with Lyran fighters. The spear-move did not come, though. His head still spinning somewhat, Dalbrin attempted to regain his focus as the three Lyrans' features sharpened in an instant, small hairs sprouting all over their bodies. The three men were obviously the tactical portion of the Lyran unit. Dalbrin backed up just a step, fully gaining his balance, allowing the other men to make the first move. They came at him all together, the two Lyrans on the outside producing metal batons from their vests. Dalbrin had to bob and weave the attacks, the upper half of his body dodging while his feet stayed stationary. He managed to barely stay ahead of the swings as they came, though one clipped him on the ear. The metal rang hard against his skin, and was searing to the touch. The Lyrans were fighting with silver weaponry, a dirty tactic among the Loren, as the metal was fatal to a large portion of the many races. This changed the engagement, but not in a way that Dalbrin could not deal with. He would simply have to become less civilized.

The Vampyr ducked under an oncoming blow, the Lyran in the middle's foot passing over his head. The move was a feint, as the two Lyrans on the outside swung in simultaneously, expecting Dalbrin to be unable to dodge their simultaneous attacks. The Vampyr slid forward, digging his claws into the middle Lyran's standing leg, lifting the man from the ground. The metal rods *clanked* together harmlessly behind him as he bullrushed forward with the man in his grip. They slammed hard into the far wall and Dalbrin released the man's leg, blood flying quickly from the artery on the side where the Vampyr hand sunk his fingers. He turned, his arm flying fast out to the side again to clear the poisonous blood from his fingers, flinging it directly into the eyes of the Lyran on his right. The man on his left swung fast, leaving Dalbrin no other option but to catch the oncoming blow. Dalbrin's hand burned as it caught the silver, his right fist coming up immediately to land a hard blow to the Lyran's nose. The Lyran's vision clouded and took a step back to keep his balance, but it was too late. Dalbrin released the metal and brought the claws on his left hand down across the man's face, then he brought his right hand around in a similar fashion, completely blinding his opponent. The man whimpered for a moment, until Dalbrin stepped forward and took the Lyran's head in his hands, shoving his thumbs hard into either eye socket. Dalbrin pushed his fingers inside the man's skull immediately, and the man's whimpering ceased as he fell lifeless to the concrete.

As Dalbrin turned to finish of the remaining third man, he was met with a direct hit from the silver baton. The flesh on his face burnt immediately upon contact, and he took a rapid jump backwards to avoid being hit again. Subsequent blows from the weapon would easily cave his entire face in. As he landed from his jump, his left eye watering uncontrollably, he saw the Lyran coming at him. The man wore a mask of rage, his fangs showing clearly in the daylight, Dalbrin's own fangs displayed out well out of a carnal, instinctual need to show he was unafraid. The Vampyr stepped forward as the Lyran closed in, grabbing the man's wrist as the baton came forward in its attack. The two struggled to gain the better balance, falling to the ground in the process. Dalbrin quickly brought one foot underneath the Lyran to disengage, as he was more comfortably fighting on his feet, but the Lyran held tight in the hold. Dalbrin's opponent rolled the Vampyr on his back, Dalbrin with one hand around the man's wrist holding the baton, the man with his hand holding Dalbrin's other wrist, the two fought with their legs and hips. Dalbrin thrust his hips upward to try and dislodge his opponent, but the man was too skilled to be thrown off. The Lyran ducked down, digging his shoulder into Dalbrin's throat, hoping to cut off his air supply. Dalbrin could go a very long time without breathing, but he could not continue to fight without giving oxygen to his muscles. There was no other option.

Dalbrin whipped his head around the man's shoulder, biting hard into Lyran flesh. The Vampyr was careful not to drink the blood, though it flowed fully into his mouth, a significant portion snaking its way down his throat in spite of his best efforts. The man screamed in pain from the bite, arching his back reflexively. That was all Dalbrin needed. The Vampyr tore the chunk of flesh from the Lyran's shoulder with his mouth, spitting the muscle and skin out and away from him. A spurt of blood released from the Lyran's shoulder and fell onto Dalbrin's chest as Dalbrin worked his feet under the man, kicking with both as hard as he could. The Lyran flew out and away, landing flat on the concrete. Dalbrin was on his feet in an instant.

Staring down at the back of the Lyran's head, Dalbrin's foot placed itself fully inside of the man's skull.

The Vampyr took one step away from the scene, turning back to survey his work. It had been an excellent battle. More fun than he'd had in over three decades, if he was honest. There were still two more Lyrans he would eventually go looking for, and he have to remember not to let his instincts take over when he did. He was, after all, meant to return with at least *some* information, he couldn't just-

Dalbrin keeled over in pain, the contents of his stomach firing themselves from his mouth in huge, explosive bursts of bile, solid food, and Lyran blood. Though his mind had nearly forgotten about swallowing so much of the poisonous liquid, his body had not. He spent more than a few minutes on his hands an knees, appearing more as someone disgused by the scene in front of him than the cause of the three dead bodies. He feared for a moment he may pass out from the strain, but was pleased to see that his body managed to fully excrete the toxins, though he was unhappy that both ends had managed to work towards the excretion. He stood again, his face and hair disheveled, and his pants fully soiled. The Vampyr took a few steps to disrobe behind a dumpster before continuing on with his day, throwing his clothing into the waste receptacle. He took one final, lingering moment to enjoy the destruction he had wrought, before vanishing not unlike a puff of smoke, happy to have found his prey and survive the forbidden drink of his enemies.

He made a note to come back for the necklace.

Chapter XVII

Spice stood patiently upon the rooftop of his favorite building in the city, the Downtown Library. He looked out at the lights of the city, which were only now coming to life, awakening as the sun above prepared to sleep. He had always been fond of the library for its view. There were other buildings with similar views, as well, but they did not afford him as easy of an access route to their top level. He did not know the building's history specifically, but it had obviously been designed with his kind in mind. A Wretched could easily travel from the sub-level of the building, through its walls, which were expansive enough that he did not need to shimmy, and up a ladder onto its roof with no trouble. He had been coming up onto the roof of the library from when he was old enough to walk around on his own. Spice had spent his entire life fascinated with the surface, and the open sky it provided. He removed his coat and stretched his arms across his chest, stretching as well the muscles in his back and shoulders. Spice leaned forward slightly then, as two large, leathery wings slid out from slits on either side of the back of his shirt. He gave his wings a stretch before stepping off the side of the library, flapping a few times before casually catching an updraft.

Like the rest of the Loren, even his own kind, Spice did not know where his wings came from. He didn't know where they went, either. His kind could call upon their wings when they wished, and dismiss them just as quickly. Even when the skin and muscle was flayed from their bones, no sign of the wings could be found. If he were shot from the sky right now, his wings would disappear the moment the life left his body. He used to spend all day when he was younger, trying to come up with an explanation for the phenomenon. Of course, he had never come up with any better reason than the rest of the world had managed. Eventually he stopped caring entirely. Now, when he had time to wonder, the only thing on his mind was figuring out why more of his kind didn't take the time to go for a flight every now and then, as he did. Even the Wretched who chose a life on the surface were, as he found them, not known to use their wings very often. More than utility, a Wretched's wings were powerful weapons, the long, sharp claws on the ends able to be used not unlike spears – providing ample distance to defend themselves from afar. But he had been there when other Wretched were being pressed, or threatened. He had seen the way they were so often treated by the other Loren, as if they were barely better than the dirt they all walked upon. He had never seen a single Wretched use their wings in defense.

He used his wings all the time.

He preferred using them for flight. As he was just then being reminded, flying had an exceptionally calming effect on his disposition. He found that most of his cares and stresses of the day fell away the moment his feet left whatever solid thing he was standing on. He didn't know how his people had come to live in underground cities. That part of history was lost to his kind. But the irony of a race capable of flight living where there is no sky above them often left him feeling disheartened to the point that he was forced to wonder if the other Wretched didn't *deserve* to be treated like they were nothing. All they had to do was step out onto the surface and flap their wings. Instead, millions of his kind never saw the light of day.

He would be sad about it, if he cared enough to be. Or if he had the time, perhaps.
As he landed, his wings appearing to slide themselves back into his body, he threw his coat back on and saddled up against the brick wall of an old building. He hadn't really been ready to land just yet, but his life did not allow for much fun and games any more. Well, that wasn't true. What he did *was* fun for him. He was passionate about his work. But still, he had felt like flying for a little longer. At least his contact was on time. Nobles are funny that way. Nice clothes and living quarters aren't the only things that separate the Celebrant nobles from the scum they often to dealings with.

The nobles are also punctual.

"Good to see you again, Henry." Spice said.

"Spice. Thank you for being on time."

"No thanks required. You've brought the other half of my payment, I trust?"

"Indeed." The Celebrant nobleman released a pouch of golden coins from his pocket. It often seemed ridiculous to Spice that anyone would take the time to deal in physical coins anymore, but who was he to refuse money? The amount of things a few coins from a Celebrant noble could buy for him made carrying the weighted sack completely worth his time, in spite of how silly he found physical money to be. More than anything else, he was glad his business in locating the Warmonger was finished. Even if the job paid well, he preferred to gather information on targets who couldn't kill him twice over before his bodyguards could even react.

"Shame about those men," Spice said as he took the coins.

"Nonsense," the nobleman replied. "Cannon fodder – nothing more. Don't bother troubling yourself."

"Oh? So the Rent band was never meant to bring you the girl's head?"

"Ha! Don't be absurd. Those two hardly won their audition. Their tactics were as weak as their disposition. They relied on simple misdirection, as if that were ever going to get them anywhere in life. No, they served their purpose. We learned what it was we needed to know."

"Well, say what you will about mercenaries, but at least they have their uses."

"Indeed." The nobleman said, somewhat curtly. The man made no attempt to continue speaking after the word had exited his mouth. Spice cleared his throat through the silence.

"Anyway, pleasure doing business with you, Henry. Do reach out if you need anything else." As if in spite of the simple pleasantry, the nobleman literally reached out then, grabbing Spice by the arm.

"Oh, no, Spice. We are not finished." The nobleman produced an additional pouch from his other pocket, filled with even more of the same golden coins. "That was your payment for the first job. We'd like to hire you for an *ongoing* contract. We want to know where the girl is at *all* times. This should be enough to get you started. You can expect another payment at the end of the month."

Spice opened the sack of coins, looking long and hard at its contents. This would be the most dangerous job he would ever take. It was also the most lucrative. It would likely get him killed.

But if it didn't…

"I'll send you weekly reports. Give me a day or so to get my people in place, and you can expect 'round the clock surveillance. Any time you want to know where she is, all you'll have to do is call. And keep the money coming, of course."

"Of course," the nobleman replied.

"Will there be anything else? I need to see a few people so I can start working on this new assignment."

"No, no. That will be all." The nobleman turned on his heels immediately. Spice watched the man walk to the end of the block, a black sedan pulling up the moment the man reached the curb. Another

Celebrant stepped out of the driver's seat to run around the side of the car to let the man in, and the car quickly sped away.

Spice knew this job might be his last. Unless the Celebrants managed, somehow, to win. Then, he might not be killed by the Warmonger.

Then, he would truly be famous.

Trajen felt a gaze upon him. The hairs on his neck stood straight, his own eyes darting everywhere in suspicion. The street looked deserted, a car driving casually past him. But in the waning light of the day, he knew he was not alone. He steeled himself with each passing step, opening as much of himself, and his senses, as he could. Then, a familiar scent passed lightly into his awareness. Something he'd not smelled since his fight in the alley.

Russel.

As the thought came to him, so too did the old man, moving much faster than his age belayed he should. Sharp red hairs sunk back into the old man's skin as he rolled down his sleeves and emerged fully from the alleyway to Trajen's left. His face grew softer in feature, and he drew a short breath with which to speak.

"Hello again, Trajen. I'm glad I caught you. May I walk with you for a moment?"

Trajen smiled. This would be his first real conversation with the older Lyran, whom he now understood was quite sly. Trajen hadn't been able to figure out how to both soak in the sun and then take on his Lyran powers, nor could he muster any other combination of powers or aspects. Russel walking with him was welcome in that moment, as he would not have to deal with the disappointment of not understanding his powers all over again. "Hello, Russel. It's good to see you outside of battle. Yes, of course, let's walk. "

"Outside of battle? That was a street fight, at best. I'll let you *know* when we're in *battle*. Speaking of fights, though, there were some things I wanted to ask you about." The two began back down the sidewalk, continuing on in Trajen's previous trajectory. Russel took a moment before he began, as if he were searching for the words. "Trajen, what do you remember?"

"Of what? Before I was here?"

"Yes. Of before I woke you, and you left LyraCorps. What can you recall from before that?"

"Not much of anything. Close to nothing, really. But I've had...dreams. Well, a dream, at least." Trajen was embarrassed to say it. He felt as though his conversation with Russel needed to be important. As though the words he shared with the man who freed him from his prison ought to have merit, or not be spoken at all. More than that, Trajen realized he was hoping this conversation might give him some purpose. He was truly sick of doing nothing. He wanted Russel showing up to mean he'd have a job to do.
Russel made no indication that he found the mention of dreams anything except serious. "Good. That's good. In the dream, what did you see?"

"It was pretty blurry, for the most part. I was in a large hall. Somewhere impossibly old. It feel like it almost might be outside of time. I was standing among others like me, though we were within our own race segregated from the others. Around us are the other races, from Morkhavians to Lyra. Even the Vampyr are there."

"And the Golems. Did you see them?" Russel's ears perked up as he asked, a curious happening because his ears were human at that moment, and already straight.

Somehow, they managed to perk themselves up ever further.

"Not clearly. I looked at them in my dream and knew that was what they were, but I couldn't make out any details. Hey, why are they called Golems? I thought Golems were supposed to be made from stone, or metals."

"Golems were the first race. It is only the youngest of them who were made from stone. The first Golems were nothing but dirt and clay. Others were made of bronze or alternative metals, you're correct in that. I don't think I understand why you're asking though. Are the Golems in your dream not made from earth or metal?"

"No. The Golems in my dream are human."

Russell found this comment particularly interesting. "Really? I've only read about such a thing. The Golems are long, long gone. But there are stories of them having...well...the term is *loose souls*. That's roughly translated, of course. The idea is that their souls can move from object to object. I suppose that could include a human body. I always imagined that they simply moved to a new shell of rock or metal. I had honestly never considered a living form."

"In my dream they look like people, at least. So, there aren't any more Golems? They're all dead?" Trajen was sad about hearing this, though he tried not to show the emotion. Russel did not seem sad that there were no more Golems, so he felt as if he should not either.

"Dead or hiding. Golems are said to be naturally solitary. Their race was the first with history, naturally. They're supposed to love chronicling things. There is are many myths from the early times of man that speak of a race of Watchers. Both the Book of Enoch and the Book of Daniel come to mind. Golems have never been involved in a single race war, choosing instead to write about them. It's in the scribing of an ancient Golemnic Tome that I read about the lightness of their essence."

The word hung hard in Trajen's mind. *War.* He hadn't asked Garrett much about why he was working with Russel to overthrow LyraCorps, and bring down the 'shadowy empire' of the Lyra. But it was starting to make sense. "Russel," he said, carefully, "Is there a war *now*? I forgot to ask Garrett about that when I told him about my dream. I think in my dream the big Lyra, with the white stripe down his head and back, is calling for war with the Vampyr. Are you and Garrett on the other side or something?"

Russel smiled. Trajen felt the slyness in the man once again. "Very close, Trajen. Well done. There was a war, but it's passed. It was The Great War. An event hundreds of years in tenure, it caused the divide among the races. It caused, as well, the eventual loss of not just the Golems, but also the Vampyr. And before you ask, yes. This time, I do mean that they're all dead. Killed a few myself, unfortunately."

"What do you mean? You didn't want to kill them?"

"Who *wants* to kill anyone? I'm no killer. I never have been. I'd just as soon run from a fight as I would stand my ground. And I never killed a man unless I had to. Other Lyra don't feel that way, of course. Even fewer Vampyr, when they were still around, would have passed on killing a Lyra. You can be sure of that. It was the way of things, not so long ago."

"So how did the Vampyr die off?"

"I see Garrett truly has told you nothing. What the hell have you been doing? I told Garrett to *wait*, not leave you completely dumb to the world!" Russel paused, obviously angry, before drawing a calming breath. The old man rubbed his eyes before he continued. "It was numbers, really. A war that long always is. Lyran women are especially

189

adept at breeding. Those of our kind who can fully take on the guise of a wolf, their females still have litters. Six, sometimes seven little babies all at once. It can really throw you off when you see it. Most of our young come out looking human. Not theirs. I've seen many Lyran doctors look to be at the point of losing their lunch at the sight of a human-looking woman giving birth to puppies. I don't blame a single one of them. Seen it myself, and I'll tell you, it's not something I ever want to see again."

Trajen began to feel more comfortable with Russel as their conversation went on. Even though he had been feeling embarrassed about mentioning the dream, with the talk of the war between the Lyra and the Vampyr, he didn't want to miss his opportunity to ask for answers from someone who, to him, was rapidly beginning to seem like they knew quite a bit more than Garrett did. "Did the Lyra declare war on the Vampyr because they knew the Vampyr were all that was in their way if they wanted to take over, as LyraCorps has? Did the Lyra always want to be in charge?"

"Yes and no. Your kind was meant to stand as the governing entity. It's natural that leaders fight for more power – for many leaders, it's a part of who they are. And honestly, in a race almost exclusively made up of dog-people, I think that need to not just be the leader of their own pack, but *all* packs, was always going to be an issue. In the history of the Loren, it was people like you who made sure no single race grew into what the Lyra, and LyraCorps, have become."

"So I've heard. But then, where are they? I'd definitely like to talk to someone like me. I have so many questions. Like-"

"Trajen." The men stopped walking. Russel's form grew stiff, his slyness falling away as he grew serious in tone. "There are none. I don't know why. I have more Golemnic Tomes than the largest Loren library, and I've never found anything that says where your people went. We found you by *accident*. You were a rumor that I'm sure the people we heard it from hardly believed. But when I went down there, there you were. I saw you...and I don't know...I just *knew*." Russel smiled, somewhat sadly, as he continued, "That's how the Lyra took over the way they did. Somehow, they got rid of your kind first. I was born into a world without any of what you are, when The Great War was on the decline, and the Vampyr were no more than a few hundred around the globe. I was thirty when we killed the last Vampyr. In a town like this one, as a matter of fact, but a whole world away. That was almost two hundred years ago." Russel waited a moment before he began walking again, his brisk pace leaving Trajen momentarily behind.

Trajen stepped quickly to catch up. "You're two hundred and thirty years old?!"

"Shush, boy. You want the whole world to hear? Besides, you look young, and I'm happy to treat you as such since you don't seem to know your shoes from the Lyran-like claws at the end of your toes, but you're probably *much* older than I am. At *least* eight hundred years older than me."

Trajen thought then of his dream. Particularly, he recalled the oversized Lyra, with the white stripe of fur down his backside. "Russel, in my dream, when I saw Mordacity...Is it the same one as the man you and Garrett are after? It can't be, can it?"

"Make no mistake, Trajen. Mordacity is unlike any other Lyra. Impossibly old. Impossibly strong. And the biggest damn dog to ever walk the earth. There has only ever been *one* Mordacity. The Tomes are clear about that. He manipulated and clawed his way to the top of the Lyra when he was young, and he's been there ever since."

"Jeez, and you guys are gonna try to fight someone like that?" The idea seemed perfectly crazy to the young Peacebringer.

"We must! And besides, no one is without weakness. It was Mordacity's hubris that started The Great War. Lyran scholars would have you believe the Vampyr cast the first stone, and that war was the only option back then. But I found a Tome that told a much different story, about a young Lyran hungry for power, slighted by a Vampyr noble with no respect for our kind. Really puts things into perspective, if you let it. To think that an entire race was wiped out because somebody made a rude comment...That's life, I guess."

Russel and Trajen reached the end of the block, the old Lyra stopping them in their journey. Trajen turned to face the man, still processing the information he'd been given. A Great War? Why hadn't Garrett mentioned any of this yet? He'd been here for almost a year. What was he doing wasting his time in school? His kind were meant for more than books.

"Russel, I've been thinking about something for a few days. I don't want to just wait around anymore. If the Peacebringers were meant to keep the balance between the races, then that's what I want to do. I want to help you and Garrett, and whoever else you're working with."

Russel smiled at the idea. "You know, I've been trying to figure out where you could fit in, but maybe it's better if we let you do that for yourself. I have to meet with some people, but we're gonna bring you in. As long as we take the time to cover the trail your scent will leave, we'll get you out to a meeting, and you can decide for yourself how you can help the cause."

"That...sounds great! There's one other thing, too."

"What's that?"

"We sort of need to teach me how to use my abilities."

"Kid, that ain't the only thing you don't know how to do. Once we get set up, I'm teaching you how to *fight*. For a member of the most powerful and versatile race of Loren, you are a sorry comrade to take into battle."

Trajen smiled.

He felt like he *needed* to do this.

He needed to get the world back on track.

From the pages of Hrath's Golemnic Tome. Vol 33.
Dayrunners.

The world had changed so much. Gone was my ability to survey the earth in my natural form. The cities had become too crowded – too expansive in their reach. Any exploration I might partake in is now and forever confined to a host form.

It was in the first true age of technological advancement, when I had my most honest experience with a Dayrunner.

I had taken the form of one.

Experiencing life through a host body is a tiresome affair. The forms of the other races are less hardy, their biology keeping one from experiencing time as anything but a stream of moments. I find hunger to be the most bothersome of things, returning as quickly as it does, especially for the Dayrunners. Unlike the Vampyr, the physiology of a male Dayrunner does not allow for more than an hour or so of satiation. Hunger returns almost immediately for many of them. At first consideration, the synergy between the male and female of the species seems so convincing. It's easy to believe that the female Dayrunners, with the ability to draw in sunlight and produce energy, would be the only thing the males of the race needed. Perhaps, in the biological sense, the relationship does work. I found, however, in my experience as one of them that life is hardly so simple.

A Golem "worth their stones" will not take a host body already occupied with sentience, which does not truly begin until the brain develops the capacity for memory. In our earliest studies of other races, we found that the only proper way to take a living host form is to do so at the earliest stages of its creation. I took the form of a female Dayrunner solely to avoid the infinite cycle of hunger the males experience. The first true railroad was being built in the year I had made my decision. I could hear the hammering of the spikes which would hold down the tracks from where I was within the earth, the shockwaves of the many hammer strikes reverberating through the ground until they reached my body. It was the humans and their creativity. I had searched for a human form that day, but a soul is not long for the world without a body. Time truly precious to a soul free of a form. Rather than return to my own that day, rather than express the patience I know my mind to have an unending amount of, I chose not to wait. Perhaps I was afraid the modernization of the world above me would pass by too quickly. Perhaps I do not have as much patience as I believe. Whatever the case, the result was that I was without a truly human form.

Being a female Dayrunner was okay.

Dayrunner abilities do not manifest until puberty. Their bodies are nearly fully grown before they have the ability to move with what a human would consider to be preternatural speed. Dayrunners call this 'The Shift.' It signifies not just the gaining of their heightened agility, but also the ways in which their lives change. Male Dayrunners become increasingly energy deficient. Their bodies begin to metabolize energy at a much faster rate than any other race. Female Dayrunners, as their bodies change, can photosynthesize sunlight. The energy they produce is not without its limits, though a single female can produce enough to keep up to three males satiated. When my Dayrunner form Shifted, my body fully through puberty, I was ready to fulfill what I felt was my purpose as I learned about the world. I would find a male, perhaps two if we bore no male children, and keep them satiated. I found out early on, however, that Dayrunner culture had not placed the same value I had in my studies on the synergy of their biology. This is a valuable lesson to any burgeoning, or ancient, observer of the world. There is often much in the way of Psychology which cannot be learned without observation. This was, obviously, something I needed to be reminded of, as I learned what I consider to be the most interesting thing about the Dayrunner race during my first few days fresh from my Shift.

Very few male Dayrunners ever commit to a female of their race. Partnerships are frequent, but they are also an extremely wistful and easily dissolvable thing when it comes to one Dayrunner being with another.

It would be dishonest for me to say that I did not prefer to be alone in the Dayrunner body I had taken. Once I had realized I would be without a mate, someone who desperately needed the energy my body could produce, I took to seeing the world and the boom of its technology. Still, in spite of knowing that I was not truly a Dayrunner, I found myself searching for a male of my species in each new city or town I explored. While many males of the Dayrunner race were willing to receive the energy I could produce, never did I find one who did not soon find themselves taking the energy of a far less bountiful race. Like the Vampyr, with whom the Dayrunners share common ancestry, male Dayrunners can draw energy from the body of a race even if their prey is without the ability to transfer that energy freely. Female Dayrunners need only touch their skin to another's to give the excess energy they have stored. A male Dayrunner can, and in my experience will, take this energy. But the energy upon which they feast is found in every race. Male Dayrunners will take it from them, as well.

The life of a vagabond is a common one for a male Dayrunner, who can gain sustenance for an entire day simply by walking through a crowded city, bumping their hand into the many they walk by, stealing bits of energy as they do so. Others, should they have the financial means to do so, often choose a life of glitz and glamour, constantly surrounding themselves with an entourage. Many male Dayrunners keep a harem of either men or women, choosing to feed only during their most intimate moments. Considering how often I found myself needing to produce sunlight to stave off my own hunger, though, it is hard for me to imagine how such individuals could possibly have meaningful lives if the only time they drew energy was when their clothes were removed.

I learned many things about the world in my time as a Dayrunner. Gone was the age of fearing the dark. The even playing field of nature had become heavily favored by the animals with the ability to reason. Humans no longer worried about any natural predators other than themselves, or the races they perceived as being themselves. I found that aspect of the state of things to be the most curious. At some point, which I imagine must have occurred while I was sleeping, there became a division among the Loren. Many of the races knew about the other, though they all kept themselves a secret from the humans. I still do not know why that was, or even how it managed to become a reality. I chose not to abide by this rule, happily revealing my alternative nature to many humans throughout the course of my life.

Perhaps that is the greatest power of the human race, along, again, with their unending pension for creativity. Perhaps they are also the most skilled at seeing only the things they want to see. I lived a long life as a Dayrunner, never meeting a single human who was aware that they were not the only intelligent race on the face of the earth. Dayrunner energy is not without healing properties, even for humans, who do not heal as quickly as other races. Yet, even humans who witnessed firs-hand my ability to take sunlight and rid them of a scrape, or even a grievous wound, never seemed to spread the knowledge. Though, I cannot say how many other humans may have believed them if they tried. The ability of the humans to spread the things they would ultimately choose believe in, though, had grown immeasurably. This was among the most important things I had learned.

I also learned that the humans and, indeed, the many sentient races of the earth, had finally grasped the importance of chronicling their history. Somewhere along the course of their technological advancements, the many races began to see the importance of tracking not only the major events of their village or city, but global events as well. In spite of the innumerable borders which had eventually sprouted and their ever-changing nature, even the humans kept record of global events. This was, and is, the most important lesson technology ever allowed me to learn. My kind was not born as the other races were, and we do not reproduce.

Our truest function is to do just this: To survey the earth and chronicle its history. To know the many races better than they might know themselves. To track their history so that it is not lost. Facing the fact that this function was no longer required of me was not easy. And I do not know if I will ever truly cease to keep an honest account of the world. But life, even at its simplest, was never meant for the faint of heart. I will adapt to my freedom. I will do what I must to survive.

But first, perhaps, I will sleep.

Chapter XVIII

Shen sat at the end of a long ornate Vampyrian-crafted table, runes in a language no longer spoken aloud carved into its base and legs. He stroked his chin in concentration, carefully considering the next thing he chose to say. Each pass of his hand down his face saw his fingers twirling a long and thin beard. After much internal debate, he addressed the other Vampyr at the table, looking directly at Dalbrin.

"It was careless," the Vampiric Elder stated. His tone was a mock anger. It was obvious that Shen was only feigning feeling anything. "Why did you do such a thing?"

"I was operating under the direction of the council, my lord," Dalbrin said with lowered gaze.

"Your orders were to gather information, Matron Dalbrin. Not to slay a Lyran enforcer. And *especially* not an enforcer in Mordacity's personal service! What were you thinking?" This was what Dalbrin hated about his race. About the *elders,* specifically, and especially when he was forced to refer to them as such. He was just as old as nearly every one of them! And at any moment in time, they might change their minds. Dalbrin knew his orders had been changed before he killed the Lyran enforcers. He hadn't agreed with the elders, though. So, like many of the choices the old Vampyr had made throughout his existence…he did it anyway. Everyone had their part to play in today's meeting. He would play his as he was expected to, his fingers still fresh with the scent of the poisonous Lyran blood.

"Forgive me, my lord. It could not be avoided. The Lyrans were out for blood. Frenzied. It was self-preservation."

"Mind yourself," another elder, Horace, said. His tone was light and mocking, to match his tiny form. Dalbrin knew better, though. Horace was angry. Horace was always angry. He was the only elder known to lose his temper, stuck as he was in his childlike form. Horace was the only elder on the council not born a Vampyr, turned when he was no more than a toddler. Horace waited a moment before continuing. "You know full well you didn't need to walk into that shop. Or track down the other two Lyrans. Own your actions, Dalbrin. You *wanted* to kill those Lyra." Dalbrin played his part mainly to appease Horace, so ferocious a Vampyr was he.

Dalbrin looked up at his elders. "Yes, my lord. Of course." Horace seemed satisfied at the admission. Dalbrin was unafraid to die, but he did calm somewhat as he noted Horace's satisfaction.

Shen raised a hand for silence. He looked sternly at Horace, and then to the other members of the council. "Dalbrin's actions were uncalled for. No one will say otherwise. This coven survives only because it is smart. Do you think the Lyra won't know one of their own was killed by a Vampyr? How could they not, with the bite you took? Do you think they didn't know about the bodies surfacing with their throats torn free, as well? So many humans. You have grown sloppy, living with your wife, Dalbrin. If you are not more careful, we will be forced to act."

Dalbrin wanted to smile at the threat. He feared Horace, but he knew the council would make no such move against him. How could they? He was one of the last Vampyr in existence. He thought to question the latter part of what Shen had said, as it hadn't been he who was killing civilians so wantonly, but his pride would not allow him to show the weakness. If they believed he was being sloppy, so be it. Only the oldest of their kind had survived The Great War. And Shen was certainly right about how they'd managed to accomplish such a feat. But there was hardly any weight behind the threat, at least with Shen issuing it. Perhaps if Horace were to threaten Dalbrin... And besides, Dalbrin had been one of their greatest generals, before their race was forced into such a paltry existence. Time could not take the Vampyr as it could the other races, but it had certainly not been kind.

Still, with the threat coming from Shen, Dalbrin knew they'd never kill him.

Shen spoke again, as if he could read Dalbrin's thoughts. "Do not be so quick to write off what I say, Dalbrin. I know as well as any the sorrow that comes with losing a loved one. It is a shame when pretty things disappear from this world. It would be a shame if Gracia were to...never...wake again. There are few things as enrapturing as when someone like your wife greets the new day's sun, as I'm sure you know all too well. I would wager you've never seen a Dayrunner deprived of sunlight. Not a pretty picture at all. So take heed, and hear when I speak to you. Do not force us to take your wife away from the only thing she might love as much as she loves you...*Matron* Dalbrin."

Dalbrin stiffened, any notion of smiling gone from his mind. He lowered his gaze again, understanding the stakes at play in the conversation at hand. If he were anything other than obedient in this moment, he'd lose Gracia. He thought about killing them. To protect his wife or stroke his pride even further, it didn't matter which. But he could not, he knew. Even if he managed to take Shen, or one of the other elders, Horace would never let him make it out alive. You could put a hundred angry Lyra in a room with the tiny vampire, and come back an hour later to a pile of Lyran skulls two stories tall. He could do nothing other than what was expected of him at that moment.

"Please, my lords. Forgive me." Dalbrin sunk his head even lower, as if trying to look through the earth itself. The elders seemed appeased with the apology, in spite of its brevity.

Dalbrin was dismissed soon after, his form practically dissolving, appearing as nothing more than a puff of smoke. It would take him an hour to reach the surface, so deeply under the ground were the elder Vampyr. But the journey would not be so bad, he knew.

There was plenty to think about.

He needed a new plan.

Dalbrin had spent so long pretending to be so many things. During the war he pretended to be human. Most Lyrans alive today couldn't distinguish a Vampyr scent from their own feet. But long ago, Dalbrin had learned to mask himself out of necessity, as keen Lyran noses often found members of his kind quite easily. He had taught others how to hide. At least, those who would take the time to learn. Dalbrin was a respected leader then. There had once been many covens, and his own pretended to be human during the war.

Theirs seemed an unconquerable town in a sea of settlements overrun by Lyran soldiers. Even after the town was lost, Dalbrin had led his coven well, themselves basically hidden from their enemy until it was too late for the dogs to strike back. And now that the war was over, he continued to assume the guise of a human. He met Gracia when he moved to the city. For a while he'd had her fooled. You can only eat dinner with someone so many times, though, before they notice you hide your food however you can, and spill more on the floor than you put in your mouth. What could he do? He had known all along that she was not human. When she found out he was a Vampyr, there hadn't even been a lapse in the conversation. She spotted a butterfly mid-sentence and immediately began remarking about how wonderful some of their migration patterns were, and how beautifully a healthy butterfly's wings caught the sunlight. It was better that way – Gracia simply accepting him as he was, saving them both the trouble of a drawn out conversation.

Dalbrin had never pretended to love his wife. That part of him was real. As real and impactful as the threats were to take her away. His loyalty to the last Vampyrian coven was as important to him as his teaching. If he never had to use his darkvision again, he could say to himself honestly that it would not bother him.

But what could he do?

He and Gracia could never *outrun* the other elder Vampyr. He could not kill all of them. Even if it came down to only him and Horace, he would never see his wife again if he chose that route.

But perhaps they could *hide* from them...

Perhaps if he gave the other Vampyr a reason not to look for him, he and Gracia could spend the rest of their time together in peace. Perhaps, he mused, if he were *dead*.

Following along with the machinations of the other Vampyr was no longer the route which he wished to follow.

Dalbrin needed to die.

■■

Mordacity sat in his office, static on each of his television screens. Where there were normally images of news anchors, or channels with numbers rapidly running across the bottom of the picture, there was now nothing more than a myriad of black and white dots, utter silence accompanying them. To the casual onlooker, their leader would have appeared to be in deep concentration. Perhaps meditating, or even in a trance.

But inside the mind of the leader of the Lyra, a great battle raged. Mordacity had been stuck in his own mind for longer than he ever anticipated he'd live, though he never had a chance to enjoy his physical longevity. He spent most of it walking a literal maze within his mindscape. Year after year he walked through the winding stone walls that seemed to make up the space that existed deep inside his consciousness, coming as he always did to its center.

It was there, always there, he found the *monster*. The being who was in control of his body, responsible for his impossible lifespan. It was the

203

monster who was responsible for the atrocities committed during The Great War, which Mordacity was forced to watch his own hands perform, and was responsible as well for the domination of LyraCorps. The two had battled countless times inside the Lyran's mind, Mordacity trying time and again to defeat the beast. Each new attempt provided the same outcome as the last. The dance, as the monster called it on occasion, had become frustratingly familiar to the oversized Lyran. But his hate was strong, and he refused to give up the fight for his body, even after centuries of failed attempts.

Mordacity hung then suspended in the air, his great claws raking the tendril wrapped around his throat. A common outcome for his fights with the beast.

What are you doing, dog? Do you ever ask yourself that?

Today is the day, monster! I am Mordacity! I am taking back my body!

What makes you so sure? Mordacity felt pain then. Trapped inside of his own body as he was, he could not remember any other sensation. He had an idea of what it was to feel warm, or cold. It occurred to him sometimes that he used to feel both of these things. But that was centuries ago. Pain was all that he felt now, otherwise he felt nothing at all. And the monster was quick to remind him how fully he could make the Lyran hurt as the tendril wrapped around Mordacity's large form, squeezing the bones of the Lyran leader's imagined body.

Ahh! Trouble me no more, beast! Be gone!

Mordacity knew his words would prove fruitless, but he could think of nothing truer to say. He was beyond desperate. The Lyran would do anything to get his body back; say anything. On more than one occasion, and there had been many occasions, the monster had made Mordacity say despicable things. He had tried to make the Lyran believe it was his idea to kill children, or otherwise innocent beings; that Mordacity had wanted to do the terrible things he was forced to watch his own hands do. Time and again, as nothing seemed to work, it always came back to this. The raw struggle of it all. A physical, hands-on fight between the two forms imagined in Mordacity's mind. His own Lyran form against the monster's writhing mass of tendrils and otherwise rounded edges. The best losses against the monster were those where he was so utterly obliterated, often times right at the beginning of the battle, that the entire fight was over in only a moment. Sometimes Mordacity managed to keep his wits about him, as he was now, and land a solid hit or two. On those times, just before the darkness came and he returned to the start of the maze, he would manage to take a chunk of the monster's flesh in his mouth. Those fights were the worst.

They gave him hope.

More pain. Mordacity's physical form began to sweat. The Lyran guards nearby could smell their leader's musk as it permeated from the room, their hushed voices speaking into the radios they wore at shoulder level. These Lyrans knew *everything* about their leader. So committed were they to the success of LyraCorps, they could be trusted not to whimper at the first whiff of their leader's scent, like so many dogs do when they don't understand the situation. The average Lyran solider needed to believe that their leader was invincible. They needed to know that Mordacity's musk never took on the subtle changes it was displaying as it released itself from his office. Even if the body was not really Mordacity's to control, when his fear of failure brought on by the hope of battle began to take hold, when the dog inside was truly afraid, his body could not hide that it happened. The monster, of course, felt nothing.

Please. You will never be free of me, dog. I own you. We've discussed this. Though, as you always seem to need a reminder, I'm happy to oblige...

More sweat. More pain. More hope and fear. Mordacity's spirit felt as if it would become nothing. His will was strong, but he knew he could take no more of the assault from the monster that held claim to his form. He'd lost again, the walls around him becoming blurred as the pain subsided and he fell to the ground. After a moment, the monster was gone. As he caught his breath, he looked up to see, again, that he was at the start of the maze. He mused, as he always did, at the futility of the exercise.

He got up to try again.

Mordacity's physical form was drenched in sweat, as the monster's concentration was back to the present. His nose burned from the smell of his own fear about the room. His sweat ceased almost immediately, as the monster had control of such things when not in the mindscape. He could slow the flow of blood with a thought, so long as he was fully concentrating as he was now. He stood, his socks pushing out sweat with a *slush* as he put his weight onto his heels. The monster turned off the televisions as Roper entered the room.

"Sir, are you alright? I smelled- Sir! You're sweating! What happened?" A question to keep up appearances more than anything else, Roper knew exactly what had happened to make the room smell as it did. He was simply waiting for the door to fully close before his conversation became more casual.

The monster wiped off his stolen face, flinging sweat off his fingertips. "I'm fine, Roper. Nothing to worry about."

"Of course. That *swine* inside of you needs to learn his place. Mine gave in long ago, you know. Almost admirable, the way yours still fights."

"Between you and me," The monster said, "I don't really mind. Every time I defeat him in the mindscape, the look he has before I send him back to the beginning of the maze makes the brief, pitiful struggle worth it for me."

The two monsters shared a laugh.

"Well, I come with less than pleasant news." Roper continued. "The men have come up empty again. They tracked the boy to somewhere in the city – this little shop downtown. All they found was the shopkeeper, though."

"And did they question him?"

"Get this – the man was a *Golem.*" The monster wearing Mordacity's face looked surprised, and with good reason. The monster had known a Golem or two, once upon a time. It did not seem possible to him that there could be any left.

"How do you know for sure?" The monster asked.

"The way the men described the scent. They said the guy smelled sweet, you know? But none of them could agree on what *kind* of sweet he smelled like. Some said candy, others said flowers. One of them is still there, I think. Stupid dog couldn't help himself. Said if he didn't stick around to eat the shopkeeper, he might go and slaughter the whole block."

The monster thought for a moment.

"Hm," he said. "You're right. Definitely a Golem, if their account is to be believed. How curious, to have a Golem nearby. Perhaps LyraCorps' domination will not remain as unchallenged as we expect it to. Too bad they ate him. There was a lot of knowledge in that body before they ripped it to pieces. Maybe if we had known, we could have kept an eye on where the soul ended up."

"That would have been something. Well, what would you like me to have them do? Everything else is still going according to plan. There have been no delays in the current projects, in spite of the loss of cargo. Would you have me tell them to keep looking? Should we go back to looking for the Vampyr?"

"No," the monster said. "The men will catch the boy's scent again, I'm sure. Maybe one of them will get lucky on their day off. But we've caused enough excitement, I think. Only a fool continues to work towards a goal he cannot accomplish. Whoever is hiding the boy knows what they're doing. We'll not find him if we continue to look. I'm certain whoever he is working with will come to us eventually. We'll see that old dog again soon, too. You know we will."

"Of course," Roper agreed. The second in command had managed to track the microphones in the executive gym back to Russel, whom the two monsters so casually referred to then. "With the information we've been feeding him from his 'bug' in the building, he'd be stupid *not* to come at us again. I must commend you again for your most excellent deception where that was concerned."

"Thank you, my friend. Let me know when the men return so I can ask them personally if they learned anything from the Golem before they killed his body. Otherwise, your job now is to ensure that our local operations continue in the manner we need them to."

Roper stood, bowing low to Mordacity, an action carried out as part of traditions from his own culture rather than that of the Lyrans, who were certainly not ever known for their formalities. The second in command eyed the guards outside the door before walking down the hallway, sharing a knowing look with each. They were good men, them. Not like the sad excuse for a strike team he was forced to train and mentor. If he could send either of the guards outside of Mordacity's office against the boy, or either of his companions, the fight would be much different indeed. If anyone came whimpering back to the building with broken bones, it would not be these men. But alas, valuable resources are not often valued because they are bountiful.

Instead, he was left to command a group who could not help themselves when something *smelled good.*

Oh well, he thought. *I could have the dumbest of their kind under my command, and it wouldn't matter.* Their plans had not been altered. Not really. The old mutt and whatever group of Loren he was working with could never hope to stop LyraCorps as far as Roper was concerned. They had already won. He wondered how long the red-haired idiot would keep trying to throw a wrench in things he could hardly comprehend, so massive was the scale of their planning.

Stupid dogs.

Stupid Loren.

He thought then about his name. They called him Roper, though that wasn't what the dog had been called when he took it. He'd never cared to learn what his body was called. It hardly mattered, he'd taken it over so young. This body was his third. And they had always called him Roper. In his native tongue, the name meant commander. From the day of his birth, his name came with respect. There was a time when he thought his name destined him to lead. He'd grasped at power, then. And when he grasped, he could no better hold onto leadership than he could a handful of sand, so strong was his true leader's following. But that was alright with Roper.

He would keep living.

Their kind could live forever.

He had made his way to his favorite chair, pulling the lever which allowed for reclining. This was his only object of sentiment. He'd had the chair reupholstered several times over the years, but the frame was the same. It was still, is still, *his* chair. Lately there was hardly any down-time. But when there was, he liked to sit in the chair, the same as he had for the last fifty years.

As he sat, he mused upon the past. He'd accepted his place long ago. He thought then about the war. All the terrible things he'd enjoyed doing. There was no more fear, anymore. He used wake up and look around at a sea of scared faces; trembling children. He recalled his most favorite, most awful memory. When his squad had found the den with the last Vampyr children to ever have been born.

He was in his second body then. Its face looked much like this one, though he'd taken a different breed at that time. One of the bigger ones, more suited for physical combat. He appreciated how much less he needed to eat by comparison. Anything more than a few thousand calories a day becomes a burden, and even for someone who can live forever, time is precious. Food for Roper's kind is fuel, and hardly ever fun, even with an exceptional chef upstairs. Eating that much had been a chore.

When he took on the Lyran aspects of his form back on that day, his features had grown much larger and very wolf-like. He'd needed the power, at the height of the war. It was amazing so many of the smaller, weaker bloodlines had survived. They'd found the children under a mausoleum. A trick the Vampyr had employed too often, believing the smell of dead could hide their own scent. Their scent could be hidden in other ways, he knew. But the Vampyr that day were not apprised of such methods. Roper's corrupted Lyran squad had torn through the tombs to the soft earth below, digging until the ground fell out beneath them. All it had taken was a whimper before his soldiers knew their prize lay below.

As the earth collapsed in around them, Roper's eyes caught a young Vampyr's. They stood, gazing at each other for a breath, a soldier raking the boy's face on the next. Roper hadn't lifted a finger that day, watching as his men tore through the few women and many children who had inhabited the space. The blackness of the Vampyr's blood coated almost every inch of the cramped quarters when the monsters had finished. It was Roper's single greatest victory, and midway through he'd abandoned his Lyran attributes. He could see better with his human eyes. When he closed them now, he heard the screams of the children, delighting in the sound as it came to him.

"Sir," a nearby solider called out, ripping Roper back towards the present. He opened his eyes slowly, knowing his break to be done with. He silently lamented he had not gone somewhere more private, that he could have milked the time some more. But he still had his job to do. Not all of their soldiers were corrupted. The dogs bred too fast for that. And so people would always come to him for their leadership in the field, especially in the times when he was trying to relax. Their true leader met with almost no one but Roper himself.

"Are we ready?" Roper asked, knowing the answer already.
"We are. The men have eaten. We can leave at a moment's notice."

"Good. Let's be off. I grow increasingly weary of this city."

Roper's name meant commander.

And such was his role in the field.

Many were the men who would never have the chance to meet Mordacity. For them, there was Roper. He passed numerous such individuals as he made his way with the soldier who had come for him. There were some who simply acknowledged his passed, while others stopped what they were doing entirely. Their empire was a funny thing, in his mind. He did not know why they had chosen the race of the Lyra so long ago, but it had certainly made for some interesting results. Theirs was a people who were not completely composed with the attributes of any single animal. Roper often found that where one Lyran solider was unfalteringly loyal to him, as an extension of their true leader, another would be wildly insubordinate by comparison. Many Lyran soldiers followed Roper's orders simply because their rational mind accepted him as their commander, rather than because of their innate pack mentality.

Roper emerged from the elevator and exited the massive LyraCorps building, another man opening his door for him as he sat himself in the limo. When he was settled he looked over to the seat across from him, at a face he'd not come into contact with as long as he'd had his current body.

"Lady Reach," said the surprised Roper, "To what do I owe the honor?"

"I need your help." The beautiful woman said. She handed Roper a picture of the Warmonger, and the monster inside the stolen Lyran body smiled.

"Yes." He said. "Yes you do."

. . . .

Shen had just finished speaking, the room then fell silent. The words he'd said were not his own. His speech had been sent to him from *her*, the only one who had ever truly led the Vampyr. Only the council knew she still existed. Their job was to keep her a secret, even from their own kind. They were hardly fit for leadership otherwise.

Shen, most of all.

He could play at having all of the answers well enough, play at commanding respect. But deep down, he'd never been more afraid. The others had won, and he worried that the time he had left was short.

"So we are meant to simply continue on?" Another councilmember asked. "Our job is to watch the boy. Nothing else?"

Shen looked to his companion. "Nothing else."

"But what of our ranks?" Another councilmember asked.

"She will provide. As she always has. Even now, she spreads across Mexico, the heat of their desert keeping her warm as she converts each human she can find. She creates more Vampyr with each passing night."

"Will it be enough? Will the war begin again?"

"It will." Shen grew solemn at that statement. He'd hated the war; hated the fighting. Not like other Vampyr, who seemed to enjoy killing the Lyrans. The fighting only made him afraid. "But only once we've found what it is we seek. Soon we will have the numbers, but they will be useless without the poison. Until we have what the monsters have, we'll only lose again. And next time, it may take even longer. What they used is the key to our salvation."

Shen understood the plan better than any of them, so entrenched was Lilith inside of his mind. She did not control his body, but she commanded his thoughts. She no longer needed sleep, so his dreams were the images she saw. Even if they couldn't trust what she said, if they thought she was lying to them, he'd seen so many of the humans she turned. With the poison, they might have a chance. All in the service of her, their queen.

Lilith would have *her* empire again.

Shen sat back as the link was released. He prayed for there to be no further questions, and to his relief, there were not. Three of the elders exited the chamber, each wearing the same frustrated look. They would have to deal with their emotions, Shen knew. Lilith would not allow for anything else. She was faster than them all, stronger than them all, older than each of them combined. She could be down to where they were in two days on foot, and she would, if she thought a councilmember meant to disobey her orders. They would have to try and run during the day, when Lilith was forced to sleep, as she was the only remaining Vampyr still affected by the touch of sunlight. She was also the only Vampyr left with the ability to turn humans into their kind. Shen had learned this personally, when he lived his first life as a man, the secret he kept aside from how utterly afraid he was at all times. The other elders thought him born a Vampyr.

Shen remembered his own transformation.

He had lived a full life as a human. That was the way it was meant to be. Only the most devoted familiars were offered the opportunity to embrace life as a Vampyr. The true elders of the race were known as Nobles. Only a Noble could take on a familiar. A kind Noble did not choose their familiar lightly, either. Shen was selected from a large pool of applicants, all more than qualified to serve his former master. In the end, of course, he had been chosen. He served his master for almost two decades, until his own health began to wane. When he could no longer keep up with the eccentricity of the Noble he served, he did what any good familiar ought to and offered to end his own life for being the burden he had become. Instead, his master had chosen to be kind, and reward him for his servitude, using a then mysterious liquid to turn Shen into a Vampyr. It had been Lilith's blood, of course. The true Vampyr Nobles knew of their queen's existence, and were trusted with such decisions. Not like the Council they had now.

The Great War was still young then. No one – at least no one he'd known – would have ever thought a petty squabble could be carried on as it was. No one he knew had ever thought almost every Vampyr on the planet would be killed.

In that moment, he mused, it didn't really matter what he thought. It didn't matter how he felt. Whether he protested or not, there were forces at work much larger, much more powerful than he was. No one could stop what was coming. Lilith was turning more humans each evening. There were hundreds of Vampyr the world had no idea existed. There would only be hundreds more to come. Whether anyone liked it or not, there was nothing to be done but wait, listen, and when the time came, find a new hole to hide in.

War would come again.

Chapter XIX

Trajen woke up, unsure what to do with himself. He'd talked with Russell, he knew it was time to understand his powers. It was time to do his job, the task he was born to do. It was time to set things right. He had no school that day, though he wasn't sure he would be going back anyway. Normally, he would have gotten in the shower, and gotten ready for work. But Arnold...

Trajen's heart ached profoundly at the absence of Arnold. He could tell that Garrett, too, was hurting. Trajen couldn't remember a time where he had felt so awful. He couldn't begin to attempt to understand how he might try to make Garrett feel better, either. If such a thing were even possible. Garrett had brought them the news as Bren had turned on the television the previous evening, only to see the exact scene Garrett was describing from multiple angles. Trajen had thought the local television coverage did well to memorialize Arnold, at least for the evening. Garrett hadn't been able to make it through the entire program, retiring to his room shortly after relaying the details he had which were left out of the newscaster's teleprompter.

Arnold hadn't just been murdered, he'd been butchered. Garrett had been told that the scene was more than just 'gruesome,' as they said on the news. It was an absolute bloodbath. Arnold had been torn limb from limb, and someone had eaten most of him. That was part that made Trajen feel the worst. He hoped Arnold hadn't suffered, but he almost wished more that the man's body had at least been left intact, out of respect.

He walked downstairs prepared to smell food cooking. Instead, he saw Garrett, sitting alone at the table with a glass of juice, a seemingly blank stare aimed at the small window above his kitchen sink. Trajen should have seen Bren instead.

"Trajen. I'm glad you're awake." Trajen saw again the apparent sadness strewn across Garrett's face. The man seemed somewhat serious, as well.

"Hey Garrett, where's Bren?"

"She got called in to work. I took a sick day." Garrett focused fully on Trajen. "Hey, have you heard from Russell? I thought I smelled him on your jacket."

"Actually, I have. He and I spoke yesterday. I actually wanted to-"

"Wait. Yesterday? Not today?"

"Well, no. I mean, I just woke up. But-"

"Trajen. Russell was supposed to check in with me this morning, but he hasn't. Grab something to eat and get dressed. We need to find him." Garrett was alive with movement. Trajen could tell in that moment that the man had obviously been waiting for a reason to get up, like accidentally shoving the doorstop out from underneath the wood of the door, Garrett was swinging into action. Every step he took was almost frenzied, as if he could stomp the pain inside out of himself and through his feet as he trundled around the house.

Trajen reached for an energy bar and walked back up the stairs. He attempted to step through the shadows to make the trip quicker, but couldn't find a shadow large enough. The energy bar did little to fully satiate the hunger that came with waking up, but it would have to do. Garrett was already grabbing his coat by the door, leaving Trajen to catch up. Hopefully they would get to talk while they looked for Russell. Trajen wanted to tell Garrett that he was ready to learn everything about his powers. All of them. Even then, he focused on trying to grow the bone in his finger, and was frustrated when he could not. He would argue with Garrett if he needed to. Convince the man that the world was too far gone for him to pretend to be something he wasn't. And besides, Russel had already agreed that he should help.

Trajen caught up to Garrett at the end of the patio.

"Garrett, listen. After talking with Russell yesterday, I realized something."

Garrett inhaled deeply, his eyes closed. If he heard what Trajen had said, he made no move to show as much. After another deep inhale, he opened his eyes. "This way," he said, directing them south along the sidewalk. "Sorry, what were you saying, Trey?"
"I said I realized something. I need to learn how to use my powers, Garrett. I need to help you guys overthrow LyraCorps and defeat Mordacity. It's what I'm meant for, you know?"

"And Russel agreed with this?" Garret asked.

"He said he'd start working on getting me out to…wherever it is you guys meet. I'm going to decide for myself how I can help, I guess."

Garrett stopped in his tracks, his smile larger than normal, and his face more angular. "That's great. Let's start now. What can you smell?"

Trajen took a deep breath, attempting to get as much scent in through his nose as possible. "Mainly the dew in the air. Must have rained last night. Smells like wet grass and pavement. I can smell you, and some other musk." Trajen grabbed at his jacket. It was the same one he was wearing yesterday. He sniffed it again. "Oh, yea. That's Russell."

"It is. Keep thinking about the scent. Breathe deep. See if you can find it in the air. I'm no blood-seeker. I doubt whatever Lyran parts you got in you are either. But I think you should still be able to pick him up on the wind, same as the rest of us."

218

Trajen concentrated as hard as he could. He took one breath, then another. On the third, he thought he caught something. On the fourth inhale, the wind rustled in the trees, and he was sure. "Yes!" He said. "I can...wow...I can smell him!" As Trajen concentrated on the scent, his eyes started to dance and focus. He could feel them trying to see something. Finally, a fog came into his vision, dancing in the air before him. "Garrett...I think I can *see* his scent."

"Purple?"

"Well, more maroon. Maybe fuchsia. Or-"

"Right. Purple. That's good, Trajen. You passed your first lesson in Lyran powers. Looks like your face isn't ever going to change. It definitely would have at this point. I was curious. You're certainly accessing your Lyran aspects, but I don't see any extra hair either. Great job though. Now, cmon. Keep the scent in your nose, but don't let it become all you focus on. And don't hunch over like that. Anybody see's us, we want them to think we're just out for a walk."

"Was that a pun?" Trajen said with a smile. He was elated to have mastered another part of himself so quickly. Garrett tried to be serious in his reply.

"We might run into trouble, you know. I hope you're still making jokes if we need to take on some of Mordacity's goons."

The pair continued on after Russell's scent, though Garrett was already sure where it would lead them.

Lilith woke as the sun was setting, the last of her race still living in fear of the daylight. It had always been that way for her, the science or magic behind her existence depriving her of the sun's life-giving rays, which

219

would for her only mean death. Lilith had made peace with the darkness in her life long ago, though. She did not miss the daylight.

She ruled the night.

The earth was warm as she left the confines of the cave, her home only for the week. The heat of the dirt clung to her bare feet as she began her nightly trek into one of the last truly small towns left in the world. Zirahuen had managed to retain its small stature in spite of Lyracorp's ability to ensure that populations and economies across the globe had boomed decade after decade. The people of Zirahuen had kept to themselves, theirs a portion of Mexico not traditionally inhabited by any of the other races of Loren. For a time, Zirahuen had become a hub for Morkhavian activity, though all of the dead-flesh eaters had now moved farther North, where the territory was more heavily run by the Lyra they worked for. The soil there was much better for their fungus-filled trees, as well. With the Morkahvians gone, Zirahuen had enjoyed a population composed entirely of humans, their small community tight-knit and prosperous. The city plays host to nearly three thousand people, though most days the streets are so empty, with the evenings so quiet, it's hard to believe the population exceeds more than two digits in number. Lilith thought it was perfect. Zirahuen's large, deep lake served her purpose exactly as she needed it to. She had searched many years for such a location. Finding it meant the resurgence of the race she had worked so hard to create. The Vampyr had let themselves become nearly extinct.

Lilith was going to change that.

Creating a Vampyr is a simple process for Lilith. Not nearly as messy as films would have one believe, or as laborious. Though she did appreciate a good film. It takes only a drop of Lilith's blood to corrupt the form of a human, turning them eventually into one of her kind. For the other races of the Loren, Vampyr blood is poisonous if ingested. Of course, Lilith knew why the change only worked with humans. It was what she had been, in the time before history and memory. She no longer claimed human heritage, of course.

She was a Vampyr.

The mother of them all; a distant memory for any who had seen her when the war with the Lyrans began.

Often, Lilith found herself pondering the what-if of it all. What if she had been active when the war began? What if she had learned of it sooner? Such thoughts left her feeling angry, often leading to becoming disgusted with herself. But she would make her race plentiful again.

The transformation process from human to Vampyr is painful. Many do not survive. When Lilith had created the first wave of Vampyr, she had been careful to select humans whom she was certain would live beyond the first day of being introduced to her blood. Further complicating the process was the mindless state of rage a newly transformed Vampyr experiences. For the first six days and six nights of a Vampyr's rebirth, they are an angry organic machine, and will feed well beyond the scope of reasonable consumption. Zirahuen's lake made this process easier. Vampyr do not need to draw oxygen into their lungs.

Lilith had taken the time to set up many simple cages and enclosures along the bed of Zirahuen's lake, which she used as storage for her newest Vampyr. On the seventh morning, upon the brink of starvation, the new Vampyr were allowed the opportunity to feed themselves. These Vampyr, with their wits about them, rarely killed more than a few people to satisfy themselves. An average Vampyr can share a feeding with another and leave their prey alive. Should one of them be released even a few hours too soon, however, the damage could be incalculable. Lilith needed this city. It would become the new mecca for her kind, where the Vampyr race was born again to be stronger than ever before. She had worked tirelessly over many weeks already.

Over half of Zirahuen were now Vampyr.

It would be many more weeks before the city was completely turned. Keeping the transformation hidden from the Lyra had been easy thus far, but Lilith could only do so much. She would need to distribute the power soon among her kind. No Vampyr could resist her will, but she could not be everywhere at once. The council existed for just such a purpose, though she knew that the council members had been elected not because they were worthy, but because they were all that was left. In her new Vampyr empire, she would need to ensure that her elected generals, the new Nobles, were fit for the task. Lilith's plan was long-term. She would need many years before she could ensure the utter destruction of the Lyran race.

She had allowed the Loren to live with a balance before. Her deal with the Peacebringers and Warmongers had been hard-struck. All it had gotten her was the near extinction of her people.

Never again.

When her plan was finished, she would see to it that the Vampyr ruled the world.

The monster was sucking on the space between his teeth as he unbuttoned Mordacity's suit jacket. He liked the noise the tongue made from the pressure. It sounded like what he heard when his kind put themselves inside of a body.

He stood at his place at the rounded table. Each of the five Members stood in their places, as well. Each Member was of a different race. It was the six of them who decided, so long ago, what they would do to finally take over. To take the world they knew belonged to *them*. Here, plans lived and died which were never spoken of anywhere else.

The only truth that truly existed to the monster was spoken in this room.

The Shadone spoke first. "My Hidden have found the boy. They wait in the shadows, but are ready to strike. He is with another Lyra."

"Oh? Interesting," Mordacity said, directing everyone's attention to the form behind them. Russell was on his knees, his face bloodied, chains around his ankles and wrists. "Tell us, *dog,* who is the other with the boy?"

Russell spat, smiling as he growled low. He had been turning his wrists in their shackles the moment he'd been chained to the wall, and continued to turn them in their place, rubbing his skin raw.

"No matter," The Morkhavian said. "Is there any reason your shadow warriors shouldn't engage?"

The Members stood silent. Even Mordacity, who desperately wanted to capture Trajen himself, said nothing. Here, he was not the leader. He played the most pivotal role in their plan, but among The Members, he was only an equal.

"I'll make the call," The Shadone said. "Is there any other business?"

"One thing," Mordacity said. The Members looked to him as one. "I've had this body a long time. Much longer than any of you have had yours. Longer than any of our kind has stayed inside the same host, I think. Tell me, do any of you know if...Well..."

"On with it, brother." The Morkhavian said. The monster instinctively curdled his nose as he caught a whiff of the man's breath. Even with his senses naturally dampened, the dog's nose was still good enough to smell the pure, absolutely rotten mess living inside the Morkhavian's mouth.

"Right, of course. I'm just wondering. Have any of you ever heard about them winning? This dog inside of me learned the maze long ago. He's never come close to defeating me in the mindscape. But still, even after all this time, he fights."

"And you're worried?" The Celebrant asked. Her tone was both playful and mocking.

"Of course not!" The monster shot back, the emotion in his voice unchecked. "Never mind. Forget I said anything. I have no other business."

"Well," The Celebrant continued. "If he *were* to win, he'd be the first. I can tell you that much. No host has *ever* gotten free from the bond we create. And it wouldn't be like when we release ourselves from a body."

"What do you mean?"

"I mean you would be less essence and more form. Being in control of the vessel is what allows the rest of what we are to stay hidden inside the smaller places in the host's body. I imagine you would be expelled, quite forcefully, and retain the physical form we develop inside of these vessels we steal. That's a pretty big dog, too. If he had his wits, there's no telling-"

"Thank you, that's enough." The monster was starting to sweat under his suit. True sweat, from his own nervousness. He had gone countless decades unafraid that the dog he shared a mind with would win out in their battles. The monster knew he would be lying to himself if he pretended any longer he wasn't curious about what might happen, simultaneously berating himself internally for not lying to the other Members about it. Luckily, none of the others could smell sweat the way Lyrans could, and he was the only dog in the room. There was no weakness allowed for the Members. They decided that long ago. This one, inside of the Celebrant – she had wanted the monster gone for some time.

He wouldn't let that happen while they were so close to the final phase of their plan.

If they could catch the Peacebringer, things would be back on track. At that thought, the monster was hopeful.

Shadow warriors were hardy. They almost never failed.

Chapter XX

"Alright, stop here." Garrett said. "What do you smell?" The pair were situated behind an old schoolhouse, deep in the woods. This was the closest Trajen had come to the LyraCorps compound since the night he'd left.

"The scent is strong now. I can tell Russell was here recently…and that he bled."

"That's what I smell too. I'm picking up something else. Do you smell…ah, here we go." Garrett seemed somewhat resigned as his voice trailed off. Trajen thought it sounded like the man was expecting what the boy now perceived as a shifting in the air, and the crunching of twigs a few feet to their left. As Trajen looked over, Garrett ripped off his pants, revealing shorts with a hole cut in the back for his hairy tail. Trajen wasn't even aware that Garrett had one of those. Garrett's body became covered in white and brown hairs, his nails extending into sharp claws. "Don't focus on their scent. That's too new to you. It'll just get in the way." Garrett no longer sounded like a man. His speech was guttural, more a growl filled with vowels than anything else.

Trajen did as Garrett instructed, focusing less with his nose and allowing the colors of the world to return to their normal hue. It was time to fight, and Trajen felt as ready as he could. He opened his ears up, hearing the familiar *bwump* he realized came when he stepped through the shadows, a fist meeting the side of his head hard immediately after. The blow knocked his head to the side, and though he did not fall his balance was completely shot. He heard Garrett growl deeply, his Lyran companion grabbing the shadow warrior and throwing the man headfirst into a nearby tree so that their enemy seemed a living missile covered in tendrils of smoke, the light and air around his body seeming to bend around him as he moved. As the warrior struck the tree, a blow sure to leave his neck broken, he disappeared with another *bwump*. Trajen wondered if his own Shadone powers could allow him to take on such a form, as the warrior seemed to bring the shadows with him, though there was hardly time for such musing.

Trajen spotted two more shadow warriors coming, both revealing shafts of wood from their sleeves. The warriors brought them up to their mouths in unison, darts flying towards Trajen and Garrett. Trajen was the quicker of the two, then, grabbing Garrett's arm and shadow stepping the two of them a foot to the right. Trajen shadow stepped again immediately after, placing himself next to one of the shadow warriors. The boy struck hard into the shadow warrior's temple, who reeled at the blow before shadow stepping behind Trajen. The warrior grabbed the young fighter from behind, wrapping strong arms around Trajen's neck. He could hardly breathe, understanding that in a moment he would lose consciousness completely. Trajen called on his Lyran powers, flipping himself forward, the shadow warrior flying through the air on his back. Trajen hoped this would dislodge his attacker, but the man continued to hold. As they landed, Trajen firmly on top of the shadow warrior, he could feel the tendrils of smoke crawling on his skin. Something about them felt different. They were like the feeling he sensed when he shadow stepped, normally a cold experience, but stinging to the touch, as if the air were frozen. Firmly planted on the ground, Trajen lashed out with both of his elbows one after another, striking as hard as he could to try and get the shadow warrior to release his grip. His assailant cried out softly from the pain, as Trajen could hear he'd broken one of the man's ribs. The grip softened as he heard the *crack* beneath the man's skin, and as Trajen rolled out of it, the blood rushing back to his head, he caught the man's scent.

It was bitter.

The shadow warrior was the first person with a scent Trajen associated with a taste since he had been around Arnold. The young man realized this too late, as two fists struck him in unison, both hits landing in each eye. Trajen's head shot backward from the blow, his legs falling out from under him.

The shadow warrior Trajen had thrown rolled sideways as he landed, standing up immediately. Trajen found his bearings just as quickly, the two warriors who had just struck him now battling Garrett. The boy was to his previous opponent in an instant, kicking the man in, then through, his chest. With a great yell, Trajen's foot caved in the man's breast plate, shards of bone cracking as they met Trajen's boot, until the treads on the bottom of his feet could be seen poking out of the man's back. Trajen tried to pull his foot out, surprised more that it was stuck than that he had just killed a man. His ankle caught on the shadow warrior's insides, and he stumbled forward, the man's body releasing his leg as it fell to the ground. Now fully dead, the tendrils of smoke around his opponent seemed to fade away, falling into the earth, leaving a normal-looking human in their wake, the light completely gone from his eyes.

Trajen drew his attention back towards Garrett, who was holding his own against another two shadow warriors. The boy watched one warrior attempt to shadow step, getting only halfway into the motion before Garrett was able to grab him by his shirt and swing the warrior into the other. The two shadow warriors took the blow hard, Trajen dashing over to help Garrett. As the boy got there, he brought his fist directly into the first shadow warrior's head, hearing the man's skull crack, blood spurting out in two directions from the pressure. The warrior fell immediately to ground, dying in the same manner as the other man Trajen had killed. Garrett grabbed the remaining shadow warrior by the throat, digging his claws into the man's windpipe before ripping out his throat entirely. The shadows faded from his form as well, leaving only another human form at their feet. Trajen and Garrett looked around, prepared for more assailants, though there were none. After a moment, Garrett's features grew softer, though he still kept much of his hair, his tail receding somewhat.

Garrett turned to Trajen, checking the boy for any wounds. "Did they get you?"

"Almost, kind of. One of them got his arms around my neck. I got him though. Then he caught my boot with his...uh...well, you can see for yourself. I'm getting pretty good at calling on my Lyran abilities, I think. At least the strength and the speed."

"Wow," Garrett said as he looked at the dead shadow warrior, a large hole in the man's chest revealing the forest floor. "I don't think that was Lyran strength. I'm strong, sure, but not put-my-boot-through-someone's-chest strong. If it was your Lyran strength, you'd have to have been channeling some kind of *huge* breed. No, that was something else. Probably-" Garrett's words cut off there, and the man fell face-first into the ground in front of Trajen.

"Garrett!" Trajen saw the problem immediately. A stray dart had managed to land on Garrett's neck. Trajen pulled it free, turning Garrett over. He could hear already that Garrett's breaths were getting shallow. Trajen didn't know anything about poison, but he could tell that Garrett was in trouble. He thought about slinging the man over his shoulder, carrying him to a hospital. But even in that moment he could feel Garrett's skin getting colder to the touch. He'd be dead before the two got more than ten feet in any direction. Trajen was suddenly without answers. Was this what hopelessness felt like?

He heard a rustling to his right, then. He was on his feet in an instant, ready to kill a hundred more shadow warriors for what they'd done to Garrett.

"None of that now," Russell said. The old man's face was covered in blood and dirt. Trajen could see the man's hands bent almost completely in the wrong direction. "There'll be plenty more fighting later. Right now, we need to save Garrett."

"Russell!" Trajen's eyes lit up as he saw the old man. "Please, what can I do?"

"Just do what comes naturally. There's plenty of sun comin' through these trees. Use it."

"Use it? I mean, I've taken it in before. But you're saying I can…what…give it to Garrett?"

"I sure hope so. One of those races you have access to certainly can."

Trajen reached his hand out, allowing the sunlight to cover it completely. Drawing in the light the way he'd captured it in Arnold's shop. It took a second, but Trajen could feel the light more fully than he ever had before. It was as if it were trying to break into his skin. At first he didn't want to let it, but when he realized what was happening, it was already too late. He could feel the light pouring into himself. As he saw his fingers begin to glow, he stopped resisting, and the light filled him up completely. Looking down, he instinctually touched his hand to Garrett's face. Immediately, the light transferred from Trajen to his friend.

Garrett's eyes shot open. The man turned his head and threw up violently, a thick black liquid shooting itself all over the ground to their right. Garrett wiped his mouth and looked at Trajen. Both of them shared a smile.

"Hey Russell," Garrett said.

"Garrett."

"Looks like you ran into those Shadone before we did." Garret coughed, the last of the black liquid free then from his body.

"Something like that. Thanks for taking care of them. Navigating this part of the forest is tough enough without those freaks teleporting all over the place." Russel held up his bent appendages, making a face at Garret behind Trajen's back. The old man didn't want Trajen to know he'd been captured, but Garret knew instantly that was what had happened.

"Freaks?" Trajen asked.

"That's what they are," Russell replied. "All those tendrils and all that smoke. That's not normal for any Shadone. Shadone look like humans, really. I guess most of 'em are a little lanky in the arms, but you really have to try and notice. Not supposed to be covered in shadow like that."

"What do you think it means?"

"Who knows?" Garrett said, getting up from the ground. "Let's all get back to the house. That was enough excitement for one day. We found Russell. We need to heal up and decide our next move. Bren should be home in a little while. We can talk about forming some kind of plan over dinner. Trajen, you think you can heal Russell's hands?"

"I don't see why not." Trajen replied. "Maybe we should get back to where it's safe first, though? Russell's right, I think. Feels like more of those Shadone could come at us any second."

"Sounds good to me," Russell replied. "About time I got to enjoy some of your wife's cooking, Garret. It'll be nice not to just have to smell it, for once. And Trajen, nice job before. I caught the tail end. You took the hits a little better than you gave 'em, but you did alright."

Trajen beamed with the compliment.

Still, he was ready to learn how to *actually* fight.

∙∙

The three men walked home with their heads held high, the two natural Lyrans with a slight prance in their step. They weren't quite sure what the plan was just yet, but they knew they'd won the day. Trajen emulated their movement out of instinct. Though, if he was honest with himself, he felt pretty good too. Russell knew about the shadow warriors. He had a lot of information for Trajen and Garrett, about the horrible things similar Shadone had done during the war. He told them these must have been newer recruits, as even one veteran shadow warrior was enough to raze an entire village; though none of them knew why the men they fought had been covered as they were in the tendrils of shadow. Russell and Garrett had never seen such a thing.

Still, they had won.

Then came the smoke.

It was Garrett who smelled it first. He took off as he caught the whole scent, his legs pumping like they were steam-powered. Trajen couldn't understand why Garrett was running. He didn't know to access his Lyran sense of smell. But Russell did. "Cmon, kid. We got more trouble!"

Trajen and Russell raced off after Garrett, unconcerned with what any casual passerby might think about how quickly they were able to move. Trajen looked for some indication as to why they were now traveling at full speed, only to be given his answer as his gaze drifted slightly upward.

The smoke seemed to puff lazily into the air, moving with a cadence much calmer than Trajen imagined the flames on the ground were burning. As the trio rounded the final corner into their cul-de-sac, Trajen could hear Garrett start to weep. Then he heard him scream.
Trajen wanted to tell Garrett to calm down. Maybe Bren wasn't home. Maybe she was out. But as he took a good, long whif, he knew it was too late. He could smell what the others could. Garrett didn't even try to run into the house. There was no point.
The smell of cooked meat drifted lazily into the air, floating just as casually as the black smoke above. The smell didn't know it was an evil

thing. It didn't know it shouldn't smell as it did, or even exist at all. It didn't know what it told the three men; it didn't know it said anything. It was just a smell. But it spoke volumes. It told them a very evil, very *wrong* thing.

Bren was dead.

....

The monster didn't like the news the lowly whelp in his office delivered. Shadow warriors weren't supposed to lose. Especially not *their* shadow warriors. Still, here they were. It made him angry. The dog before him was not one of theirs, but he was of a loyal breed. A real give-him-orders, type. The man standing before the monster would gladly lay down his life before sharing the information he'd brought to his master.

The monster had to get his anger out somehow, though.

Long tendrils shot from his mouth as he released his human form. His body grew larger in an instant, the Lyran soldier impaled just as quickly with his strong, flowing body parts. He pushed them further inside of the Lyran, extending the spikes in the tendrils as he did to cut the man's flesh from within. The soldier stayed loyal even then, hardly whimpering as he met his brutal ending. The monster spun each tendril in opposite directions, emulsifying the bone and muscle around them, before pulling them outward and away from each other, splitting the Lyran solider nearly in half. The man's organs fell to the floor in a steaming pile, landing with a loud *plop*.

But it was not enough.

Killing the dog certainly felt good. But the monster's anger was too great to be satisfied with such a quick thing. It was time he put down his own dog as well. No more navigations through the maze. It was time, after so long, he claim this body fully for himself.

Sitting down in his chair, he travelled immediately to the mindscape he shared with his host. Still the wolf was traversing the maze he'd set up, already nearly to the center once again. *Good,* the monster thought, *let us end this.*

As the real Mordacity appeared, the monster could sense his eagerness. The filthy thing was always ready for a fight. Lyrans were so stupid. He lashed out immediately with his tendrils, uninterested in trading words or pleasantries. He would destroy the oversized mutt completely on this day. The monster had always been content with beating Mordacity unconscious, thinking eventually, surely, the dog would give up the fight.
This time would be different.

Each swing of his tendril hit Mordacity hard, one strike nearly breaking two of the wolf's ribs. He shot one tendril straight out, intending to impale the beast the same way he'd caught the soldier before, though the dog was too quick for the move. He struck out again exactly the same as a feint, intending to sweep out Mordacity's legs with an ulterior tendril, as he'd done so many times before. Though, as he did, the monster was surprised to see Mordacity dodge the attack. The large wolf jumped over the tendril with ease, grabbing onto another of the monster's grotesque limbs in his mouth so firmly that the tendril lost all feeling and was ripped away from the monster's body.

This made him even angrier.

The dog, foolish thing, pressed its perceived advantage. Mordacity came on strong, raking with his oversized claws, nearly jumping over the monster's huge form in a single bound to scratch its face with his feet. Deep gashes formed all over the monster's forehead, cheeks, and lips as it thrashed every which way, momentarily blinded by the wounds Mordacity had inflicted. The monster flung his tendrils wide, expecting one to catch the wolf so that he could crush him to death. Miraculously, the dog managed to avoid the swinging appendages completely.

Then the unthinkable began.

It took hundreds of years for the monster to lose his fight with his host, the real Mordacity proving that sometimes an iron will is all you need to win a war, even if you've lost every battle. Mordacity's huge jaws clamped around the monster's neck, ripping large chunks of flesh free from its body, until he'd managed to remove everything but the bone. As the last bit of light faded from the monster's eyes in the mindscape, Mordacity felt his own consciousness drift as well.

When he realized what had happened, he realized as well he'd forgotten what color looked like, knowing in that moment that the mindscape had been a place of black and grey. Everything around him was so vibrant. And the clothes he wore…it felt so wonderful to have the cotton on his skin again. Though, he could do well without all the noise.

An alarm sounded. The third one that year. The people in the compound, hardly any of them human, understood that the alarm meant their leader was in trouble. Some of them understood, as well, the true implication of such an alarm, and moved even quicker than others to respond. Four of the Members would be angry. The Celebrant woman would be pleased.

Mordacity could smell the other monsters coming. They didn't smell like the other Lyrans his nose detected. He knew that now, after such a long time smelling the monster. He could smell something else, as well. Something *different* from everyone else around him. Different even from the monsters making their way to his office. He knew in that moment he had to find her. That she could help him take back his race.

She was far, but he could make it.

As he leaped from his office, crashing out of the third-story window, Mordacity knew he had to find the Warbringer.

They had to save the world.

Epilogue

Dalbrin watched as Trajen and the man he lived with left their home. The Vampyr hadn't come prepared with much of a plan. He knew the council thought Trajen was important, so he'd worked out thus far that whatever he did to get away, it ought to involve the boy. Beyond that level of detail, he had nothing. He'd spent an hour already watching the man of the house sit impatiently in the kitchen, waiting for someone to come home. As Trajen and he were leaving, Dalbrin contemplated following the pair. Perhaps he could engage them? Find a way to feign a fatal injury. But then, the possibility remained that the two Loren might *actually* kill him if he attacked. Dalbrin thought the man, whom he had seen a few times before, had a crazed look in his eyes.

Dalbrin didn't mean to linger around the house where Trajen lived. It happened mostly on accident. He'd been lurking in the shadows around the house for at least twenty minutes, when the woman that lived there had arrived home from work. Dalbrin saw her walk confidently from her car into the house. She was certainly beautiful, for a human. He could see why the Lyran that lived there was with her. The Vampyr snuck in through the backdoor, guided by instinct more than anything. The woman was on the phone, her inflection not unlike the way Dalbrin recalled Gracia talking to him. He could just make out the man's voice on the other end. It was not the man who lived here. And he was coming by.

This was good.

Dalbrin waited not much longer. The man must have been nearby when he'd called. As he walked in, Dalbrin could see him for what he was, and the old Vampyr grew elated at the sight. Only Loren can accurately identify a Dayrunner, the foil race to the Vampyr. Dalbrin was not surprised to find that it was a Dayrunner enabling this woman to commit adultery.

237

Promiscuity came with the profile. Where Vampyr often kept the same mate for multiple lifetimes, some bearing no offspring ever, Dayrunners were notorious for operating in an opposite fashion. And this one was no different, it seemed.

Dalbrin knew that Dayrunners had been somewhat culled during the Great War. All of the races had, of course. Many Lyrans believed that if you weren't with them, you might eventually be against them. There came the point for many Loren, at the establishment of LyraCorps, that you either worked with the Lyrans or were killed. The Lyrans spared only the humans in this regard. Dalbrin knew that many Dayrunners who fed on human energy did so exclusively to the species, as energy from each race was different. If this one fed on humans, it was likely he was completely alone in the city. No one would miss him if he were to disappear.

Thanks goodness for that.

Dalbrin studied the man as he sat down on the couch, appearing alluring in his own way. *About the same height as me,* Dalbrin thought. *Similar build, though he looks like he may have fallen into that weight-lifting, health craze.* The Vampyr could see the woman struggling with something. She kept beginning to speak, stopping, and continuing again; her car of a tongue sputtering down the road with her broken sentences. Finally, she got the words out. The affair was over. She couldn't do this anymore.

The Dayrunner was displeased.

Dalbrin watched the man stand up, and the woman shirk back a step. The Dayrunner began to yell, his hands flying as he talked. A moment later, they flew at the woman. The sound the Dayrunner's hand made as it struck the woman of the house in her cheek seemed to echo. The sound in the room then ceased, the situation clearly on the precipice of being over or getting much, much worse. Dalbrin didn't care for this sort of thing. Domestic violence was a real issue for any race. He had killed plenty of living things in a fit of passion as a younger Vampyr. But just because he could relate with the Dayrunner's position, didn't mean he agreed with it. For Dalbrin, harming things weaker than yourself was a waste of time if you weren't going to eat it. And while Dayrunners still possessed their fanged teeth, Dalbrin knew this one was too young to consider ever feasting on a human. He was only there for the energy.

The Dayrunner raised his hand to strike again, but Dalbrin had seen enough. He was in between them in an instant, his hand clasped around the Dayrunner's mid-swing. He felt such little resistance as he held the other man at bay, their age difference must have been great indeed. It was possible the Dayrunner was, in actuality, only as old as he looked.

The woman stepped back, frightened now more by the strange man in her living room than the thought of being struck again by her lover. Dalbrin pushed the man into the couch forcefully, the piece of furniture sliding back as the man landed on it.

Dalbrin turned to look at the woman. "I just don't appreciate wanton use of power." He said.

"I...thanks." Bren said, clutching her cheek with a free hand.

"Oh, no. I'm sorry dear. You see, doing damage because you *can* – I don't agree with that. But doing it when you need to? It's a man's responsibility to protect his family."

Bren didn't understand, but it didn't matter. Dalbrin knew there was a gallon of gasoline in the garage. And he was right about the Dayrunner.

The man's clothes fit him perfectly.

Thank you for reading The Loren - Trajen. I hope you enjoyed reading it as much as it was to create. Since you took the time out to buy the book I have added an extra treat if you turn the page.

JENTRA

Chapter I

Her eyes darted around in the dark. Opening suddenly hearing an increasingly loud sound. All of a sudden the sound was gone. She could hear footsteps from several directions, but unable to discern how many or where they were from. An inordinate wanting to close her eyes came upon her swiftly and like before her eyes closed. The light vacating the area and the sound quelled around her.

Several minutes pass and suddenly her eyes pop open again. There was still no sound, but this time when her eyes open she could see everything around her, every detail. Hinges on the cage in front of her appeared to be bent in several different directions. Her hands firmly clasped with some material stronger than folded steel around her ankles and feet. They would not bend; she was held fast in place.

Then with a thought, she felt the restraints loosen and suddenly with one deft motion her cage is suddenly no longer a problem. The crude manacles lay at her feet in a state of disrepair.

She took a step forward, stumbling slightly before getting her bearings. She notices several more cages lining the halls, but something inside of her compels her to look at the empty cage in front of her. It was barren, but one word formed within her head, "Trajen."

Trajen? What or who was that? The word rung inside her head like a childhood nursery rhyme. A familiar face appeared in her head. The name, the face, they were connected. She scanned the floor near the cage in front of her, as well as the surrounding areas. Small pieces of metal were strewn across the floor.

Then there was this smell. A scent in the air. Flowers. Dandelions. She smelled dandelions.

Turning towards the long walkway she spotted a door still slightly ajar, she begins to run, barely noticing that her feet are not even touching the floor. Behind her she feels her shoulders pumping. Gusts of wind moving across her face. It wasn't until she had made it into the next hallway she noticed the shadow of wings on the floor below her; moments later she finds herself outside.

Wings? She remembered this sensation. Flying. The young lady thought to herself.

Her feet touching the ground a sense of coldness creeps up on her. The color white covered the ground in all directions up to the tree line in front of her. The scent of dandelions was so strong in that direction she could almost taste it. Her feet start to move towards the horizon and follow the smell she is drawn to, but the air shimmers slightly, a blinding light shoots out and a pair of translucent arms reach out of nothingness and pull her into the light before she has a chance to think.

The air still and no longer shimmering. The young lady no longer standing on the snow. The only reminder of her presence, a set of footprints in the snow.

In the distance you can hear the screech of tires on a slippery snowy road.

••

Her head felt like it was going to explode. She could hear a large pop, followed by a suction sound as the bright light faded. When the light subdued she frantically glanced around. Several people now looking in her direction.

Looking around she stood in a room with several chairs arranged around an oval table.

Almost a dozen faces are looking on of various degrees at her in one fashion or another.

"It's ok. We aren't here to hurt you. We were actually looking for you, well I mean we have been for quite some time. Ever since..." The young woman speaking paused for a beat." ... We can talk about that later. I am Blake." She started to motion around the room for more introductions.

"Jentra?" A questions asked semi rhetorically.

She didn't know her name. For some reason she was having trouble remembering that. The question directed towards her seemed less of a question and more of an inquiry. The name more than a little familiar, like a melody heard over and over, and then like a balloon popping she remembered.

"Yes." She nodded acknowledging the person speaking.

"Where is the boy?" A fairly deep voice spoke from the head of the table. The question didn't seem to be leveled directly at Jentra, but at a small group of people huddled together.

Three people closest to the new arrival, looking very gaunt and out of breath replied in unison. "Gone. We sent out the hands and there was no sign of him."

One of the people was tall, very tall, almost two whole heads higher than the other two, and to make it even more awkward he was stooped over.

His features hidden, by what looked like a soot all over his face and hands. A film of dark grey prevalent everywhere. If it weren't for the blinking it would almost appear as if they were coal shaped statues.

The next person seemed female in appearance and was tall for a woman, but nowhere near as tall as the first person. She was staring at.

Lastly, there was a more rotund man next to the woman. He was large horizontally like the first man was vertical.

A sigh escaped the another gentleman at the table a couple of seats from the head of it. All across the room seem distraught at that last piece of news.

"For the time being we are spent. I can gather the clave again in a few weeks and we will start looking again Carmac. Now that we know what to look for we can find him easily as well as the others. I will not r...e...st." The tall man stammered and tried to regain his composure.

He raised his hand as if to speak again, and almost on queue fell to the ground writhing in noticeable paid.

The man at the head of the table ran towards him reaching out, right before his last breath.

"No, we are so close, we have to fix it. Please Kkaz don't pass, we have much to do."

Kkaz Asem one of the most powerful Elders to live, and this one's best friend. Disagreements a plenty marked there hundred-year friendship, but the loyalty these two shared was unbreakable.

Over a hundred years ago, they sat in a room similar to this one. Each one's parents looking on explaining to them that they were different from other kids. Kkaz spent the half of the night telling Carmac that dragons were real and Carmac spent the other half of the night debunking the theory; the latter being incorrect. Since then they had quarreled like the tightest of brothers, laughed as the best of friends and at times even wept together.

It was times like these that weeping would be in order. The room went into a frenzy. People were running around the room. Some murmuring things Jentra couldn't understand. Lights popped all around the room. Symbols appeared out of the air. She saw women and men come running in holding all manner of items she couldn't even begin to ascertain.

Jentra stood mouth agape trying to comprehend what has going on, but before she was even able to sort it out took a few steps to walk over to the fallen man. She placed her hands on him and suddenly his eyes opened. A glow surrounded him and his chest began to rise and fall slowly and steadily. She wasn't sure what just happened, her memory foggy at best, but several things about these people began to become clear. In an instant one word came to mind.

Magic.

TO BE CONTINUED...

Make sure you check out www.theloren.com for more information on the different races that make up the Loren or just to drop a line. Don't forget to check back for our next in the series set to release in 2016!